K.L. ARMSTRONG is the pseudonym of a popular author.
She lives in Ontario.

Also by K.L. Armstrong

Every Step She Takes

Wherever She Goes

THE LIFE SHE HAD

K.L. ARMSTRONG

DOUBLEDAY CANADA

LIBRARY AND ARCHIVES CANADA CATALOGUING IN PUBLICATION
Title: The life she had / K.L. Armstrong.
Names: Armstrong, Kelley, author.
Identifiers: Canadiana (print) 20220162859 / Canadiana (ebook) 20220162875 |
ISBN 9780385697668 (softcover) / ISBN 9780385697675 (EPUB)
Classification: LCC PS8551.R7637 L54 2022 / DDC C813/.6—dc23

Cover design: Matthew Flute
Cover images: (woman) Hans Neleman, (house) shaunl, (sky) Yefta Madari / EyeEm, all Getty Images; (smaller woman) Tyler Nix, (sand) Marcos Rivas, both Unsplash

Printed in Canada

Published in Canada by Doubleday Canada,
a division of Penguin Random House Canada Limited

www.penguinrandomhouse.ca

10 9 8 7 6 5 4 3 2 1

THE LIFE SHE HAD

ONE

CELESTE

My mother used to tell me that I can't run away from myself. At thirty-three, I still have no idea what the hell she meant. I only know that it wasn't intended as a gentle warning. It was a slap in the face.

No matter how hard or how fast you run, dear daughter, you cannot escape yourself.

The last time I heard those words, they'd dripped with smug satisfaction. Twenty-one years old, and I'd literally just escaped from a nightmare. Found a damned pay phone—the only one in the county—and, fingers shaking, dropped in the coins and dialed a number that made tears stream down my face, buttons blurring until I had to blink them back to continue.

I-I got away, Mom. I finally got away from him. Can I come home? Please?

Those words ignited the last shreds of my dignity, burning them to ash at my feet. I remembered the girl I'd been five years before, furious at a world—and a family—who blamed me for a tragedy that had nothing to do with me. I'd made mistakes, endless mistakes, but I hadn't done *that.*

He'd believed me. The boy I met online. He'd believed me. Sympathized with me when I needed it, and raged with me when I needed *that.*

Come stay with me. Start over. They don't deserve you. They don't understand you. I do.

At twenty-one, I cringed at the girl who'd fallen for such obvious bullshit. At thirty-three, my anger is aimed where it belongs: at the asshole who'd targeted a desperate teenage girl. And at the mother who picked up the phone five years later.

You can't run away from yourself.

She said that and then hung up. I never contacted her again.

Today I *am* running. Not from myself. *I've* never been the problem. It's the rest of the damned world that just keeps boxing me in. This particular box was supposed to be my den, my safe hideaway. Now, once again, the comforting barriers between me and the world threaten to harden into cage bars. The urge to flee is overwhelming, but this time, I recognize that the problem isn't a place. As always, it's a person. I've finally started to realize that the answer is not *escape.*

Don't abandon my safe den. Deal with the person holding the damn keys.

Twelve years ago, I fled Aaron, and what did that get me? Twelve years of running.

Don't run from the threat. End it.

First, though, I need to keep from getting killed myself, and today the threat comes in a package as ridiculous as rust-speckled pickup trucks. Two have already spit gravel at me, their drivers honking and yelling.

They see me. They're just making a point: roads are for driving on. Even when I jog on the shoulder, I swear they swerve *toward* me. At the last second, they veer and hit the gas to send black smoke billowing.

The worst, though, are the dogs. Around here, I'm jogging a gauntlet of snarling canines who've only ever seen a runner when someone's making off with the family Xbox.

I pass my neighbor's house. Kids race around the yard with toy tomahawks and six-guns. Even thirty years ago, born to parents who weren't exactly models of liberal thinking, I knew better than to play this particular game. When the *pop-pop-pop* of gunfire sounds, I instinctively skid and drop to one knee, and the towheaded children erupt with laughter, pointing at the silly city slicker who doesn't know the difference between a handgun and a cap gun.

When I can breathe again, I squint over at the kids. There are at least four of them, all in hand-me-downs, with scraggly hair. The oldest can't be more than seven and totes an air rifle.

Dear Lord, I can hear the banjo music already.

The oldest kid—a girl, it seems—points her rifle straight at me. She fires, and the plastic pellet skids through the gravel beside me. I wheel, ready to march over and have a word with her parents. Then I see the girl's father, beer in hand, lounging on the front porch, watching everything. He lifts a hand in mock greeting.

As if on cue, the roar of a pickup sounds behind me, and I am tempted—damn tempted—to stride into the middle of the road.

I won't let you intimidate me. I'll stand my ground, and I'll make you pay . . . forced to clean my blood and bits from your front grille.

As much as I'd like to think my untimely demise would haunt my killer, there are people around here who'd only sue my estate for the vehicular damage. Not that it would do them much good. After a cheap burial, my estate would consist of a ramshackle house in rural central Florida. If someone does hit me, I almost hope they sue . . . and end up stuck with a money pit of a house, perched on land not even worth the cost of demolition.

That house might not be much, but it's more than I have ever had. A respectable job. A place to live. A piece of land. A life that is actually worth fighting for.

I resume my jog. When gravel crunches, I turn, expecting to see an asshole driving on my shoulder. Instead, this one stays on his side as he slows to pass me. I brace for what will come next—some witticism about how he can help me get my exercise . . . in the back of his pickup. That's when I recognize the vehicle and know no innuendo is forthcoming.

The truck is an antique Dodge, driven by the owner of the only business in Fort Exile—a combination gas station, automotive garage and convenience store.

As the pickup passes, I struggle to keep my gaze forward.

Don't look. The view may be very nice, but don't . . .

I look, of course. Tom Lowe is the hottest guy in Fort Exile. Granted, it's a town of under a hundred people, half of them over fifty. Anywhere else, Tom would be a seven edging in on an eight. Dark hair, worn country-music-star long, dark-brown eyes, a crooked nose and a grin that shows off excellent dentition to full advantage. Add a scarred cheek and broad tattooed biceps and Tom's body tells the story of a guy who grew up destined to work under the chassis of a pickup, sweaty and grease stained.

The fact that one of those tats clearly comes from a prison stint should erase the appeal of the rest, but . . . I call myself a reformed bad-boy magnet. The problem is that Tom Lowe is the walking model of a reformed bad boy. Exactly the kind of man I could fall for, with the bonus that, like me, he's past that stage of life. He seems like a genuinely sweet guy, one who pulls over for joggers, runs a legitimate business, and is a respected member of a community that grants respect as grudgingly as praise.

I know I shouldn't slow when he passes. Shouldn't look temptation in the face. Fortunately, I don't have to, because that window only goes down long enough for a friendly thumbs-up. Then, as the truck rolls past, Tom points at the sky. I squint to see dark clouds.

"Thank you!" I shout.

Tom flashes another thumbs-up and keeps going. I tell myself that's for the best. Like an alcoholic with a ninety-day pin walking past an open bar, I feel a twinge of regret but mostly a wave of relief. Tom Lowe would be my bender, sending me tumbling back to rock bottom.

I peer up at the sky again. Those clouds are rolling in fast, and storms here strike hard, especially in late August as hurricane season hits the coast. The first time I'd been caught in the rain, I'd nearly done a jig of glee, imagining the cool water sluicing the sweat from my body. Instead, the rain lashed in bruising torrents, the humidity doubled, and the sweltering temperature didn't drop one damn degree.

I turn around to head back. I'm passing the neighbor's house when he shouts at me from the porch.

"Done already? You weren't hardly out for a minute, girl."

His laughter fades behind me as I reach the blessed quarter-mile gap between our houses. Cows graze under a moss-draped live oak. The pasture ends in a snarl of kudzu that has swallowed the fence between our properties. On the other side, my land devolves into brush and swamp. I'm passing the edge when I catch a flash of motion in my backyard.

I freeze, half hidden behind a gnarled cypress. The moment I stop moving, mosquitoes descend, and I swat two before steeling myself against the bites and peeking around the tree trunk.

The first thing I see is the house—a two-story clapboard box with peeling white paint and a crooked front porch. Whatever movement I saw, though, it wasn't at the house. It was in the backyard, which is huge. An acre, according to the local kid who cuts the grass and smirks as he overcharges me. Probably a half acre in reality. Still huge, and it's close enough to that swampy brushland where I spotted an alligator in my yard last month, which is why I'm frozen here, peering into it.

The yard is still and empty.

What had I seen? I struggle to remember as I swat at another mosquito. It'd been well above ground level, whatever it was. Definitely not an alligator. A person? Yes, I'd had the impression of a person moving behind the shed.

I squint at the shed. It's a dilapidated wooden building that looks as if it has served time as a small barn, garden shed, chicken coop and now, in its dotage, a structural eyesore, begging me to put it out of its misery. The only saving grace is that it doesn't sit in the middle of my lawn, howling for release from its rotted bonds.

Whoever cut the lawn before had granted the shed a dignified dotage by not mowing within ten feet of it, that extra space now consumed by long grass. I can barely make out the building. Yet I know it's there, and no matter how often I tell myself it's a charming addition to the property—the sort of rickety rural structure that photographers clamor to capture—all I see is an eyesore.

Right now, though, I see more than an eyesore. I see a place where someone could get within a hundred feet of my back door unseen. That's a chilling prospect for any woman living in the country alone. For me, it could be a death sentence. The only thing that would make my current situation worse is if my past nightmare returned.

If Aaron has finally caught up with me.

At twenty-one, even *thinking* I saw someone in my yard would have sent me running. I wouldn't even have stopped in the house to pack a bag.

By twenty-six, I'd have told myself I was seeing things. I'd have walked into the house, locked the doors, closed the blinds and pretended everything was fine, just fine . . . and then spent the next week sitting awake all night with a gun in my lap.

Thirty-three-year-old
illusion, one that can be
By an email. By an en
for a headstone engrav
credit card.

I hide behind the
ing heart. When I re
blown sprint for the
upstairs. Get the gun
door, gun hidden at

It's a masterful p
from the overgrown
lot slower as I scan for the telltale shift of the
gator." At least the gun will help with that, too.

I pick my way through the overgrown strip until I reach the shed. I circle it once as I listen for any sign of life. None. At the door, I pause and listen again. Still silent.

The door lost its handle years ago, and now a nailed-on piece of rotted wood is all that keeps it from banging in the wind. Or the wood *was* rotted. It isn't now. Yet it's the same rusty nail and the same makeshift design.

Someone replaced the crappy wooden stopper with a slightly less crappy wooden stopper?

I snort at the idea. Clearly, I'd formed a general "rotted wood" impression of the entire shed, which extended to this scrap. It isn't as if I've been out here in the past two months. Who uses a shed surrounded by knee-high Florida swamp grass?

I swing open the makeshift stopper and yank the door. With the rusted hinges, I could barely open it the first time. When the door flies open freely, I stagger back, nearly landing on my ass.

So someone not only replaced the door stopper but oiled the hinges? Nicest hired killer ever.

at's ridiculous, of course. Aaron would
That would take all the fun out of watch-
or my life. Also take all the fun out of killing

ges clearly loosened up after I wrenched it open last
end to the ground, looking for footprints. The problem
ground is hard, and despite the promise of rain, it's been
a week. Even my own sneakers leave no marks on the dirt.
push open the door and use my cell phone light to look inside.
don't expect to see anything. No one would be using the shed in the condition it's in, the interior filled with broken pieces of tools I couldn't even identify the last time. Rusted metal and rotting wood and—

I blink and lean in for a better look. The metal is still there, and the wood, and it's still scattered around, but it looks . . .

As if someone tidied the shed while leaving junk lying about?

I give my head a shake. No one Aaron sends is going to replace the door stopper and oil the hinges and tidy up while leaving junk artfully strewn about to make it *seem* untouched. That's the sort of hired killer Hollywood envisions. Anyone Aaron sent would just hole up in the shed until nightfall, bust in the back door and drag me back to his boss.

No one is here, and no one has been here in a very long time.

I back out, shut the door and peer up at the sky. Black clouds creep inexorably toward me, a stealth storm hidden under cover of bright sunshine.

I peer at the shed again. Then I shake it off. No one is here. No one has been here. The only thing I need to worry about is battening the hatches before the storm strikes.

I take one last look around before heading inside.

TWO

DAISY

Shit, shit, shit! The words pound through my head each time my sneakers smack the road. Well, no, to be honest, it's actually *Ew! Ew! Ew!* complete with schoolgirl squeaks of disgust, but no longer being fifteen, I'll pretend it was the far more age-appropriate *shit.*

And just as I think that, what do I step in? A big ole pile of literal shit—canine—at the side of the road, which has somehow avoided melting in the rain. So now I really do have a reason for my girlish squeaks.

I made the mistake of wearing socks in my sneakers. Both are soaked, and as I run, each foot comes down with water squishing between my toes.

I dart under a cypress and brace one hand against the trunk to pull off my socks and shoes.

Uh, tree? Lightning?

Hey, a bolt of lightning might grant me superpowers. Like the ability to grab the runaway train of my life and thrust it back on track.

I'm working on it.

I sidestep onto the grass, yank off my sneakers and stuff the sopping-wet socks into the toes. Tie the laces. Loop them over my hand, and off I go. So much bet—

A pickup flies past, sheeting me in water, and all I can do is sputter a laugh. Typical. Fix one problem, and the world slam-soaks that split second of accomplishment. Oh well, it's not as if I wasn't drenched already.

I'm about to step back onto the road when I realize the pickup has stopped. The reverse lights flash on. Backing up to apologize? Or to soak me again? Either seems equally likely.

The pickup idles there, the reverse and brake lights candy-cane smudges through the downpour. I squint to see the truck better, but the rain's driving too hard for that. Then both sets of lights go out, and the pickup accelerates, fishtailing in the mud before roaring off.

Okay, that was weird.

I shake it off and hit my own accelerator as I break into a run. My feet crash through puddles, water spraying, rain cascading over me, and it is glorious. The skies have opened and baptized me in a Florida downpour, making me realize how much I've missed this part of the world.

I lived in Florida, once upon a time. Before a tragedy brought our family of four down to three, and then two, as Mom left for Pennsylvania with me in tow. I remember waking in the city one February morning and crying as I looked out at the gray slush. The thunder of highways. The crush of people. The stink of pollution. The endless fields of concrete where once I'd gazed out at orange trees and everglades calling me to adventure.

I swore I'd come home the moment I turned eighteen. The dream of a girl who thinks such things are simple. Then eighteen comes, and that dream bleeds away with all the other childish fantasies. I'll be a veterinarian! I'll own horses and a kennel full of dogs! I'll marry the sweet boy next door and raise children even more adorable than our puppies! By eighteen, I realized that dream was as likely as me becoming a unicorn-riding knight and marrying a handsome prince.

I could have come home to Florida sooner. I should have. This is where I belong, running along a hard-packed dirt road, hot rain soaking my clothing as my face turns upward to meet it. My legs burn, and my pulse races, and I am ten again, running in the downpour as someone on a front porch shouts at me to get out of the rain.

When an actual voice booms, "Get out of the rain, ya damn fool!" I think it's the memory, but then I glance to see a skinny guy on a porch, beer can in hand, a passel of blond children craning to watch the storm.

I wave, and he laughs, and I run faster, and I am home. God, I am finally home.

Tears mingle with the rain. I should have caught that bus at eighteen. Emptied my bank account, bought a ticket and come home. So what if I had an invalid mother counting on me, all her burdens heaped on my shoulders?

My back eventually broke under those burdens. *I* broke. And for what? An obligation I did not owe. But at eighteen, you're in such a damn hurry to grow up that when your mother leans on you for support, it makes you feel strong, mature, recognized. The truth is that it meant nothing except that I was young, naive, malleable.

I veer onto the property. Through the trees, I see the two-story white-clapboard house and imagine it through the eyes of old friends from my suburban life. I haven't seen any of them in a decade, but I still drive by their social-media pages. They're unrecognizable to me now, those girls who'd snickered at their mothers' ordinary lives. They've inherited those lives, their wild dreams corralled by homeowner associations and corporate-cubicle careers.

Those drive-by viewings always leave me unsettled. I could sneer at those old friends trapped in the very lives their teenage selves had railed against. Yet their desperately happy updates cast me into uncomfortable quicksand bordered by relief and sadness and something like longing. I tell myself I don't want their lives . . . but I'm never completely sure I believe it.

If they saw this house, their minds would flip the channel to one of those destroy-and-decorate shows, with rangy men wielding quips and sledgehammers, knocking down walls and ripping out floors, telling themselves they're "fixing it up" when, really, they might as well take a wrecking ball and start anew.

This house doesn't need that. It requires the deft lover's touch of a carpenter who sees the beauty in its craggy old face. Each time I look at it, my fingers twitch like a pianist spotting a grand piano. The keys beneath *my* fingers are sandpaper and sawdust. Not a pianist, then. A plastic surgeon, gazing on this weathered and sagging face and thinking, "I could make you beautiful again."

It looks as if the woman who lives here is already planning a little cosmetic repair, with cheap vinyl siding resting along one wall. I shudder at that—it's the renovation equivalent of plastering on an inch of makeup over bad skin. Address the structural concerns first, and then worry about the cosmetics.

As I circle through the shrubby wetland to the shed, I keep an eye out for anything slithering through the foliage. I follow the path, mud squelching between my toes. It feels like childhood, playing in puddles and mud. I splash through a few patches of both. When a light flicks on upstairs, I duck behind the shed and watch the window. The curtains open, and the woman peers out.

She seems to be looking right at the shed. Did she spot me? Huh. That would be a problem if I were just a squatter in need of shelter. In this situation, though . . . ?

No, this situation is very different, and I won't accomplish my goal by hiding in this shed forever. Time to step from the shadows and say hello.

Soon. Not quite yet. But soon.

CELESTE

The storm didn't strike for nearly two hours after I came inside. I had been working in my second-story office with the window open. Yes, having the window open and the AC blasting is money flapping out into the wind, threatening an electric bill I cannot afford. I'm watching the shed, though, and the open window lets me listen, too.

At first, the black clouds seemed to move on, clear skies chiding me for pouncing on the excuse to abort my run. The sky had been robin's-egg blue and cloudless, the sun ruthless. Then, before I could blink, dark clouds blew through like the wake of a passing jet.

Now rain smacks the old siding, rat-a-tatting like machine-gun fire. I make the mistake of reaching through the open window, and rain hits my wrist so hard it bends backward. I yank my hand in. It's dripping wet. No sign of hail pellets. Just rain.

I peer out as I close the window. The shed squats there, peeling white paint seeming to glow in the darkness.

There's no one in the damned shed. That's what I have been telling myself ever since I came inside. I'm being paranoid. Hell, the entire reason I'm trapped in this "arrangement" is for protection from Aaron. That was the devil's bargain I made with Liam.

Let me take care of you. Aaron will never find you here. I'll give you whatever you need to be comfortable. And you'll have me. That's not such a hardship, is it?

It *hadn't* been a hardship . . . until I realized our arrangement wasn't a decent man protecting his lover. It was a calculating bastard doing what he did best. Controlling and manipulating. Putting me securely under his thumb.

You don't like our arrangement anymore? All right. I won't make you stay. I'm not that kind of guy. Go on. Just run fast. Run fast enough that Aaron won't catch you once I set him on your trail.

The shed is empty. I already established that.

What about the door stopper? The hinges? The tidy interior?

My memory had overexaggerated the poor condition of the shed, that's all.

I'm about to turn back to my laptop when light flickers inside the shed. Breath stops as my chest seizes.

I sit paralyzed in the crosshairs of that open window. Everything in me screams to move. Drop to the floor. Lunge from my chair. Get the hell away from the window. But I cannot move. I don't dare.

It only takes a few heartbeats for the panic to subside under the cold anger of that internal voice telling me to stop being so silly. I thought I saw a light coming through the cracks between boards, but now I see nothing except the pale shape of the shed itself.

Still, when I do move, it is excruciatingly slowly, inching my rolling desk chair to the side until I am behind the faded brown drapes.

Deep breaths. No one is there. Everything is fine. When the rain stops, I'll go out and nail the door shut to be sure I never need to worry about this again.

More deep breaths. I eye my laptop on the desk. I have work to do, but I cannot bring myself to cross in front of that window again.

At least twenty minutes pass before I've chastised myself enough to make the journey back to my desk. Inch by inch again, even as that internal voice sighs and grumbles at me for being such a child.

It's even darker outside now, the storm turning the late afternoon to night. I focus on the pounding of the rain as I move back in front of the window and—

And there is a light in the shed. There is *undeniably* a light.

I stumble off the chair and fall on my ass, pain slamming up my tailbone. When I can blink back the pain, I creep to the desk and take the gun I left beside my laptop. Then I rise on my knees just enough to see out the bottom of the window.

Light glimmers through the cracks in the shed, and there is absolutely no mistaking it for anything else.

Someone is in my shed.

I reach to pull my phone from the desk. Then I scuttle until my back is against the wall. I lift the phone and stop, fingers poised over the numeric pad.

Who am I calling? The police?

It's Celeste. Maeve Turner's granddaughter? I inherited her house a few months ago? Right. Well, um, I hate to bother you, but there's someone in my shed. Could you, um, swing by when you have a chance? Talk to them?

Normally, I would be more direct, but I've learned to dial it down in Fort Exile, where I'm an outsider. Even caring for Maeve on her deathbed hasn't earned me any credit with the locals.

I know how that call will go. They'll point out that it's a storm. Someone probably needed to take shelter for a few hours, and am I really going to roust them out into the rain?

Folks around here are a bit more hospitable, Miz Turner.

Even if I could trust them to help, do I *dare* summon the police? Dare call attention to myself? Dare suggest that there's a reason I'm freaking out over someone "taking shelter" in my shed?

My fingers move to the contact list. To Liam's name.

I pull back as if burned.

Hell, no. This is just what he needs—another excuse to lock my cage even tighter. He's already hinted at having me move in with him. This arrangement suited him fine at first, but I'm becoming a bit too . . . What's the word? Independent. Can't have that, can we?

I don't dare do anything that gives him an excuse to push harder, to exert real pressure, the kind that comes with the vise grip of threat.

I will not call the police, and I absolutely will not call Liam. I'm trying to find a way out of this trap, not ensnare myself more.

I can handle this. I'm not the sixteen-year-old girl who left one nightmare to tumble into another. I'm not the twenty-one-year-old who fled Aaron and cowered in corners for years. I'm the woman who thought I was in control of this situation and, yep, found out otherwise in one hell of a hurry, but I'm also the woman who learns from every mistake and gets better, gets stronger.

I crawl from the window and then march downstairs, where I double-check every lock and close every drape and blind. Then I make a pot of coffee, fill the biggest mug I have and sit on the sofa, gun in hand.

It is going to be a long night.

THREE

DAISY

This is more than a summer rain. It's been raining for hours, with no signs of letting up. There must be a hurricane or tropical storm closer to shore, and we're getting steady rain accompanied by a wind that threatens to send the shed Dorothy-express to Kansas.

I pull a finishing nail from between my teeth and use a rock to pound it in. Then I squint up at the roof. One never truly appreciates the phrase "leaking like a sieve" until one experiences it. I'd done a cursory examination of the roof when I arrived, and it had seemed solid enough, but it seems I missed half a dozen small holes. No matter. I can fix them.

I've been a carpenter since I was seventeen, conned into a Habitat for Humanity project by my suburban friends. They'd quit after a week. I was the one who stayed and discovered a passion.

It wasn't veterinary school, but by then, I knew just how foolish a dream that was for a girl who struggled to get Bs in science. After my mother got sick, those grades plummeted. When graduation came, I clutched my diploma the way others might clutch a doctorate degree.

No veterinary school for me. No college at all. I needed a job that let me care for my mother as cancer dug in its claws and we ran out of belongings to pawn.

Discovering both a talent and a passion for a trade was like fate handing me a gift, more precious even than I realized at the time. No matter what fresh hell life dumped on me, there was always work for a carpenter. Even here in this shed.

I paw through my box of scraps and tools. The wood and nails come from a collapsed tree fort two properties over. A city dweller might have looked at that heap of half-rotted wood and declared it free for the taking. They might even tell themselves they were doing a good deed, hauling off a mess that the owner couldn't be bothered clearing away. Knowing better, I'd assessed the value of the scrap and tucked ten dollars into the owner's mailbox. Those people were not the woman in this house. *They* deserved to be treated fairly.

I select two more rusty finishing nails and give them a quick sanding. Then I use a small hatchet to chop a shingle-sized piece of wood from a chunk of lumber. The hatchet—along with a few other decrepit tools—came from a property where someone had been repairing a fence and left the tools out. They'd been there for years, half-sunk into the earth, which convinced me I could safely borrow them.

I've been fixing leaks all day in hopes of a semidry sleep. Night's falling, and I'm finishing up by the sickly glow of my flashlight. At least I don't need to hide it anymore. The woman knows I'm here. Knows and doesn't give a shit.

That's good, right?

Sure.

Don't tell me you're actually annoyed because she's ignoring you.

Part of me is thrilled that she isn't alarmed enough to even call the police. It is the best possible response, and I will take full advantage of it. As soon as this rain stops, I'll move faster.

I'm about to tap in another nail when something crackles outside the shed. Even as I go still, logic demands I ignore the noise. It's a storm. Of course things are crackling. Lightning. Broken branches. We even had hail earlier.

Still, something about that particular crack isn't right. It sounds like something moving through the undergrowth, twigs cracking in its wake. Except, well, after hours of rain, nothing's dry enough to crackle like that.

There's a rotted spot along one wall, big enough to put my fist through. I have only loosely covered it to leave a peephole. I lift the board and peer out.

Something passes in front of the hole, and I fall back, stifling a yelp. I strain to listen, but all I hear is the pound of rain. I inch back, lift a floorboard and pull out my gun as I keep my gaze trained on the door. Then I crawl back and lift the board again.

Nothing.

I can't see—

Someone steps right in front of the hole. My breath stops, and all I see is denim. One leg of worn blue jeans. Then the squelch of mud under shoes as the leg moves. I side-creep to the door and rise until I'm standing.

Silence.

I glance at the open hole. Through it, I see only the hazy green of distant ferns. Another squelch. Then a creak, and the door moves, boards creaking inward. I hold my breath, gun in both hands. The door moves again. This time, it hits the makeshift stopper I've set up so no one can enter without me knowing it. A solid shove, though, and it'll pop open.

The door creaks. Whoever's out there is testing it. I brace for the slam that'll send it flying open, but all that comes is that creak. Silence. Then the squelch of retreating footsteps.

I count to ten and then ease open the door just enough to see footprints in the mud. Men's prints, at least a size ten. A heavy work boot tread. I slip out to get a better look, only to have them disappear before my eyes, washed away by the rain.

CELESTE

It's dawn, and I have drunk enough coffee that if one of Aaron's goons came crashing through my window, I doubt I could shoot straight enough to even hit him. I've been on this sofa all night, waiting for the doorknob to turn, a window to shatter, even a call on my cell, Aaron's deceptively soft voice telling me to look out my back window. Instead, I've heard nothing but the steady pound of rain and that relentless voice telling me I'm being silly, being *stupid*.

You never were the brightest bulb, were you?

Whose voice is that? Aaron's? Or my mother's? In my memory, the two swim together in a single current that washes over me on nights like this.

Stupid. Weak. Silly. Worthless. Pointless.

Were we wrong? Look at yourself. Spending all night on the couch with a gun because you saw someone taking shelter in your shed during a storm. Because you're convinced that a guy you left twelve years ago still cares enough to want you back.

Pathetic.

No, I'm not deluded enough to think Aaron wants me back. He wants to punish me. I humiliated him, stole from him, and he's killed people for a hell of a lot less.

I have reason to fear, and I need to stifle that voice that says I'm being silly and weak.

I remember those early days with Aaron, when he was still playing savior. Okay, so he wasn't eighteen, as he'd claimed online. Wasn't in college, as he'd also claimed. And his money sure as hell didn't come from rich parents. But he *was* handsome and charming, and he owned his own business . . . if one called drug-dealing a business, which he certainly did, and I did, too, in those early days.

I remember late nights at the kitchen table, helping him with his accounting books—I was always good at math. If I made a mistake, even one I caught myself, I'd fall over myself apologizing, and he'd rub my back and tell me I was doing great.

I'm not your mother, baby girl. I think you're brilliant. Brilliant, gorgeous, and tough as nails.

All the right things to say, at least for a little while. He used to laugh about my mother, ask what she did for a living. High-powered defense attorney, right? Or former military? Maybe a CEO? Some profession that had turned her into such a battle-ax. That made me laugh. My mother was what they'd called, at that time, a home-maker. Gave up her career for her family. Whatever that career had been. I didn't know, but she'd never let me forget that she'd given it up, and for what? A daughter like me? Spoiled and silly and stupid?

But I proved her wrong in the end, didn't I? I did something that made my mother long for that spoiled, silly, stupid girl. I helped kill a girl. That was the story anyway.

I banish the voices that tell me I'm being ridiculous, sitting with this gun on my lap, jittery from mainlining caffeine all night.

There'd been a time, maybe five years ago, with a little extra cash in the bank, that I'd invested in something that would have horrified my mother. I'd gone to therapy.

I'd only been able to afford a few sessions, but I'd found gold there in the kindness of a stranger who, yes, was being paid to be kind, but sometimes, that is still a nugget of gold, sparkling in the dirt.

You know that it was in Aaron's best interests to make you feel small and insignificant. To convince you that you couldn't survive without him. Is it possible your mother did the same? That she needed you to need her? That they both taught you not to trust your own instincts, because it benefited them?

Who did it hurt for me to sit here with a gun on my lap? To stay up all night? I was self-employed as a graphic designer—I didn't have a job to get to in the morning. How much worse would it be if I listened to that mocking voice, went to bed and woke up to one of Aaron's goons looming over my bed *after* I already realized someone was in my shed?

Soon I make breakfast, keeping the gun within reach. It takes another cup of coffee before I work up the nerve to go into the screened back porch and look out. I can see the white shed through the rain, which has let up a little. As I watch, the shed door opens. I snatch up the gun so fast I fumble and drop to one knee catching it.

The shed door stays open, as if someone is looking out, and I bend the other knee until I'm low enough not to be spotted. A head appears. Then a figure holding a partial sheet of plywood up as a makeshift umbrella. For a moment, I have to blink, certain I'm seeing wrong. Knowing Aaron's taste in evil goons, I'm expecting a hulking behemoth, and with that in mind, this figure looks like a child.

It's not a child, though. It's a woman. A young woman, slightly built, wearing a T-shirt and shorts, her feet bare.

The young woman slips out and behind the shed, only to return a few moments later. A bathroom break. In moments, she's back in the shed.

Once that shed door is closed, I rise and head inside to think about what I saw.

I've been working for a couple of hours when the phone rings.

"Hey," Liam says when I answer. "Just checking to see how you're holding up. Storm hitting hard there?"

I answer in kind, playing the role of girlfriend, even with no one around to observe the performance. That's what men like Liam expect. He's not some lowlife drug dealer. He's a lawyer, damn it. A respected and respectable member of the community. If he's inclined to treat me like a real girlfriend, then I'd damn well better appreciate that and respond accordingly.

The worst of it is that Liam isn't just expecting me to play a role. He really does consider me his girlfriend. He takes me to work functions, sends me flowers, acts as if it's a normal relationship. That's how he sucked me in at first. Compared to what I was used to, it seemed normal. *He* seemed normal.

"How about I come by after work?" he says. "Bring dinner. We can hang out, watch a movie, weather the storm together."

It sounds like a suggestion rather than a demand. I know better, but as long as he's phrasing it as optional . . .

"Another time?" I say. "It sounds awesome, but I had a rough night, and I'm running on half power today. I expect to be hanging out with my laptop into the wee hours."

"Then we'll just make it dinner."

Dinner and sex, he means. Also, a movie and sleepover, if he decides that's what he wants. Normally, I'd give in. This isn't worth the fight. But if he comes over, he could see the girl in the shed, and he's not going to just ignore her. He might invite her in for dinner because it would amuse him.

"I wish I could," I say, managing something akin to genuine regret. "But I'm really feeling off. I don't think I could stomach dinner."

"It's ten in the morning. You can't possibly know how you'll feel by dinnertime."

"I just—"

"I want to come over. Tonight."

"I just—"

"Is this really the choice you want to make today, Celeste? Think about it. I'll give you a minute."

"Yes, it's the choice I want to make, Liam. Not tonight."

"You have a headache?"

His tone has changed. It's deceptively light, almost teasing.

"Yes, actually, I do have a headache, but that's not why I'm saying no. I'm tired and under deadline, and I'm asking for a night to myself. I'll make it up to you."

"I know you will."

I try not to grind my teeth. "May I have the evening off, Liam? Please?"

"You may, Celeste. I need to head to Miami for a couple of days next week. I was going to invite you along, but you're obviously busy."

"Miami?"

He laughs, pleased by my feigned dismay. I roll my eyes. I have no interest in going to Miami. I'll appreciate the time to myself so much more. But I know how to play this game.

"Too late," he says cheerfully. "You missed your chance. I'll see you when I get back."

"All right," I say with an audible sigh. "I really do need to work, so I suppose it's for the best."

"And you'll make it up to me next weekend."

"I will."

"Oh, that wasn't a question, Celeste. Not a question at all."

He hangs up, and I'm left looking down at my phone. The urge to run slams through me, but I stifle it.

No more running. This is my home. My house. My job. I could finally have a place in the world, and the only thing standing in my way is Liam, holding a guillotine blade over my head. He is the keeper of my secrets—all my secrets. He *owns* me.

I have two options. Run from the threat or eliminate it. I am tired of running.

I sit at the window, watching the shed and thinking. After about a half hour, the door opens again. The girl taking another bathroom break.

The more I think about the girl, the more I have to wonder what prompts a young woman to sleep in a shed. She looked like a backpacker. A modern-day hippie. What would make someone decide to backpack by herself through rural central Florida? Is it a choice? Or one of those situations where you pretend it's a choice, to hide the truth that you've run out of choices, that you're alone and desperate.

How desperate might this girl be? How *alone*?

An idea plants itself in my brain. It is a grublike thing, barely pushing from the earth. It needs more to grow. More time. More data.

It is possible, just possible, that this girl is a gift from an indifferent god. An answer to my prayers. I need to get free from Liam, and this girl might be my way to do it.

FOUR

DAISY

I'm tacking up another piece of wood when a shriek cuts through the steady pound of rain. I drop the hammer, which manages to hit both my elbow and knee on the way down. I barely slept last night after that intruder outside my door. I told myself it was just a local poking around. The excuse would make a lot more sense without the torrential downpour.

I ease open the door and peer in the direction of the cry. Movement flickers near the house, but that's all I see.

"Help! Anybody? Help!" a voice shouts.

I shake my head. *Anybody?* The nearest neighbor is a quarter mile away. The only person who is going to hear her cry is me.

From the sound of the shout, the matter is of medium urgency, somewhere between "Help, I've skinned my knee" and "Help, I am currently on fire." No need to race out in my only dry shirt, then. I switch to the still-wet yellow one.

I dash into the yard to see the woman on the lanai roof, waving her arms as if signaling passing aircraft.

I jog across the lawn, yelling, "You okay?" The first time, a blast of wind whips my words away, and I have to shout again. When I do, she gestures to the side, where I spot a fallen ladder. She pulls an "I feel so silly" face, and I laugh.

I'm not laughing at the self-deprecation, though. I'm laughing at her predicament . . . or lack thereof. She's on a sturdy lanai roof, the edge barely six feet off the ground. She could dangle and drop onto rain-soft earth. As emergencies go, this one lands alongside "Help, I've skinned my knee."

Still, I run over, resurrect the ladder and hold it steady as she descends. Then, without a word, she jackrabbits through the back door, leaving me staring before she reopens the door and beckons for me to follow.

I step halfway into the lanai and hesitate. She's grabbed a beach towel from a stack, and she's drying her dark-blond hair. When she sees me, she waves again.

"Come in, come in."

I take exactly one stride, shut the door and then stand there as rainwater pools around my bare feet. When she notices, she tosses me a towel, repeating her singsong "Come in, come in" of welcome.

Am I welcome? I'm not so sure. After I ran to her aid, she can hardly leave me in the rain. However . . .

I do need to get into the house. To get close to her. To gain the woman's trust. This isn't quite how I planned it, but it could work.

I towel-dry my hair as she strips out of her tank top and shorts. With a shudder, she steps free of the wet garments and envelops herself in a fresh towel. She turns to me, and I sincerely hope she doesn't expect me to follow suit. I'm already feeling vulnerable here.

She hands me a second towel and then scoops up her soaked clothing, saying, "I'll find something for you to wear, and we'll get that dried for you," as if I am a neighbor who stopped by to help.

She disappears into the house, and I wait. I'm still waiting ten minutes later, my teeth chattering as AC blasts through an open window.

I sponge off my face, which is a mistake. The threadbare towels smell as if they've been in the lanai since the turn of the century. Still, I'm about to borrow a couple and make a run for the shed when the door opens, and she walks out, smiling breezily.

She passes me a sweatshirt and shorts that look as old as the towels. I take them with thanks. When I hesitate, she laughs and turns around. Feeling like that girl in gym class who changes in the bathroom stall, I strip and pull on the dry clothes as fast as I can.

When I finish and clear my throat, she turns and puts out a hand. I shake it, and she laughs again.

"I was reaching for your clothing, but yes, we should introduce ourselves. I'm Celeste."

"Daisy," I say.

As I gather my wet things, I take a better look at Celeste. Dark-blond hair. Hazel eyes. She's a few years older than me. An inch or so taller. Maybe thirty pounds heavier, with a generous figure in a tank top and shorts.

"Would you like something to eat, Daisy?" she asks.

My spine crackles as I tense. Celeste isn't offering coffee or iced tea, like a proper southern hostess. This is charity, and it knifes through me.

Uh, you are sleeping in her shed, remember?

True. I force my hackles down and murmur, "No, thank you. If I could dry my things, I would appreciate that. Then I'll get out of your hair."

Her lips twitch. "Dry them so you can run back into the rain?"

"I'd take a spare umbrella, if you have it. I'll return it, of course. A garbage bag will work, too."

"You rescued me. I'm not sending you back into that storm." She walks into the kitchen. Again, when I don't follow, she gives an impatient wave, as if I'm a not-too-bright puppy.

Celeste hits the button on the coffee maker. Then she opens the fridge door and pulls out a Tupperware container, which goes into the microwave.

"What were you doing up there, anyway?" I ask.

"Trying to fix a leak."

I choose my words with care, making sure my tone is free of anything that could be interpreted as sarcasm. "You probably need to go onto the house roof for that. Not the porch one."

Celeste sighs. "I realized that once I was up there. The leak is in the wall, so I thought it was a hole there. Can you tell I'm not an architect?"

"It's the roof leaking down the wall. Either way, you won't want to be fixing it in the rain. If there's an attic, you can temporarily repair it from the inside. That's what I was doing in the shed."

Which leads to the elephant in the room that she cannot ignore, so I plow on with, "I've been staying there. I'm sorry to trespass. I thought the house was empty."

I settle onto a kitchenette chair. "Someone over in Sun City mentioned this place. They said the old woman who lived here passed away and left the house to a granddaughter who lived out of state. I'm guessing that's you?"

"It is. No longer living out of state."

I nod. "I've been making my way across Florida, and I figured I'd see if that old woman's house had a barn or a shed I could hole up in. I didn't notice the lights on in the house until the storm hit."

Celeste smiles. "Well, thank you for choosing the shed instead of the house."

"I wouldn't have done that," I say evenly. "I realize I'm trespassing, but it was an emergency. I just needed a roof over my head."

Awkward silence stretches until the microwave dings, and Celeste busies herself taking out what smells like lasagna.

"I've been repairing the shed," I say. "That's no excuse for trespassing, but I wanted to give something in return. I'll be gone as soon as the rain clears."

Celeste scoops the Tupperware contents—yes, it's lasagna—onto a plate and puts it in front of me. Then she pours two cups of coffee and passes me one. I take it with sincere thanks.

"I could fix the roof leak, too," I say as I cut into the food. There's a slight chemical smell that tells me, despite the Tupperware, it's not homemade. It's hot and it's free, though, so I take a big bite before continuing, "I've worked construction for years. No pressure, of course. I'm not looking for an excuse to stay."

"If you could look at the leak, that would be lovely, thank you."

I resist the urge to smile, and dig into my meal.

CELESTE

The woman from the shed has a name. Daisy. I almost laughed when she said that. Do people still name their kids Daisy? In truth, though, the name suits her, and I don't mean that in a bitchy way. It's a crunchy granola kind of name, perfect for a woman who sleeps in sheds as she makes her way . . . across the state, she said? Hoping to "find herself" on the open road? Or fleeing those poor life choices I know so well? That isn't a first-conversation question. I'll get to it soon enough.

Data. I need so much data. Like evaluating a candidate for a job. A role I need filled.

When she offers to fix my roof leak, I realize that poses the small problem of not actually having a leak to fix. But I can remedy that, and if she's done construction, as she says, that opens up a bigger possibility. An excuse for having her stick around for a few days.

"I'll start tomorrow then," she says when I agree to have her look at the leak. "What tools do you have here?"

"The basics are in the basement crawlspace," I say. "My grandfather's, I guess."

"Or your grandmother's," she says with a smile. She sips her coffee and looks around. "It's a nice old house."

"Needs a lot of work," I say and immediately want to smack myself. Too fast.

Fortunately, she doesn't seize the opening and only says, "Old places always need work. Florida might not have winter weather, but the elements can be tough on places like this. They weren't built to last centuries."

"You're a Floridian?" I ask.

"Once upon a time. My family moved when I was young. I haven't been back in years. So this was your grandmother's house?"

I nod. "I came back last fall for a visit that turned into something more."

I pull out a chair and sit, coffee in hand. I take a moment to shove past the wall that warns against sharing data. I must open up if I expect her to do the same.

"I don't know if you have any experience with elderly relatives," I say. "I didn't. I hadn't seen my grandmother in years—family squabble—and I wanted to reconnect. I foolishly imagined her as one of the snowbirds over in Sun City, darting about in the golf carts, soaking up the sun in an active retirement. Not exactly what I found."

"She was in ill health," Daisy says. "That's what I heard at the diner."

"She'd lost most of her sight. Untreated glaucoma. By the time I got here, it'd progressed too far for surgery, and she had too many other issues to risk it. Unmanaged diabetes, high blood pressure, arthritis . . . Luckily, I'm self-employed, so staying wasn't a hardship."

"That was good timing for your gran," Daisy says. "Not just getting help, but getting a chance to know you again."

I relax into my seat. "Yes, and even better, I got a chance to know *her*. She was a tough old bird. Lived here alone ever since my grandfather died. I don't even remember him. I barely remember her, to be honest. But I'm glad we had the opportunity to reconnect. She was a remarkable person."

"She sounds like it," Daisy murmurs.

"She had deep roots here. That's why she wouldn't move to Sun City. That and the expense, which is one more reason I wish we'd kept in touch. I could have helped."

There, that should be enough. I inwardly sag with relief, as if I've been standing naked on a firing range.

"It must have been difficult," Daisy says.

I shrug. "She was my grandmother. I owed her that much, and I was happy to be there."

She rises, dishes in hand, glancing around for a dishwasher. Before I can say there isn't one, she rinses her plate and mug and puts them in the stack of unwashed dishes.

"May I see the leak?" she asks. "I'll fix it while my clothing dries. Then I can leave you alone." A glance at the window. "It'll be getting dark soon."

"Then the leak will need to wait until tomorrow," I say. "The attic is a disaster. I swear Gran hasn't gotten rid of anything in fifty years. That's why I hoped to fix the leak from the outside. I'll need to clear a path for you."

"We'll wait for morning. Hopefully, the rain will stop by then, and I can climb onto the roof and do a proper job of it. Is it all right if I borrow this clothing and an umbrella?"

"Force you out for another night in this storm?" I give what I hope is a hearty—and not false *at all*—laugh. "What kind of person would that make me?"

"It's all right. I've fixed the leaks, so the shed's dry."

Her gaze darts toward the door, as if she's eager to be gone. I hesitate. I need to get to know her better, but I don't want her staying in my den. Maybe just a token protest, positioning myself as a good person, before accepting her next refusal.

"No, no," I say. "You must stay. Especially if you're going to help me fix *my* leak."

Daisy hesitates. "I wouldn't mind sleeping in the lanai, if you were okay with that."

"The . . . ?"

She smiles. "The screened porch. That's one thing I recall from my Florida days. They call them lanais."

Perfect. I can get to know her better while not actually having her in the house.

"If you're sure . . ."

"I am. Thank you."

I lift my coffee mug to my lips to hide my smile.

FIVE

DAISY

Well, this is awkward.

Celeste has gone upstairs without a word, leaving me on the main level. Am I supposed to head into the lanai now? If so, she could have subtly herded me that way.

I'd offered to wash dishes, and she went upstairs, and it's been long enough for me to realize that she's not coming back. Does she expect me to just retreat when I'm done with the dishes?

Weird and awkward.

Let's face it, this whole thing is weird and awkward, and if I really was just passing through, I'd hightail it back to my shed. But while staying in the house wasn't what I had in mind, it is useful.

Useful and dangerous.

Damn.

I look around. It's a proper country kitchen with plenty of room for cooking and preserving and parties that stretch into the night.

I swear I can hear echoes of the past, voices getting loud with drink and laughter, cards slapping on the table, the room filling with humid night air and the smell of late-night fried chicken.

I run my fingers over the chair back, worn smooth by decades of touch. There isn't an appliance or a piece of furniture here that isn't older than me. Same goes for the wallpaper, lemon-bright yellow faded to a muddy mustard and stinking of cigarette smoke. A sunny yellow rectangle and empty nail shows where a calendar must have hung for years.

I tiptoe into the living room and look around. The basement door beckons, but there will be time and opportunity for that. Celeste mentioned the house needing repairs, which it obviously does. I resisted the urge to offer help. Too soon. Too suspicious.

I have things to do here. Plans to set in motion. I need a bit of time, though, to adjust to this new situation. To make the best possible use of being in the house, with access to my target.

My gaze strays to the sofa and armchair. Both are ancient, their fabric worn shiny. They're as misshapen and spring-shattered as walk-in medical clinic furnishings, but I've been sleeping on the ground, and my knees weaken at the thought of stretching out on that sofa.

And you will be just as comfortable on the lanai lounger, without the fear of Celeste looking at you like you're a transient leaning against her car.

True enough. I walk to a crooked bookshelf devoted to things other than books. Celeste has piled papers and unopened mail between the dusty knickknacks. I touch a plastic cat, smiling as I lever its tail, making its eyes move back and forth. Letters lean against it, and my play dislodges one addressed to Ms. Celeste Turner. As I return it, I thumb through the others in the stack. Junk mail, mostly addressed to Maeve Turner.

A creak sounds overhead. I drop to one knee, so if she comes down, she'll see I'm just checking out the books. There's only that one creak, though. Then all goes silent.

I scan the single row of books. Half are old historical romances, and I pull out one showing a windswept redhead in the arms of a shirtless kilted man. I imagine curling up on that lumpy sofa with a yellowed paperback that smells of mildew and cigarettes, losing myself in the tale of a dashing Highlander and his spirited, reluctant bride. Memories of my own youth wash over me, whipping through pages of books like this, pulse racing as my eyes widened at the hidden delights.

I move along the shelf to a small collection of children's classics. My smile widens as I tug out a copy of *Black Beauty* with a cover that has very clearly been gnawed by tiny toddler teeth. Crayon scribbles decorate the first pages. Then, in painstakingly careful letters: "Property of Celeste Turner." The penciled words actually say: "Propurte of CeCe Turnr," but someone has used a pen to correct it.

The doorbell rings, and I topple backward, book flying to the floor. The chime box is right over my head, and the jingle rings like a brass bell at my ear. I grab the book and rise as I wait for Celeste to come down the stairs. I'll ask to borrow it before I retreat and leave her with her guest.

Instead, the bell sounds again, and as I turn, I realize I'm in the sightline of the front-door window. A man stands on the other side.

An image flashes. The man outside the shed in the storm. A denim-clad leg, and boot tracks in the mud.

The man smiles and waves. The upstairs toilet flushes. Damn. I shouldn't answer Celeste's door, but I can hardly flee while this guy is looking straight at me.

I open the door, chain engaged.

"Hello?" I say.

The guy is around forty with silver-templed dark hair. Handsome. Dark-blue eyes and a trim build. One glance tells me he knows Celeste—he looks equally out of place here with his pressed trousers and golf shirt and blazing white smile.

"Hey, there," he says. "Is Celeste around?"

The bathroom door finally creaks open above, and her shoes *tap-tap* toward the stairs. She sees the door still chained and waves for me to open it.

"Sorry," I murmur. "I was just—"

"—being safe," she says, and she waggles a finger at the man as he enters. "As well you should with this one." She kisses his cheek. "I thought you weren't coming over today."

"Surprise!" He spreads his hands.

My skin creeps as he gives that too hearty laugh.

He isn't a smarmy, stereotypical used-car-salesman guy. He's something worse. Polished and affluent, reeking of designer aftershave and razor-honed charisma. A used-car salesman can only sell you a lemon. This guy can convince you to empty your 401(k), mortgage your house and max out your credit to invest in his scheme. After all, he drives a luxury car and has an uptown office address. What can possibly go wrong?

I realize I'm assigning a personality type based on a thirty-second acquaintance, but he reminds me too much of my stepfather, and I can still see my mother's face when she first told me about him. "He works in an *office*," she breathed, the way others might say, "He's a cardiac surgeon."

Mom never graduated high school. Pregnant and married at eighteen to a guy who put more heroin in his arms than food on the table. A cheerful, scattered boy, endlessly caught up in whatever dumbass criminal enterprise his friends talked him into. After the tragedy, she took me north and met Keith, a pharmaceutical rep with a closet of suits, a corporate office and a BMW. She thought her suffering had been rewarded. Instead, it'd only just begun.

I murmur something unintelligible to Celeste, lift the book to show I'm taking it and start for the back door.

"Am I going to get an introduction?" the man calls after me.

I turn with what I hope looks like a genuine smile. "Sorry. I just didn't want to interrupt." I put out a hand. "Daisy."

His brows arch. "Like the flower?"

I laugh softly. "I wish. My parents named me after the *Dukes of Hazzard* character. I think Dad liked her short shorts. It was nice to meet you. I'll just slip out—"

"Liam," he says, walking to me with a hand extended. "We forgot that part. I'm Liam Garey."

I smile and shake his hand, and before I can escape, he says, "So you're local?"

Before I can answer, Celeste smoothly cuts in. "Daisy is hiking across the state. She took refuge in that old shed out back. I invited her to wait it out in the screened porch."

Liam's brows arch. "The lanai? Why not the spare bedroom?"

Celeste tenses. She tries to hide the reaction, but I see it, and I don't blame her for it. There's something in Liam's tone that makes my hackles rise.

"I prefer the lanai," I say quickly. "I appreciate the hospitality. You two have a good night, and we'll discuss that leak tomorrow."

"Leak?" he repeats.

Celeste waves it off. "You know this old house. Nothing but problems. Good night, Daisy, and if there's anything you need, help yourself."

My gaze slides to an old blanket on the sofa. She snatches it up with "Absolutely. Take this."

"I'm sure we can do better than that, Celeste," Liam says.

The use of *we* makes my hackles prickle again. That plural is presumptive and territorial. But Celeste only promises to bring me a pillow and other bedding later.

I thank her and escape as fast as I can.

CELESTE

"Inviting strangers into your house now?" Liam murmurs as the back door shuts behind Daisy. "You are a woman of hidden depths."

I resist the urge to say—again—that he agreed not to come over. Once is enough. He's in a good mood, and it's in my best interests not to spoil it. So I just roll my eyes and continue up the stairs. His laugh follows me, echoed by his footfalls.

At the top, he grabs me, still laughing as he pulls me in for a kiss.

"Let me guess," he says, nuzzling my neck. "She's your secret lover, clumsily passed off as . . . What was the story? A hitchhiker crossing the country?"

"A hiker crossing the state. And I'm tempted to say, 'Yes, you've guessed correctly,' just to see your reaction."

He laughs and takes my hand, leading me to my room.

See, just an ordinary couple goofing around. Nothing to see here. Nothing at all.

I tell Liam about my leaking roof and Daisy's rescue. He is as amused as I expected, his blue eyes dancing at my apparent predicament.

"So now you're stuck with her in your lanai," he says.

"Better than the spare room."

He takes off his shoes and stretches out on the bed. "I knew she wouldn't accept. She's a timid rabbit, couldn't wait to bolt. What do you know about her?"

I shrug. "Not much. I don't dare ask. If she tells me a tale of woe, I'm liable to offer her a job fixing up the house." At his look, I say, "She's a construction worker."

"That little thing?" He looks over at the broken window screen. "Still, it wouldn't be a bad idea, hiring someone like that to fix up the house. Cheap reno. And a temporary lodger. That would be safer, living out here."

How thoughtful of you to suggest it, Liam. Remember now, it was all your idea.

"I'll consider it," I say as he pulls me down onto the bed.

DAISY

I wake in tears. Or that's what it seems as I startle awake to find my pillow damp. Then a warm drop falls on my cheek, and I look up to see a rivulet running down the angled lanai roof. Another leak. I still check my eyes to be sure it's not really tears. I wouldn't be surprised—too many memories resurrected, too many regrets for all the things I didn't do when they needed to be done.

Plink. A drop hits me square in the eye. I sigh and rise to move the lounge chair. As I do, my back crackles. I rub stiff muscles and grimace. Two nights of sleeping on the ground, and when does my body complain? When it actually gets a bed.

Except it's not a bed. It's a lounge chair that had looked fine from a distance. Up close, it became clear that my hostess is not the sort to drag a chair into the yard and soak up a few rays. I'd used a damp towel to clean the brittle plastic weave, only to have it crumble under my touch. She'd provided two blankets, and I'd lain between them, my head resting on a pillow so flat it could slide off the lounger and I'd never notice.

I do a few stretches as I contemplate the possibility of sleeping on the floor. Yeah, no. Even two blankets won't muffle the damp cold of concrete. I lift my face and listen to the pound of rain. Darting back to my shed would be a whole lot more appealing if I wouldn't get soaked.

I rise, rolling my shoulders, and realize I could use a trip to the toilet. Which is mostly just an excuse to grab another living room blanket. If I set my watch alarm, I can return the extras before Celeste notices.

I walk to the door, turn the knob and . . .

It's locked.

Well, damn. I don't actually need to use the bathroom that badly, but now I'm annoyed that I can't. No, let's be honest, I'm annoyed that she felt the need to lock that door. It's not as if she's alone in the house. Last I saw, Liam's Land Rover was still in the drive, suggesting he was spending the night.

I grumble under my breath and move to the window, shading it to measure the distance to the shed. When I see a bobbing light, I squint, struggling to see through a rusted screen and rain-streaked glass.

Someone's moving fast through the thick trees, circling the house. My hand clenches reflexively, reaching for the gun I keep under my sleeping bag. The sleeping bag—and gun—that I've left in the shed.

I glance around for a weapon. There's an old spade in the corner, trussed to the wall by spiderwebs. I slip over and shake it loose, only to have ancient dirt spatter my feet.

I heft the spade as I follow the light through the trees. It's the bluish glow of a cell phone. I move as close as I dare to the window. At first, I see only a figure. Then I notice a tan jacket held over a head, the cell phone light glowing beneath it.

Breaking into a house with a cell phone for light . . . during a tropical storm. Not exactly a world-class thief. Still, this *is* the state of the greatest superhero who ever lived: Florida Man. Skim any newspaper across the nation, and you'll find tales of his exploits. "Florida Man Charged with Assault after Throwing Alligator through Drive-Thru Window." "Florida Man Robs Store Wearing Transparent Bag on His Head." "Florida Man Gets Tired of Waiting at Hospital and Steals Ambulance to Drive Home." When it comes to criminals, Florida breeds them unique.

In defense of my native state, I'll point out that part of the blame lies with the open-records laws, where nothing is held back in a criminal incident, leaving all the weirdness as fodder for enterprising headline writers. But this is still the land of guys—and gals—who get drunk and wrestle wild alligators on a dare.

As I watch, the figure slows near my shed. When he glances toward the house, I stop breathing and resist the urge to backpedal. I'm safe here in the dark.

The man's gaze skips, almost incidentally, over the yard, confident that he won't be seen. Then he ducks into my shed.

I remember the guy outside my shed last night. It must be the same one. This time, though, I'm not trapped in there, at his mercy.

I'm going to get a better look.

I ease open the back door. It's pouring rain and pitch black, and all I can see is the moving glow of that cell phone.

Wait. It's dark because the porch lights are off, yet they'd been on when I went to bed. I know because I'd had to flip over to find darkness. Then I'd woken after midnight, and they'd still been on. Yet they're out now.

Someone inside the house turned out the porch light, setting the stage for a nighttime shed invasion. I can make out the jacket now. It's the tan overcoat Liam was wearing when he arrived.

Hello, Liam.

What are you doing in my shed?

What has you out there in the rain? In the middle of the night?

Only it's not *my* shed. It's his girlfriend's. Celeste may have asked him to take a look and check my story.

I've hidden the gun well. I'm always careful about that.

I run through the list of what Liam is likely to find there. The answer is "nothing important." I've traveled light, carrying only the essentials that will suggest I am exactly what I pretend to be.

Liam spends at least fifteen minutes searching, and I grit my teeth, imagining him pawing through my belongings, through my clothing.

Memories flash, and they don't stop flashing. I blame this place. Being back in the state my mother fled, determined to start over, only to tumble down a rabbit hole too dark for her to see that she wasn't the only one suffering.

She'd suffered with my father, too. As much as I loved him, I don't deny that. Battling one's demons is a cliché, but when I first read those words, I pictured my father locked in mortal combat with the drugs and the poverty that ruled his life. Yet in my mind, he didn't fight to save himself. He fought to save my mother and me, to give us a better life. He tried. God, how he tried. He loved me and protected me, and I never really realized just how much until we left him and I was alone with Mom and with Keith.

Cracks in the shed walls glow blue with the light of Liam's cell phone, and in my memory, I'm fourteen, in my bedroom watching a flashlight bob around my backyard playhouse.

I slipped out armed with a kitchen knife only to find Keith pawing through my box of treasures—the glossy shells and cheap jewelry and pretty rocks strewn over my playhouse floor.

I stormed in, seething with righteous fury. "What are you doing? That's mine."

"If it's on my property, missy, it's mine. You're too old for playhouses, and I intend to find out what you're doing in here. Your mother is worried. After your dope-fiend father—"

"I have never even smoked weed. Test me if you're worried. I'm clean. Always."

He shrugged. "What's bred in the bone . . ."

I didn't understand what he meant, but I stiffened and said coldly, "I come here for privacy. That's all."

He fished out a romance novel with a clinching couple on the front. My cheeks burned as he flipped through, pausing to chuckle at the dog-eared pages.

"Well, well," he said, "our little girl really is growing up."

"That's Blaire's. She borrowed it from her mom."

He lifted his flashlight to one of the pages and began reading aloud. With every word, my cheeks flamed hotter.

"Curious little thing, aren't you?" he said.

"It's Blaire's. Those are her marked pages." True. "I skip them." Not true.

"It's natural to be curious," he said.

I didn't answer. My favorite teacher—Ms. Nanak—had caught me reading one of those books, and she'd said the same thing. When she'd said it, though, it'd been reassuring, making me feel like just a normal girl, normally curious. We'd had a long talk about how both boys and girls are curious, but it's only considered "natural" for boys. Here was Keith saying the exact same words, and yet it made my fingers tighten on the knife.

"Are you curious, peanut?" he asked. "You don't need to be ashamed of it."

I said nothing. If there is such a thing as a female instinct, it screamed that no good would come of any answer I made.

He set down the book and laid a hand on it, almost reverently. "If you have questions, I'm here for you."

My whole body twanged, a bowstring ready to snap. I wanted to run, and I also didn't want to run—I wanted to brandish the knife and show him all the ways I wasn't my mother. If he laid a finger on me, he'd lose it.

But that voice kept whispering in my ear, telling me again that I was doing the right thing by standing firm and saying nothing. *Wait it out.*

That's what I did, all those years ago. Waited it out and then walked back into the house, shoved a chair under my door handle and went to sleep with the knife beneath my pillow.

Now I'm watching that blue glow bob around the dilapidated shed, and I tell myself this is not Keith. I am not fourteen. I am not helpless.

That reassurance, though, doesn't keep me from imagining Liam pawing through my underwear, as Keith used to under the guise of doing the laundry for Mom. He'd gather a basket with my bras and panties displayed on top and bring it to my room and sometimes hold up a piece and tell me that I needed to replace it, that I'd obviously outgrown it. Just being helpful.

By the time the blue light bounces from the shed, I'm white-knuckling the spade handle. I watch the light as it circles the house. Then the old house shudders as the front door snaps shut, leaving zero doubt who was out there.

SIX

CELESTE

There are two dreams set on perpetual pause in my subconscious, the Play button waiting to be pressed whenever my life hits a moment of upheaval and stress.

You think what's happening right now is bad? That's nothing. Remember this?

I am sixteen, waking on a Sunday morning to the sensation that someone is in my room. I startle up and see my mother in my doorway. She orders me out of bed. I'm past the age of obeying without at least a snarky comment, but that morning, I'm too sleepy to argue. I roll out of bed, and then, with the unreality of dreams, I'm already downstairs in the living room, where two uniformed officers wait.

"Where were you last night?" the female officer asks. In the dream, they are amorphous shapes, distinguishable only by a male and a female voice.

"Uh . . ." I blink. I'm still in the doorway. No one has asked me to come in and sit down.

"She was out with her *friends*." Mom twists that last word, contempt dripping. "She got in after we'd gone to bed."

No, I was back by ten. My parents had been in the living room with the neighbors. I try to say that, but the words won't come. They don't come because they won't help. In the real version, I *had* argued. I'd pleaded with my mother to remember seeing or hearing me. If she hadn't noticed me come in, she could have pretended. She did not.

"Tell us about your evening," the female officer says. "You were out with friends between what hours? And what did you do?"

Nothing. I did nothing.

That was the problem, wasn't it?

Someone laughs across the room. With a start, I turn to see my friends at our kitchen table, Starbucks cups in hand. I glance quickly at my mother and the officers, but they don't see them.

I stare at the trio. Three girls whose names I no longer even remember, but they'd been so important to me then. My new friends, the popular clique who'd seen fit to admit me when Denny Lamar said I'd come back from summer "hot."

Now they're at my kitchen table, which isn't my kitchen table at all. It's our regular corner spot at Starbucks. They're bored and shit-posting on a school message board about their current favorite voodoo doll, a girl named Jasmine Oleas. I wasn't into it. By no means did I defend this poor girl. I just didn't see the point in tormenting someone like Jasmine, whose only "crime" was being poor and bused into our school on a scholarship.

"Hey, you," one of the girls says, waving across the room at me. "You're in two of her classes. Are there any guys she likes?"

I should shake my head. I *want* to shake my head. Instead, I call over to them, saying, "Brad Moore."

"Seriously? That geek?"

I shrug. "He's nice to her."

"Post something about Brad," one says to the girl with the phone. "No, post it *from* Brad. About her."

"No!" the third says. "Text Jasmine. Pretend to be him."

Beside me, the female officer asks, "Do you know a girl named Jasmine Oleas?"

My friends keep chattering at the table. They're asking Jasmine to meet Brad. She agrees, and they set up the meet on the old pier, the one where kids used to hang out until the cops blocked it off.

"Do you know a girl named Jasmine Oleas?" the officer asks again, in the same tone, as if on a loop.

"Sure, she's in my algebra and chem classes. I don't know her well, but she seems nice."

The male officer turns to face the girls at the table, who keep chattering and texting. He speaks in droning recitation, as if he's on a true-crime show. "At 11:14 last night, police received a call. A witness reported seeing a group of girls on the old pier. According to the witness, it seemed to be some kind of hazing ritual. Three or four girls tormenting another one. We responded to find the pier empty. Two hours later, Mrs. Oleas reported her daughter missing. Mrs. Oleas had gone into Jasmine's room at midnight and found it empty. Calls to Jasmine's phone went unanswered." He pauses there, and I wait, unable to breathe. "At 5:11 a.m., we pulled Jasmine Oleas's body from the water cove."

In reality, I'd freaked out. In the dream, I stand motionless, as if on trial.

The male officer continues his TV-show recitation to my three friends, who are still giggling at the table. "Her mother says she was being bullied by four classmates. These four." He points to the three girls at the table and then at me. "We found her cell phone, and we traced those calls to one young woman's phone.

We believe these four lured Jasmine to the pier by pretending to be a boy she liked."

I open my mouth to protest that I wasn't there. Nothing comes out.

The officer continues, "The coroner's preliminary report says someone held Jasmine's head underwater. These four girls lured her out there, and then killed her."

The spell breaks. I spin on my mom. "I was in by ten. Tell them."

She just stares at me, and in that stare, I know what she's thinking. What she's already decided. That I did this. I helped kill this girl.

The male officer continues his droning report. "Witnesses place the four teenage girls at that Starbucks until 9:30 p.m. They can identify all four girls. They saw them climb into a car and leave together. That same car was seen parked near the beach an hour later."

"But I wasn't with them. They dropped me off at home." I turn to my mother one last time. "Mom, please. You *must* have heard me come in. Or Dad did. Or one of the neighbors."

"I told you not to hang out with those girls. I told you they would get you into trouble."

"I wasn't there!" My voice rises to a wail. "I swear it. I was here, in my bed!"

Mom turns to the officers. "My daughter was not responsible for this poor girl's death."

My breath catches, heart fluttering with hope.

Mom continues, "My daughter is a follower, not a leader. She's easily led. Easily manipulated. If she was there, it was as an observer only."

I stare at her, open mouthed. "Mom?"

"We're going to need to take your daughter down to the station for further questioning," the male officer says.

"Of course." Mom rises. "I presume I should contact our lawyer?"

"Mom?"

"We aren't quite at that point yet," the female officer says. "But yes, that is your right."

She walks past me. Straight past me, her gaze ahead, as tears pour down my cheeks, and I'm left whispering, "Mom?" like a little girl, as she continues on into the next room.

I bolt awake, my face damp with tears. That last moment—the one when my mother gave up on me for good—lingers, making me struggle for breath.

I'd been accused of helping murder a girl, and nothing I said or did ever convinced my mother that I hadn't been there. Even when the police declined to press charges, it hadn't helped. They'd decided against charging any of us. Not enough evidence. In other words, they didn't believe I was home in my bed; they were convinced all four of us did it but just couldn't prove anything. That condemned us as much as an actual conviction. To the community—to the entire city—we were killers. Mean girls turned murderers.

My so-called friends didn't help. They sure as hell weren't going to say I hadn't been there if it meant admitting they had. Nope. According to them, we all left that coffee shop together, and we were dropped off one by one, starting with me. Sure, they texted Jasmine, but they never actually went to the pier. That was the prank—to have her show up alone. Having a bit of fun at her expense, and we were all in on it. Hell, I gave them the name of her crush, didn't I?

Two of my friends' families moved away within a month. The third one went to live with her grandmother. That left me to stand trial in the court of public opinion. To be the target for other bullies. To be kicked out of every school club on the vaguest of excuses. To become the most hated girl in town. That's when I started noticing a kid following me around. A thin-faced girl of about ten. Jasmine's sister. Stalking me. Staring at me. Leaving notes wherever I might find them.

I know what you did.

I hope you die.

I hope someone holds you under the water until you drown.

I fell apart, and Aaron swooped in as my savior. The one who understood. The one who knew I hadn't been there that night. The one who believed me.

Three months later, I took that stack of notes from Jasmine's sister, and I burned them. Then I shoved everything I owned into my dad's biggest suitcase, and I walked out the door and climbed into the cab Aaron had called for me, a cab that would take me to the bus station, onto a bus that would take me to him.

What resurrected that nightmare tonight? Is it because I'm thinking of using Daisy to escape Liam? Does she remind me of Jasmine in some way? I suppose, subconsciously, I'm feeling guilty. I can't, though. Jasmine died, and that wasn't my fault. Daisy can look after herself. I have no reason to feel guilty.

No reason at all.

SEVEN

DAISY

I forgot to set my alarm last night, and when I wake, it's dark enough that I'm ready to return to sleep before I make the mistake of checking my watch. It's after nine. I groan and lift my head to peer at the gray beyond the windows. It's still raining, and that sound wipes away any chance of sleep as it reminds me that I need to use the bathroom urgently now.

With another groan, I roll off the lounger. Concrete damp and chill beneath my toes, I stagger to the door and find a note taped to it.

Daisy,
Good morning! Please come in and help yourself to coffee.
I had to go to Tampa for business, but I'll be back after lunch.
I can clear a path for you in the attic then if you're still okay with fixing the leak.

Celeste

I grab the doorknob and turn—

Nothing happens.

I try again. It's locked.

I spend far too much time jangling the knob, certain I'm mistaken. The note very clearly says "come in." What kind of passive-aggressive bullshit—

I squeeze my eyes shut. She made a mistake. That's all. She's a woman living alone in the countryside. Locking doors has become habit.

The fact that the note says "come in" means I'm welcome to find a way in. An open window is a pipe dream. It's Florida, and it's raining. When I was a kid, Dad always threw open the windows in this weather, and we'd sit in the sauna-heat, drinking lemonade and watching hurricane winds flatten the grass as Dad regaled me with some adventure from his youth . . . until Mom got home and gave him hell for the windows and didn't he know what that humidity did to her hair? He'd close them without a word of complaint, just a wink to me, that wink saying there would be other hurricanes, other storms to enjoy. There were . . . and then, suddenly, there weren't.

Celeste isn't me, though, or my dad. She'd have taken my mom's side in that argument. No open windows, then.

As I look around, I spot a single plant by the door. One thing I've always loved about lanais is the greenhouse feel of them, often stuffed to overflowing with tropical plants. This one holds only a single pot, and the fern inside is holding on by sheer obstinacy. As someone who does a lot of home renovations, though, that lone plant screams a message.

Just go ahead and let yourself in. There's a spare key.

Under a decorated rock.

Beneath a single paving stone.

In a lone planter.

I lift the pot from its chipped dinner-plate base and . . . Nothing.

Just as disappointment surges, there's a sharp clink as a key drops from the planter bottom onto the plate. I chuckle under my breath.

I unlock the door and return the key to its spot. I will presume that Celeste locked the door by accident. If not, well, her note did say to come in, and apparently, the door wasn't quite shut because it swung open for me. Really.

I slip inside and call, "Celeste?"

Silence. From the lanai, I could see that Liam's Rover was gone, but now I check for Celeste's little Toyota. Also gone. I exhale and head to the kitchen. There's coffee in the pot, and I pour a cup and reheat it in the microwave as I survey my breakfast options.

The note said coffee.

It did not mention breakfast.

A twinge of irritation at that, doused as I remind myself that I need to get my back down if I'm going to pull this off. I will presume that she did not intend to lock the door and that by *coffee*, she meant *breakfast*. To be polite, I will only fix myself toast. And I'll wash the dishes she and Liam left, which should adequately compensate her for two slices of toast and a spoonful of peanut butter.

Breakfast devoured and dishes washed, I pour one last cup of coffee before cleaning the pot. Then I head upstairs for a shower. Yep, the note said nothing about availing myself of the house's amenities, but washing off the stink of that shed is in everyone's best interests. I bathe, and afterwards I clean the shower and take all the towels to the laundry. Again, this seems adequate payment for some hot water and shampoo.

Once the washer is running, I stand in the living room, gazing up the stairs.

You aren't actually debating your next move, are you?

This is an opportunity I never imagined. If I saw myself in this house, with access to everything within, I'd have envisioned I got there by breaking in.

Now I have the chance to avoid that *and* accomplish a critical part of my mission, and I'm hesitating. I'm making breakfast, I'm washing dishes, I'm showering, and then I'm doing laundry while this house lies open to me, my time alone ticking past.

A deep breath, and I check my watch. Eleven a.m. Celeste said she'd be back after lunch, meaning I want to be in the lanai by noon.

I grip the railing and head upstairs.

CELESTE

She's been in the house.

I realize that the second I step inside to hear the dryer tumbling. Outrage pulses through me. Outrage and fear, too, the reactions of an animal who has returned home to find her den violated, her privacy shattered.

I locked the back door. Put out a note welcoming her to grab coffee and then locked the door. I'm not proud of that. I'd rather have just stuck a bottle of water and a few granola bars outside with an apologetic "Hey, I had to take off, but here's something to tide you over until lunch." That made me seem like a bitch, though, so instead, I'd actually *been* a bitch, inviting her in and locking the door.

I hate this push-pull of being a woman, always walking the tightrope line between assertive and "bitchy," while knowing that line moves for every person on the receiving end.

Be direct in your emails, but soften the blow with smiley faces.

Stand up for what you believe in, but remember that others have opinions, too.

A woman putting that bottle of water and granola bar outside is rude, suspicious, and that most dreaded of sobriquets: Not a Nice Person.

I follow Daisy's trail through my house, like a wolf tracking an intruder's scent. She made breakfast and did the dishes; then she showered and washed the towels. I understand that, in cleaning up, she was trying to mitigate the trespass, but it feels like even more of an intrusion, as if she's making herself at home.

The back door creaks open, and Daisy sticks her head in as I fix on my most politely neutral smile.

"Hey," she says, staying out on the porch. "Just wanted to let you know that I used the shower. I threw the towels into the wash. Hope that's okay."

"It's fine," I say, my tone as neutral as my smile.

"Is it all right if I borrow an umbrella for a walk to the store? I'm short on supplies in the shed, and I don't want to impose any further."

The correct response here would be to offer to drive her to the store.

No, the correct response would be to assure her that she's welcome to my food and other necessities *while* offering to drive her for anything else she needs.

"I'll get you an umbrella," I say.

She waits, holding the door ajar. When I hand her an umbrella, she says, "Just let me know when you want that leak fixed. I really am fine with whatever state the attic is in. It can't be worse than I've seen."

The leak. Damn it.

"I'll have you take a look when you get back," I say. "The storm seems to be clearing up, so maybe it doesn't need to be fixed."

"Sure, just let me know."

As she takes the umbrella, I glance at the door.

"I'm glad you were able to get in," I say. "I got to my appointment and started freaking out, worrying that I'd accidentally locked it."

"Nope. Which is good, because I really needed that shower."

I close the door and stand there, thinking. Had there been a pause before she answered? A sign that I *hadn't* forgotten to lock it or had left the door not quite shut? Did Daisy break into my house?

I turn the lock now and double-check it. A few moments later, the outside door slaps shut, and through the window, I watch Daisy jog off, red umbrella bobbing in the rain.

Once Daisy is out of sight, I head upstairs and make my way to the attic door. There's no lock on it. There should be, but everything in this old house is so rusted and worn that any visitor would notice a new lock and wonder who the hell locks their attic.

I ease open the door. Narrow stairs ascend into an eerie twilight, lit through filthy dormer windows. With every step, dust whirlwinds around me. I should change into my sweats. I'm turning to retreat when I remember that I lent them to Daisy.

I climb to the top and peer through the motes of dust dancing in the dim light. Stacks of boxes line every wall. Furniture covers the floor. I wasn't lying when I said it was a mess. It looked like this when I arrived, and while I'm tempted to see whether there are any antiques I can sell, the clutter is more valuable as cover for everything I need to hide.

As I step onto the top landing, I catch a soft plinking noise. Is that . . . water?

Dripping water?

I actually have a leak up here?

Of course I do. Well, that saves me the trouble of making one. I crest that last step and reach for the light. Before I flick the switch, something on the floor catches my eye. It's covered in a layer of dust, but that's nothing new. What *is* new? The fresh footprints tracking through it.

DAISY

The umbrella breaks halfway to the store. It's already ancient, creaking as it opened, rain dripping through tattered holes. Then a gust of wind grabs it, and I fight for control as the umbrella flips inside out. When I battle it around, it flips the right way . . . and two rusted struts snap.

I remember Celeste standing there with a dripping black umbrella in one hand as she gave me this ancient red one.

I shake my head and hold the umbrella up as best I can while I make my way to the corner store. It's exactly what I expect from a settlement so tiny it doesn't appear until you zoom the map to full size. According to my research, Fort Exile isn't even a town. It's an honorary name for a cluster of homes that never earned the status of town, village or even hamlet.

The story goes that there was once nothing here but a government outpost so far from everything else that its two-person staff dubbed it Fort Exile. The name stuck. As for why it appears on maps at all, I chalk that up to whimsy. It brings the occasional tourist this way . . . who will discover nothing here except this one store, a low-slung building that combines a gas station, corner store and garage. Also bait shop, post office, coffee bar and, if the sign can be believed, "tax services."

When I'd first arrived, I'd visited the store and found the contents as expected—an overpriced assortment of basic commodities for those who don't care to make the ten-mile trek to Sun City.

As I walk in, a bell chimes, and a male voice calls a greeting from the garage.

There's no sign of the middle-aged clerk, and the lights are dim. I glance back at the sign on the door. The Closed side faces my way. Okay, it *is* open.

The voice comes again, as if interpreting my silence correctly, "Glory called in sick. Just grab what you need, and come get me to ring you through."

I smile. In a town like this, when your employee doesn't show up, you run double duty and trust that whoever's in your shop won't fill their pockets and run.

I gather what I need and set it on the counter. Then I walk into the garage. It's even darker than the shop. The only bright light shines from beneath a pickup raised on a jack. I spot a work boot, presumably from the guy underneath the vehicle. One tanned arm peeks out, skin bathed in reflected light. Rolled-up sleeves show a tribal tattoo that makes me scrunch my nose. This, too, is not unexpected—people pick whatever symbol catches their fancy, whether it belongs to them or not.

"I have cash," I say. "I could leave it on the counter with a list of what I took."

"One sec," he says. "I just need to . . ."

A grunt and a crack, and another grunt, this one of satisfaction. The dolly wheels squeak as he rolls out. One look at his profile, and I realize my mistake. That tattoo isn't taken from another culture. His light-brown skin is more than a Florida tan.

That's when he turns my way, and recognition slams like a fist into my gut. In my mind, I hear a boy's voice say, "Yeah, my mom's half-Seminole, and my dad's all asshole."

No. Please, no.

It's been so many years. I'm mistaking him for a boy I knew. It cannot possibly be—

Cannot possibly? That's really what you're going with? The impossibility of returning to Florida and seeing someone from your past?

Months of planning shatters at my feet. If I've recognized him, he's recognized me, and I am undone.

"Hey," he says as he rises, his friendly smile sparking into true warmth. "I know you."

If I have any chance here, it is to confess. Spill my story and pray for understanding.

I open my mouth.

"You were in a few days back, right?" he says. "I caught a glimpse as you were leaving, and Glory said you were just passing through. You passing back? Or waiting out this damn storm?"

I hesitate, not believing my reprieve. But he stands there, his smile warm and friendly and nothing more.

He doesn't recognize me. Why would he? It's been twenty years, and it's not as if I returned to this part of the world without taking precautions with my appearance.

I only remember him because he occupies a bigger space in my memory than I would in his. A boy who'd been kind when I needed kindness. A man with that same kindness in his eyes, despite biceps big enough to lift a car and tattoos that tell me he's spent time behind bars. I grieve a little, seeing those prison tats. Grief for the inescapability of his fate, the fate of so many who've lived our life. We wanted out, he and I. A better path to better places. I'm not sure either of us found it.

"Tom Lowe," he says, extending a hand. Then he sees the grease streaks and pulls back with a rueful laugh. "Mmm, on second thought, better stick to hello."

"Daisy," I say. "Daisy Moss."

"Nice to officially meet you, Daisy Moss. I hope you found someplace warm and dry to wait out this storm."

My gut instinct is to say something noncommittal. For the past month, that's been my response to questions as innocuous as "So, where are you from?" Yet the words that leave my mouth are "I took shelter in a shed, but the homeowner was kind enough to let me stay in her lanai."

"You must mean Celeste," he says, as if this is the only answer.

He walks to the bench and takes a glop of cleaner from a jar, rubbing it on his hands as the sharp tang of orange fills the garage. "Good. She's new around here—inherited the place from her granny a few months back."

"So I heard."

"Glad she took you in. This storm's a real witch. Never seems to end. Hurricane season, huh?"

As he dries his hands on an old towel, I glance at the workbench.

"I don't suppose you rent tools," I say.

He looks over, brows rising.

"Celeste has a leak, and I've promised to fix it. From the looks of her house, though, I have a feeling any tools there belong in the last century."

He chuckles. "*Middle* of the last century more like. Sure, we can work something out. Or I could swing by and fix it myself."

"I owe her," I say. "And I know what I'm doing. I'm a carpenter by trade, but I've spent more time repairing leaks than crafting fine furniture."

"I know what that's like. I'm an aviation mechanic, and I pay the bills keeping these junk heaps on the road. Gotta go where the jobs are." He waves me into the shop. "Let's get you rung through, and then we'll talk tools."

EIGHT

DAISY

I won't be fixing the leak until tomorrow morning. I checked when I snuck into the attic this morning, and the leak is bigger than expected. Even if Celeste's tools would do the job, she doesn't have the materials I need.

Before dinner, I put on a temporary patch to stop the constant drip of water behind the interior wall. When I point out the drywall damage to Celeste, she curses, but I assure her it won't need to be replaced immediately. Soon, though, to avoid mold . . . which I can already see growing in a few other spots. She's not thrilled by that, but it's not as if I'm here as a contractor, pointing out "problems" in hopes of making a few extra bucks. My task is the leak, and I'll do it tomorrow, after picking up the tools from Tom's shop.

With any luck, Tom himself won't be there when I do so. I won't pretend it wasn't good to see him. I've often wondered where he ended up in the world, and the answer might not be what I'd wanted for him, but he's running his own business and seems happy, so I'm pleased.

I'm even more pleased to see he hasn't changed. I've known other kids raised in our hardscrabble lives who've ended up falling into the patterns of their parents, like cars that veer from the track, only to be towed back onto it.

Those kids grew up into adults I barely recognize. Disappointment changed them. Hardened them. Sapped out their kindness as it stole their hopes. That doesn't seem to be the case with Tom, and if I could cast the die of fate and choose whether he'd achieve his goals or remain himself, I'd pick the latter. "Both" would be the best answer, but we so rarely get that option. I certainly didn't.

Tom landed on his feet, and I am pleased to see it. Now I will withdraw from his life, like a ghost who flits past only to check on those she knew.

Speaking of Tom, I bought food at his store to ensure I wouldn't use Celeste's. Is that consideration? Pride? Or self-defense, warding myself against the evil eye of her grudging hospitality? A little of all three, I think.

Also, I can't afford to piss her off. I need to be the perfect houseguest, helpful and unobtrusive. I can't afford to give her any reason to kick me out.

Tom's shop isn't exactly a supermarket, but I'd put together a package that would give me a chicken dinner, a pasta lunch, and an omelet for breakfast using the leftover veggies from the first two. I offer to make dinner for Celeste, and she agrees, though she eyes my sad grocery selection doubtfully. She can't hide her surprise when the result turns out to be lightly fried chicken thighs on rice pilaf with a vegetable medley, all cooked from memory.

After dinner, I clean up, over her protests, and then I retreat to the lanai with a book that I found in the shop's second-hand collection. I curl up, and I'm asleep before dark falls.

CELESTE

She's in the house. It's past midnight and had I been asleep, I'd never have heard her. But I'm restless tonight, on edge. When the steps creak, I bolt upright, blinking. I sit there, straining to hear and—

Another creak.

I should have locked the back door. I'd been about to, and then I hesitated. Having admitted that I "almost locked it" earlier, does that give me an excuse for doing so again? Or does it negate that excuse? In the end, I left it open.

And now she's in the house.

Another creak on the steps. There's no reason for her to come up here. The bathroom on the main level is tiny and crude—installed when stairs became too much for an eighty-year-old woman—but Daisy has been using it.

I slip from bed and ease open the top drawer of my nightstand. There's a gun inside a sleep-mask sack. I used to keep a weapon under my mattress, only to learn that's the first place someone will look. The problem with my current solution is that I need to get it out of the bag first.

I pick it up, bag and all, and scoot behind my door, where I carefully unwrap the gun as I listen. The footsteps hesitate outside my door, and I hold my breath, gun in hand, watching the knob. It doesn't turn. Ten long seconds of silence. Then the footsteps back up.

Is Daisy in retreat? Does she realize I'm awake . . . or was she listening at my bedroom door to see whether I'm asleep? Her destination answers that question—the footsteps pause at my office. I press my ear to the door. A squeak of shoes as she heads inside.

A drawer opens. Papers whisper as she riffles through them.

There's nothing incriminating in my office, no sign of my past life. That's all in the attic, and while my stomach still clenches at the thought of her being up there, I don't believe she'll find anything, and there's nothing in my office except my legitimate work as a freelance graphic designer.

That doesn't mean I'm about to return to bed. She's trespassing. Worse, she's snooping, and I have every right to barge out there, gun in hand, and catch her in the act as I pretend that I mistook her for an intruder. I won't shoot her, of course, but I can still scare the shit out of her.

Scare the shit out of her *and* frighten her off, which I don't want to do. She will be useful. Yet if she's a threat, it's better if I let her go. Find another solution to my problem.

I turn the doorknob, as quietly as I can, and I'm easing open the door when there's a bang. Not a gunshot but a crash, as if something fell. I still freeze, and that's all it takes. A dark figure streaks from my office, no more than a blur before it's at the stairs, galloping down.

I race into the hall, but she's already rounding the midpoint landing and—

"Hey!" she shouts.

A smack. A raised voice and the thud of a falling body.

"Get back here!" Daisy yells.

A hiss of pain underscores footsteps thumping down the hall. A yelp, high-pitched and breaking off into curses. The footsteps recede, and the screen door slaps shut as Daisy shouts.

I make my way carefully down the stairs, gun in hand. At the bottom, the front-door rug is askew. My laptop lies atop it.

I flip on the living room light. There's glass on the floor. Blood smears continue to the back door.

As I stand there, staring at the bloodied footprints, Daisy comes back in, huffing and wincing, hand to her side. She's barefoot, and blood smears in her wake as she jogs toward me. I quickly swing the gun behind me, out of sight.

"Are you okay?" she says. "Did he—?" Her gaze travels up and down me, dressed in my chemise.

"I'm fine," I say, carefully, my brain still processing. "What happened?"

"I came in to use the bathroom," she says. "Then I heard footsteps overhead. I went to the stairs to let you know it was just me down here, and someone came barreling down and knocked me flying. I managed to get that"—she points at the laptop—"before he took off. I followed . . . and accidentally discovered how he broke in."

A wry twist of a smile as she points at the broken glass. She lifts her foot to examine the damage and then continues, "I followed him out, but the glass slowed me down enough that I lost him."

"You're okay?" I ask, a little belatedly.

"I think so. If you have bandages, I'll look after my foot while you call the police."

I nod toward the upstairs bathroom. She gingerly makes her way around the glass and heads up. I stand there, surveying the scene as my heart thuds.

This is no random break-in.

I can't call the police, but I do need to notify someone, or it'll seem suspicious. And the person I need to notify is the last person I want to run to: Liam. But if I don't tell him and he finds out, that will only make things worse.

So I make that damn call, as hard as it is.

Save me, Liam. Protect me.

I wrap up the story with, "It seems that when Daisy startled the intruder by coming inside, he grabbed my laptop and ran. But she got that back, so the only damage is a broken window. Is it going to look suspicious if I don't call it in?"

"Not if you notified me and I advised you against bothering to file a report."

"That's what I thought." I pause. "It is just a random break-in, right? Someone looking to pawn my laptop for drug money?"

Silence.

"It can't be Aaron," I say, a little sharper. "You've made sure of that."

"I'm handling Aaron as best I can, but he isn't the only trouble you face, is he?"

And whose fault is that? I want to snap the words, but I know how to walk this balance beam. There are times I can call him out, like a normal girlfriend, and there are times when I'd best just keep my bitch mouth shut, as Aaron always said.

Liam knows he's the cause of the other "trouble" I face, because he set the damn thing in motion himself. That was the point. Lure me in, trap me and then come to my aid, setting himself up as my protector.

"It was just a break-in," I say, firmly now. "Probably one of my damn neighbors looking for dope, which is another reason I don't want to report it. And I really am fine, thanks to my houseguest."

"Well, then, I'm glad she's there. Maybe you shouldn't be in too big of a rush to get rid of her. While I'm sure it's uncomfortable having a stranger there, think of her as a watchdog. A small and ferocious stray terrier."

I have to laugh at the image, which strangely fits.

You think I should let her stay? Well, it's not my first choice, but if you insist, I guess I have no option but to keep her around.

He continues, "You know, I was already thinking it'd be good to have her do some work around your place."

"You've said that. I'm still considering it."

"Maybe, though, *you* don't need to be there."

"What?"

"You just had an intruder. Maybe this is the perfect time to go all in. Hire Daisy. Let her live there. Come stay here with me."

I stiffen, but only shift the phone to my other ear and lower my voice. "I'm fine here. Also, you do realize you're suggesting I leave a young woman alone in my house after a *break-in*."

"She can look after herself. I care about you."

I want to argue. I want so badly to argue. I know better, though. I have learned this lesson well.

"We'll talk," he says. "Now get some rest, and call me in the morning."

The break-in happened after three a.m. By the time I tell Daisy that I'm not reporting it, it's almost five, and she decides to stay up reading while I go back to bed. I expect surprise at my decision not to call the cops, maybe even annoyance—after all, she got knocked down and walked through glass. But she only says, "Whatever you think is best," with no hint of judgment. I'm not sure what to make of that, though I spend far too much time trying to figure it out.

Daisy's brewing coffee as I return to bed, where I get a couple hours of sleep. I come down to find the rain has stopped. Had it stopped before the break-in? I try to picture Daisy coming back in after giving chase. I remember she was trailing blood in her wake as she walked.

Water and mud, too? She said she'd gone after the intruder, yet if she'd run outside, she'd have gotten her feet dirty.

I'm not sure whether there was mud on the floor. I can't recall it, but I didn't pay enough attention. There's none of that on the floor now, but she cleaned up the blood, so if there'd been mud, she'd have cleaned that up, too.

I'm in the kitchen, chewing toast and considering this, when a vehicle rumbles into the drive. My gut sinks as my first thought is *Liam*.

It's not Liam's Rover, though. I realize that even before I look out the kitchen window. The rumble of the engine gives it away.

Tom's truck.

I smile, my mood lifting as I munch down the last of the toast and run a hand through my hair. Then I remember that this is not the reaction I'm *supposed* to have to that particular vehicle in my drive.

Damn it.

The pickup door clangs shut, and I slip outside and shut the door firmly behind me.

"Hey," he says. "Is Daisy around?"

My heart thumps. "What?"

"Daisy? Your houseguest? She is staying here, right?"

"Yes, of course. I'm not sure where she is right now. I slept in, and she seems to have stepped out."

He nods. "I'm just dropping off the tools she's borrowing to fix your leak."

He looks over his shoulder, squinting into the morning sun. Then he walks to the pickup gate, opens it and tugs out a wooden box.

"Thank you for bringing the tools," I say. "I hope it wasn't a bother."

"Happy to help," he says. "She seems like a sweet kid."

Kid. I don't miss his use of that word, and I relax.

"Good of you to give her a break." He meets my gaze with a smile that sets my stomach flip-flopping. "I'll make sure folks around here know what you did for her."

That flip-flop turns to a thrill of victory as I murmur platitudes of "It was nothing, really," and "It's the least I can do." Dear God, am I *simpering*?

I could claim I'm faking it. That's bullshit, of course. This is pure flirtation. Tom Lowe ticks every box I have plus a few new ones.

He leans to shut the truck gate, and I notice the fall of his hair, the ripple of his biceps, the set of his jaw, the self-mocking half smile when the gate doesn't quite close right and he has to slam it harder. I notice the slight squint of his eyes, the lines forming around his mouth, the dark shadow of a missed shaving day, even the smell of him as he leans my way, a mix of shampoo and grease and the faint smell of . . . oranges?

Is he standing closer than he needs to? Leaning in to speak to me when he doesn't have to? Are those brown eyes twinkling just a little extra?

Good Lord, how old am I? Twelve?

He heads for the house with the box of tools. I realize then he must have said something like "I'll carry this up for you."

"No, that's okay," I say, jogging after him. "I'll take it in."

He stops but doesn't turn my way. He sets down the box and walks toward the house, stepping carefully through the empty garden. Then he stares up at the broken window.

"I had a break-in," I say. "Last night."

He turns, brows scrunching, as if he heard wrong.

"Someone broke in. It's okay. They didn't get anything. Daisy scared them off."

"Is she okay?"

"She's fine." *Mmm, no, better correct that, or it'll seem as if I'm brushing off her injuries.* "She was pushed down a few stairs and stepped on glass."

He swallows. "Shit."

A long pause, and then he shoves his hands in his pockets. "Well, I hope she's okay. You're going to need this window fixed, though. I'm sure Daisy can handle that."

I don't reply.

"I wouldn't call this a dangerous neighborhood but . . ." He shrugs. "Sometimes people get desperate. Might be a good idea to keep the kid around a while."

I make a noncommittal noise. Seems like everyone's trying to saddle me with a roommate today. They're all just so terribly helpful.

"It'd be a mutually beneficial arrangement," he says.

Do I sound awful if I suspect this is a term he's picked up and uses because it sounds smart? Our brief exchanges haven't suggested he's a well-educated guy, and the words trip awkwardly off his tongue, as if this is a speech he's rehearsed.

He continues, "This house could use a carpenter's touch, and Daisy looks like she could use a place to stay for a bit."

"Did she put you up to this?"

A flash of annoyance, quickly doused. "Course not. I just thought . . ." He waves at the window. "At least she can fix that. Maeve left the place in bad shape, and I know you were scraping to put together funeral arrangements, so I'm guessing there wasn't much life insurance."

He lifts his hands. "I'm not prying. But I've had enough cups of coffee in this kitchen to know exactly what kind of condition the house is in. I helped where I could, but Maeve was a proud old bird. Maybe offer Daisy a few days' work and see what she says. I bet—" He stops and grins as his gaze moves over my shoulder. "Speak of the devil."

I turn to see Daisy coming across the lawn, a half-eaten orange in hand.

"Don't tell me you swiped that from the Hanson place," Tom calls. "You know what'll happen if Old Mr. Hanson catches you?"

"He'll rise from his grave and demand payment?" she says.

Tom laughs.

Daisy tosses him an orange from her other hand. He catches it as she says, "Celeste's neighbor told me there were a few trees still producing over there and the owner's been dead for five years, so I figured it was safe enough."

"It is. Meager pickings this time of year, but take whatever you want." He returns to the box and hefts it. "I brought the tools. Point me in the direction of the leak."

"I can fix it."

"Not disputing that. But I'm here, and Glory's managing the shop, so put me to work." He waves Daisy on ahead. Once she's to the door, he turns to me and whispers, "I'll mention the other thing and get her take on it."

I open my mouth to make a token protest, but he's already striding after Daisy.

NINE

DAISY

As I walk back to the house and see Tom in the drive, I think, *Well, that wasn't my best idea.*

I believe this will be my refrain for the next few hours. Possibly days. I can only hope it falls into the same category as standing under a tree during a lightning storm—you realize it's not the wisest idea, but ultimately, the chance of an actual lightning strike is rare, and it does provide temporary shelter from the storm. That tree is Tom. Temporary shelter that I'm far too eager to embrace. Perhaps not so much a tree in a storm as a blazing fire on a bitter cold night, luring me with the promise of warmth and light. A dangerous fire that I need to keep my distance from. Which works so much better when the fire stays in its hearth . . . and doesn't hop in its pickup to come looking for me.

It's a very fine pickup, too. Yes, I realize how much I betray my roots in saying that, and I don't care. I check out his restored 1978

Li'l Red Express with lust in my heart. In other words, the same way Celeste is checking out the Dodge's owner.

Her obvious appreciation catches me off guard. I have to squint and take a better look at Tom, which is laughable, really, because he's obviously good-looking. But I knew him as a chubby boy and then as a gawky preadolescent. By the time I reached "that age," Mom had taken me up North. Admittedly, there'd been a kiss or two—okay, four—during our last summer together, but we'd been ten, and it'd been a case of curiosity and availability, nothing more.

I can be forgiven, then, if I have to clear my mind and consider whether Tom is an attractive man. Yes, he is. Celeste notices, too, which surprises me. She's dating a guy who is more conventionally handsome, and Tom really doesn't seem like her type. Maybe it's a fantasy for Celeste—that old chestnut of the uptight business-woman getting down and dirty with the local grease jockey.

As for my not-so-great idea, it's sitting on the ground. A wooden box, presumably holding the tools I asked to rent. Yesterday, I'd dodged a bullet meeting Tom and not being recognized. So clearly, my next step should have been to flee his garage and never return. *What? No, that's silly. Let's ask to rent his tools. It's not as if he's a nice guy who'll bring them over first thing in the morning.*

If there's a saving grace here, it's that he's too distracted to notice me while Celeste is batting her lashes at him.

Guess I'm not the only one who wants to rent his tool.

I chuckle under my breath, and I'm still too far away for them to hear, but Tom turns, as if he caught the sound.

His face lights up in a grin. "Speak of the devil." He notices the orange and nods at it. "Don't tell me you swiped that from the Hanson place. You know what'll happen if Old Mr. Hanson catches you?"

"He'll rise from his grave and demand payment?" I say.

He laughs, and I toss him another orange. He catches it easily, and that grin flashes broader still, a glitter in his eyes that sparks memories of the two of us sneaking into gardens, pillaging summer huckleberries.

Be careful.

Be so careful.

I explain that the neighbor told me about the abandoned trees. Celeste frowns. Doubting my story? It's true. I don't quite catch what Tom says, but then he's heading toward the house, box in hand, as if he's going to fix the leak himself.

"I can do it," I say.

"Not disputing that. But I'm here, and Glory's running the shop, so put me to work."

He waves for me to go on.

Dangerous ground.

Such dangerous ground.

But how do I argue without it seeming suspicious? Without him wondering why I'd refuse free help? In the end, I proceed into the house, and he follows a moment later, having paused to speak to Celeste.

He starts to close the door behind himself, mouth opening to speak to me, but then Celeste's there, and he says, "Sorry, didn't mean to shut your door in your face. I thought you were going out."

She says something. Again, I don't catch it, too focused on how to escape this predicament.

You can't.

And you shouldn't. You could use an ally here. You trust Tom.

That was a very long time ago. I'm not foolish enough to think that means I can trust him now.

What if I do or say something that sparks a memory? Even tossing that orange to him had been a risk.

Really? Because you're the only one who's ever thrown fruit his way? It's been twenty years. Two-thirds of your lives. He very clearly does not recognize you.

True. I'm not even sure that it'd be different if I showed up looking like myself. It'd be like when an old classmate friends me on Facebook, and I peer at their picture, struggling to see something I recognize, to form an image of the person they were, already faded in my mind.

"It's in the attic," I say, a little foolishly. Where else would a leak be? "It's not exactly clean up there." I cast a quick look at Celeste and hurry on, "Being an attic, obviously. I really am fine doing it myself."

"Do I look like I'm worried about a little extra dirt under my nails?" He flourishes a hand. "It never comes out, however much I scrub. Same as this." He lifts a work boot, showing grease on his faded blue jeans. "I'm not exactly wearing my Sunday best."

"I just don't want to impose."

"You aren't. Now lead the way."

He follows me up the stairs. As I reach for the attic door, Celeste comes up the stairs, and Tom leans around the corner to see her.

"Why don't I help Daisy?" she says. "I'm sure you've got better things to do."

"Nope." Tom tosses her a conspiratorial smile and stage-whispers, "I'm kinda hoping to win a little tit for tat from Daisy here."

At the look on Celeste's face, I bite my lip to keep from laughing. I think Tom doesn't notice . . . until I catch the glint in his eye.

He continues, "The back door on the garage has been jamming so bad I gotta come in the front way all the time, which makes it damn hard to slip past Glory. I love that woman, but she does talk my ear off. My secret plan is to help Daisy with your leak and then casually mention my door problems, hoping she'll take pity and offer to fix it."

"Sure," Celeste says. "But I really don't mind—"

"We've got it," Tom says. Then he braces one arm against the wall, muscles flexing as he leans toward her.

"Have you ever had Glory's cinnamon buns?" he asks Celeste. "She sells them up at the shop. Gotta get there early, though. They're gone by ten."

"Uh . . ." Celeste says. "Okay. I'll have to try them."

"Well, you can, 'cause I brought a box. Could you grab them from the truck, maybe stick them in the fridge before the icing melts? I thought you and I might have a coffee break after I'm done here, if you're not too busy . . ."

"I'm not," she says quickly.

"Great. Then if you can bring those in, we should be done up here in about an hour."

Celeste is still looking our way, backing up, as Tom shuts the door. I start to climb and then realize he isn't behind me. When I look back, he still has his hand on the knob, listening as she retreats. Then he trots up the stairs, wooden toolbox in hand. At the top, I take it from him. As I turn away, he catches my arm.

"I heard about the break-in," he says. "She says you got knocked around fending off the intruder. You okay?"

I shrug. "Bumped and bruised, that's all."

He glances down at my feet. "I also heard something about stepping on glass."

"Just a small cut."

"Huh. And then you happened to walk through a puddle of cherry Kool-Aid on your rambles this morning."

"Hmm?" I frown and then follow his pointed gaze to my sneaker. There's a pink stain on the white canvas.

I'm about to say it's fine, but he waves me to an old chair and insists I sit. He reaches for my shoe, and I tug it off before he can. He lifts my foot, his callused fingers scratching my skin.

"Shit," he says as he peels back the blood-soaked bandage.

"It's fine."

"No, it's not." Anger ripples through his voice. Then he straightens. "Come on. I'll run you to the ER."

"I'm fine," I say firmly.

"Is it an insurance problem? If it is, I know someone—"

"It doesn't need medical attention. It just needs me to clean it, and bandage it up and keep an eye on it."

He eases back on his haunches and studies my expression so intently I squirm. Then he pauses, mental wheels spinning as he thinks.

Don't let the small-town-boy persona fool you. He's always been so much smarter than he lets on. It's camouflage. Blending into a world that expects a certain persona from him, and as long as he projects it, he can coast and fit in.

I know all about that, don't I?

"I'm *fine*," I say firmly. "Can we just take a look at that leak?"

He nods and puts the mangled bandage back on. "We'll fix your foot later. If you won't let me drive you to the doc, then let me patch you up properly."

He rises as I pull on my sock and shoe, and he walks to peer up at the leak.

"Speaking of patches, you've done a nice job here."

"Only because it stopped raining."

"Well, let's get her fixed up. Then your foot. Then that window."

"Yes, sir."

I've removed the patch, and I'm examining the hole. Below, Tom's holding the ladder and chattering away, a light stream of conversation that ebbs and flows with the enviable rhythm of a natural storyteller. I remember this about him, too. Memories of hot summer days, sheltered under a live oak tree, positioned exactly right to catch a breeze, my eyes closed as he talked.

"Dad says I talk too much. He calls me Chatty Cathy. Says I talk as much as a girl."

I open one eye to peer over at him, his face shadowed, knees drawn up, a soda bottle wedged between them.

"Do girls talk more than boys?" I ask.

He shrugs. "He thinks so. But you hardly talk at all."

I take a draw on my orange soda. "What does your mom say?"

"Tells him to shut up. Says she likes my stories."

"I like them, too."

He's talking about the neighbors now—naming the kids and explaining how I can tell them apart. I ask a few questions, and he answers, but mostly, I just listen as I used to.

Then he asks, "You met Liam yet?"

I nod, realize he can't see it and say, "Yes."

"Thoughts?"

"I . . . am reserving judgment."

He chokes on a laugh and says, "Well, at least you didn't say he seems like a nice guy. Don't bother reserving judgment, Daisy. Whatever intuition he's sparking, lean into it. You know those lawyers you see on TV, ambulance-chasing sharks? That's him."

"Huh."

"Liam's daddy was from Sun City, a lawyer who worked out this way. So folks consider Liam a local boy done good. Which he's not. He just plays on that to drum up clients. That's how he got Maeve's business."

"He was her lawyer?" I say.

"Yeah, Liam handled the estate. Against my advice. I'm never afraid to stick my nose where it doesn't belong. Maeve liked me and usually listened to me, but she shushed my concerns on Liam. The old bird might have been half-blind, but she could still spot a good-looking man at thirty paces."

I smile at that. "I bet he can be charming, too."

"Yep, and she was not immune." He purses his lips. "Well, no, I think she knew him for what he was, but she was past caring. It wasn't as if there was an estate he could con her out of. Just the house, and as you can see, it's in lousy shape."

He peers up as I finish peeling off the patch. "Shit, that's some leak. It's a wonder she didn't notice it before now."

"Has it been raining much?"

"No. Guess that'd explain why she didn't notice it. Which reminds me of a story . . ."

He launches into it, but I miss the first part. I'm busy fingering the edges of the hole. I hadn't paid much attention until he mentioned it, but it *is* a big one. The roof is obviously in rough shape, so I'm not surprised that there's a leak, but . . .

I'm something of an expert when it comes to leaks. Repairing the damage from one is a common reason to hire someone like me. Also, I'm at the age where if my friends have houses, they're probably old with bad roofs that they can't afford to replace.

No matter what the cause, a roof leak means that water drips relentlessly onto the drywall below, and you get a wet spot that eventually breaks through. What you end up with is a soggy hole.

This is not soggy. The edges are sharp and jabbing upward, as if someone found a damp spot and jammed something through it . . . to *create* a hole.

TEN

CELESTE

Apparently, I have a new handyman. Or handywoman. Is there a gender-neutral term for that? I have no idea. I only know that I now have one, and she's also my new boarder. Better yet, it wasn't my idea.

As promised, Tom broached the subject with Daisy. He says she wavered, but only because she didn't want to impose. He convinced her that the help she provided would more than cover room and board, and she agreed. Without me needing to do anything like, oh, I don't know, actually offer her the job?

Tom meant well with his matchmaking. A woman alone in the countryside, unpopular with her neighbors, already the victim of a break-in, and in possession of a house requiring repairs. Another woman who's pretending she's out seeing the world when, as Tom suspects, she's down on her luck, maybe even temporarily homeless.

A woman in possession of skills that would allow her to repair the first woman's house.

A match made in heaven. Or so it seems to both Tom and Liam.

Thank the Lord for overprotective men. Now I have Daisy in my house, primed to solve my problem, and I argued with both men who suggested the arrangement.

Do I still wonder whether Daisy created the leak she's fixing? Yes. And that's fine. I understand desperation. But that won't keep me from making an entry in my journal, elaborating on my fears and suspicions. It may come in handy later.

Now I'm sitting in the lanai with Tom, enjoying a coffee break. I even went so far as to invite Daisy to join us. Just being considerate, not wanting her to feel left out.

I snort at the thought.

Yes, I know myself better than that. The only thing I was considering was that, as much as I enjoy time with Tom, it's a luxury I cannot permit myself. Yet Daisy demurred, and Tom didn't second my invitation. He just made sure she got a cinnamon bun before she headed out to examine the broken window.

We're sipping coffee and eating the buns, which I will admit are delicious, if a little sweet for my tastes. While I wouldn't exactly call Tom the strong, silent type, there's a hint of that to him. A guy who can hold up his end of the conversation but doesn't initiate. That's my job, and I do it while he listens and eats.

"You know," he says as conversation ebbs, "maybe with all this work Daisy's doing, she'll find Bill Turner's treasure."

I hesitate a split second before shaking my head with a low laugh. "I wish. Trust me, there's no treasure."

"You've looked, then."

Oh, hell yes, I've looked. I've decided that the only "treasure" is the house itself. That's what I got from Maeve, and I am happy with it. I wouldn't turn down more, but I have priorities, and treasure hunting is not currently among them.

Bill Turner's treasure is local lore. Apparently, Maeve's husband had been a shady character who struck the criminal jackpot shortly before his death, pulling off some heist and then double-crossing his associates. Legend says that, on his deathbed, he told Maeve where to find the money, only she didn't want tainted goods and left it in place. On *her* deathbed, Maeve told me where to find it, too. Not a place, but a clue I was supposed to understand. A clue that meant nothing to me.

"Well," he says. "Probably better it's never found. If it ever turns up, I suspect it'll be a disappointment to all. What counted as a small fortune to folks around here forty years back would barely pay for a few new windows. Speaking of which, I should get back to work on that." He rises, mug and plate in hand. "Thank you for the coffee and the company, as always. It's nice to talk to you, Celeste."

I murmur something suitably demure as he collects my dishes and takes them to the sink.

DAISY

No one broke into the house. The window *was* shattered from the outside, presumably with something soft, muffling the noise. But in minimizing noise, the "intruder" also minimized breakage, leaving a hole so jagged that no one could climb through without slicing themselves to ribbons.

I don't know what to make of this.

Who has the key? As far as I know, only Celeste. Liam rang the bell when he arrived.

That intruder wasn't the only one inside last night. I told Celeste that I just happened to be using the bathroom. That's a lie. I'd been poking around the basement crawlspace when I heard footsteps on the stairs. I'd stayed where I was until I realized the sounds came from the upper level. So I'd snuck up to the main level and gone into the bathroom in case I was caught. The intruder must have heard me and begun his flight.

I recognized the sounds of running footfalls and reached the base of the steps just in time to be smacked by a figure, who then raced to the back door. By the time I got onto the rear steps, the yard was empty.

I didn't see who struck me. I only glimpsed a dark figure barreling down the stairs and sending me flying. By the time I recovered, the intruder was on the run. Then I stepped on glass, slowing me further, too much to get a closer look.

The window suggests this wasn't a normal break-in. Yes, the intruder *did* grab the laptop, the most valuable—and pawnable—thing in the house, but a laptop has value beyond its ability to be wiped and resold. I've been snooping around, looking for information that might answer my questions. If I'd been thinking faster, I could have hidden the laptop and pretended the thief got away with his treasure.

My bigger concern is that this wasn't an addict looking for items to fence. If it was a professional, that suggests I'm not the only person following this particular trail.

I missed an opportunity last night. Several, in fact. I can't let that happen again.

ELEVEN

CELESTE

I head downstairs for lunch, only to be greeted by a smell that slams into me with the force of a thousand memories. Grilled-cheese sandwiches. When I'd been maybe seven or eight, Mom spent every Saturday with friends, and I'd be trundled off to the house of a woman who had a girl roughly my age, a girl who struggled to make friends, and so her mother was happy to babysit me in return for the "gift" of a bottle of wine.

I can't remember the girl's name. We'd spend the day sitting in the same room, doing our separate things, barely speaking, while her little sister read in a corner. I do remember lunch, though. Grilled cheese, made specially for me. I'm not sure which I liked better: the gooey, rich sandwiches or the idea that someone had cooked something for *me*.

I walk into the kitchen to find Daisy at the stove, flipping a sandwich.

She glances at me. "Please tell me you like grilled cheese. I know I should have checked, but I hated to interrupt your work."

I hold out a plate, and she laughs.

"Guess that's a yes," she says. "They're a little basic. I usually go all bougie, with three kinds of cheese and heirloom tomato, but the only thing Tom's store carries is . . ." She holds up a processed cheese slice.

"American cheese," I say. "The taste of childhood."

"Right? It only needs one more thing."

She takes a bottle of ketchup from the fridge, and I squeeze a small mountain of it on the side of my plate as she scoops out a sandwich for me.

While we eat, Daisy asks about the renovations I need done. I start babbling, trying to pull my thoughts together, and she lays a pad of paper on the table.

"I did a rough survey," she says. "As if you were selling the house. I don't know if that's your plan . . ."

"Eventually, yes."

"*Eventually* soon or *eventually* in a few years?" She lifts her hands before I can say anything. "I'm not prying, and I'm not angling for more work. What I'm proposing is an evaluation of the property, with a list of work that you'll need to hire a contractor for, as well as resale scenarios."

"Hold on. I need carbs." I take a huge bite of my sandwich, making her laugh. "Try that again, and see if I understand better."

"Sorry. I've worked with house flippers, so I'm rushing ahead. How long do you intend to live here?"

"A few years, maybe? This isn't where I'd choose to live but . . ." I shrug. "I'd like to see if I can make it mine. If I can't, I'll sell."

"All right. So dual scenarios. If you stay, you'd want to reno it to your own specifications. If you move, you'd need to consider resale value. The problem is that old real-estate mantra. Location, location, location."

"This one sucks."

"It's not economically prosperous. Which limits the amount you could hope to get. Also, it was an inexpensive home even when it was built. While she's a lovely old sow, she's never going to be a silk purse. In some areas, you might consider bulldozing her for the land. Not here."

I munch on a strip of crispy bacon. "So what's the prognosis, doc?"

"Good, actually. She has great bones, and there's plenty of life left in her. She's just never going to be a dream home for wealthy retirees. We circle back, then, to the question of timing and intention. The big issue is making sure you don't put more into her than you'll get out. Not to pry, but is she mortgaged?"

"No, thank God. Free and clear."

"That will help. I don't suppose there was an inheritance that might go toward renovation? An unexpected windfall of cash?"

I snort. "No. My grandmother didn't believe in life insurance, and there was only enough money to pay for her funeral."

"That means any money that goes into renovations is straight out of your pocket, balanced against gains if you move, or a future mortgage if you don't." Daisy pushes the pad toward me. "Here's a preliminary list of work that needs to be done. I'll need to do a more thorough inspection to give you a better idea of costs. This page is the basics—problems that will bring resale down more than they cost to fix. The next page is extras—work that will show some profit, but it's all relative."

"Got it."

Daisy rises, water glass in hand, and nods at mine. I lift it, and she refills both as she talks.

"Let me look around," she says. "Take measurements and assess the plumbing, the wiring, the roofing . . . I don't want to be intrusive. If there's any place you'd like me to stay out of, just say the word."

"That attic is a disaster, as you saw. I don't know if you'd need to assess anything up there, but if so, just ask me to give you a hand, and we'll put on some old clothes and move boxes."

"Sounds like a plan." She hands me the filled glass. "Let's take a look at the list and see where I can start on repairs."

DAISY

I spend the rest of the day poking around the house, half assessing for renovations and half assessing for my own purposes. After dinner, I head for Tom's shop to fix his door. Am I hoping to arrive after he's done for the day? Yep, I am. I do find the store closed for the night. I head around the side to see a door held shut by an old chair. I move the chair, and the door swings open. Definitely broken. Inside, Tom sits on a stool, eating a sandwich while staring at an old minivan.

"Interesting choice of dinner companion," I say as I walk in. "Is she holding up her end of the conversation?"

"She is not," he says. "One might argue that I can manage both sides by myself, but in this case, I was really hoping she'd talk to me."

"Huh." I walk over and pat the ancient beast. "What's her story?"

"Family heirloom." He takes a swig of Coke. "A hand-me-down to a single mom with five kids who really needs this old lady up and running, and I cannot figure out why she isn't."

"Mysterious ailment."

"Nah. Just old age—so *many* ailments that I don't know which one is keeping her bedridden. The mom can't afford service, so I offered to 'take a look,' hoping I could quietly fix a few things and get her running and then say, miracle of miracles, all she needed was a couple twists of the wrench, and she started right up. But the old girl's got so much wrong with her that I can only start fixing things and work my way down the list."

"Which the mom is going to figure out and not appreciate the charity."

"Yep. It is a conundrum."

"You could barter it out, like you're doing with me." I walk over and peer in the minivan window to see two child seats. "Any of her kids old enough to wield a broom without breaking child-labor laws?"

He smiles. "As a matter of fact, the oldest is twelve. Old enough for odd jobs. That's a fine idea."

"Speaking of bartered labor, I'm guessing that's the door you want me working on?" I point at the one I came in.

"Nah, the broken one is much worse." He catches my look and grins. "Kidding. Yep, that's the one. It won't close, as you can see. I've played with the hinges, and I think I just made it worse."

"I'll take a look, and you can go back to communing with the minivan."

I've fixed the door. It was the hinges plus warping from the humidity. Well, I suspect the hinge issue came from Tom trying to fix it, but I don't say that. With his help, I plane down the wood and adjust the hinges. When I'm ready to take my leave, he says, "I owe you a drink for that."

"No, you don't."

"Can I get you one anyway? I have cheese puffs."

I smile. "How can I resist?" Which is true. I can't think of a way to refuse without being rude. It isn't as if I need to rush back to the house.

"Excellent. I will even show you my secret sunset-viewing spot."

He opens a closet door at the back of the shop to reveal metal steps, and I'm about to joke about taking me to his room. If there was anything flirtatious in the invitation, I *would* make the joke. Not to reciprocate the flirting, but to force him to make a response—either insist that's not his goal, or test the waters. Either would give me the chance to shut him down before expectations rose above sea level. Yep, I know all the tricks.

There have been zero flirty vibes, though. He's treated me exactly the way he did when we were kids—as a fellow human he likes hanging out with. His dad had taken our friendship as one more sign that his son wasn't as masculine as he should be. And by "not masculine," he meant "probably gay." The flirting with Celeste suggests that's not the case.

Either way, I don't comment, and Tom leads me up. At the top, he swings open a hatch to let the evening light filter down, and I may emit a girlish squeal.

He grins down at me, and the falling light catches his hair, the red highlights glittering like sunset streaks in a dark sky. His eyes glitter, too, the warmest deep brown. Then there's the smile. That smile is a crime against nature. It should belong to a less attractive man, the kind of guy who, when he smiles, you notice he's not so bad-looking after all.

Nope, doesn't matter. He can make my insides flutter and my heart skip and my body ignite, and it doesn't change a damn thing. He's off-limits and, better yet, not interested, thank God.

He climbs through the hatch, and I follow to find a bachelor hide-out, complete with a recliner and a mini fridge powered through a very dicey power-cord setup.

He follows my gaze. "Uh, not exactly up to code?"

I shudder. "My own code isn't going to let me walk away from that without begging you to let me fix it before the whole shop goes up in flames."

"I accept your offer if you'll let me help with the reno work over at Maeve's place."

"You don't have to do that."

"Tit for tat. As a professional, you are honor bound to fix my fire hazard, and therefore I am honor bound to help you with the house. We're stuck with each other." He points me to the recliner and pulls out a lounge chair for himself. "Grab something from the fridge."

I open it to see rows of soda.

He glances over my shoulder. "Er, by *drink*, I probably implied at least beer, didn't I? I'll grab one from the store. Do you prefer Bud or Bud?"

I smile and take out an orange soda. "This is perfect."

"I don't have a problem with alcohol," he says. "In case you were wondering."

"I wasn't."

I suspect he *does* have a problem with booze, the sort that comes from growing up with a mean drunk for a dad. I don't drink often myself, for an adjacent reason.

My parents both drank too much, but it never made them mean, much less abusive. When Dad drank, he regressed to an irresponsible teen, which wasn't much different than his usual self. When he'd been drinking, he'd wake me at one in the morning to come and listen to coyotes with him, and then spend the night telling me stories, forgetting that I had school the next morning. As for Mom, drunk was the only time she told me she loved me, hugged me, giggled with me. I *liked* my parents drunk. So I grew up drinking a little more than I should, and while I never reached problem status, I saw it on my horizon and set hard limits. I suspect—given Tom's experience—his own limit is zero.

From the trunk, he pulls out the promised cheese puffs, along with pretzels and peanuts. "Party in a box. I don't do much entertaining out here, but I like to come up myself most nights. Watch the stars instead of the TV. Maybe listen to a podcast."

"Which ones do you like?" I ask.

I've never listened to one in my life, but it's a way to get him talking, and I *am* interested. I figure podcasts are like books—which ones a person likes tells you more about them than their tastes in music or sports. As we settle into our chairs, he talks about his favorites. History is his thing, apparently. Not true crime—I hear those are popular—but real history, long and detailed retellings. When he raves about a ten-hour history of the Mongol invasions, I listen, my eyes closed, more relaxed than I have been in months. The smell of the swamp wafts over on a breeze so humid I could drink it. A truck roars by, country music blasting, gravel spitting. Somewhere in the distance, a woman laughs, and a man joins in.

I am home. Sitting on a rooftop in the evening heat, listening to Tom, sipping my orange soda and licking cheese dust off my fingers.

He peppers his conversation with questions. Nothing intrusive. Just "getting to know you" stuff that I can honestly answer. How did I get into carpentry? What do I like best about it? What kinds of projects do I prefer?

I turn the questions back his way and only get to "How did you get into auto mechanics?" before he pauses. I quickly add, "I know you said you studied aviation mechanics," to show I'd been listening, but he still hesitates.

I glance over, wondering what I've said wrong. Then I have the answer to my question as my gaze drops to his arm. To a prison tattoo.

I'm about to change the subject when he sees where I'm looking and gives a wry chuckle. "That's not as inconspicuous as I like to pretend, is it?"

"Hmm?" I say, taking a handful of pretzels.

"You can tell I didn't get it in a tattoo parlor."

I shrug. "I work in construction. I've seen a few. I'm sure most people don't know what it is."

"So I tell myself. The truth is . . ." He shrugs. "Most people save their pennies for a new car or a European vacation. I'm saving mine for tattoo removal."

I smile. "Regretting that decision, are you?"

"I regret a whole lotta decisions. That one, though? There wasn't any choice involved."

I go still, soda bottle halfway to my lips. Then I glance over. "I'm sorry. That was flippant and thoughtless."

"No, it was the reasonable assumption. I usually go along with it. Better than admitting I couldn't stop someone from doing it to me."

"I'm still sorry. For the comment and for . . ." I nod at his arm.

"Thank you. There was a time when I didn't give a shit. I committed the crime and did the time, and it made me a better man. Smarter one, at least. I already had this one." He points at a gorgeous small design that turns the state of Florida into a stylized tomahawk. "I added a couple others later so the prison one would just blend in, you know? But it doesn't blend. It'll come off in a few months."

We sit and look up at the sky filling with stars.

"You're not going to ask, are you?" he says finally.

"Ask what?"

He gives me a look. "You're not asking why I was inside because you're being polite. But you gotta wonder, too, being up here alone with me. Knowing why I went to prison would be helpful."

"Were you in for anything that would make me hightail it back down those stairs?"

"Nope."

"Then I'm good."

He nods, leans over and takes out another Coke. He passes me a second orange soda without asking, and we crack them open together.

He takes a slug of his Coke. "The answer to 'where I learned a trade' is 'in prison,' which is why I hesitated to answer. I wasn't going to keep it a secret, but I hoped to bring it up myself."

"Sorry."

"Stop apologizing," he says, swinging his bottle my way. "Yes, I learned aviation mechanics inside. Prison can give you job skills, but that doesn't mean anyone wants to hire you later. I ended up apprenticing for an auto mechanic in Tampa, and then my folks helped me buy this place where I don't have a boss to give me side-eye for having a record."

"Good plan."

"Not the original plan, though. That was a college degree in accounting."

He goes quiet. I glance over with a smile and say, "Ah, so you're the guy who does the taxes as advertised on the shop door."

"I am," he says, carefully, and he's watching me, as if expecting something.

I arch my brows. "What?"

"This is the point where you laugh, certain I'm joking about the accounting, and then it gets really awkward when you realize I'm serious."

"Well, I'm glad we skipped that part." I nibble the salt off a pretzel. "Awkward is so awkward."

A snorted laugh. "So you're not going to tell me I don't look like an accountant?"

"Pretty sure if I did, it'd be a compliment." I glance over. "You going to tell me I don't look like a construction worker?"

"Construction, no. Carpentry? I can see that."

"What's the difference?"

"A carpenter has a more refined look. More creative."

I roll my eyes, and I almost make a comment about remembering how much he liked math before I shove the pretzel in my mouth to stifle it. Then I say instead, "What happened to the accounting?"

"Turns out I have a creative side myself. At least when I need money. Second year of college, a few guys I knew from high school asked me for advice on how to clean up proceeds from a criminal enterprise."

"Money laundering."

"Yep, and the worst thing is I didn't understand that what I was doing was illegal. I didn't steal the money. I didn't *touch* the money. I just investigated options and advised a course of action in return for a fee."

He rolls his head my way. "I insisted that the fee be paid from legit money. I actually thought that kept my hands clean."

"Doesn't work that way, huh?"

"Apparently not. I made enough to pay off my college debt, and I was in my final year when the cops came calling. Felony charge. I'd helped launder over a hundred grand, which is first degree, meaning I was looking at up to thirty years."

"Holy shit."

"Yep. I pled out. Got third degree and three years. Paroled as early as possible—I was a very good boy—but that was still two years in prison. No hope of an accounting job with *that* on my record."

"So you didn't finish your degree?"

He smiles my way. "Actually, I did. So I am a college-educated man, with a degree I can't use. Still have it framed on my wall. First Lowe to go to college. Not the first to go to jail, though."

I lift my hand for a high five, and he slaps it with a laugh. We chat a bit more; then, I realize the time, and we arrange to work on the window at the house tomorrow.

TWELVE

CELESTE

I'm alone in the darkening house, sitting in the living room with my gun, unable to shake the image of myself. I want to laugh and joke that I'm finally fitting into the neighborhood, one step away from rocking on the front porch with a shotgun across my legs. I can't laugh, though. I'm too frightened for that.

Frightened.

I have spent ten years facing down that emotion with dragon fire. Planting my feet and looking it in the eye and saying, "No."

I will not let you rule my life ever again.

Every time I think I've vanquished the beast, it rears up again, mocking me for my naivete and my weakness.

I'd been in my office, anxiously watching the sun set, when the doorbell rang. I'd crept downstairs with my gun in hand, only to discover a delivery woman with a bottle of single-malt scotch from Liam.

In my surprise, I forgot to tip the deliverywoman, and that had me running down the driveway, waving a ten like lifesaving medicine. That's what happens when I am afraid. I cross my t's and dot my i's with a panicked mania, as if one faux pas will sentence me to the Reaper.

Now I sit in the living room, glaring at that bottle and cursing Liam. I was already on the edge, and that doorbell sent me tumbling over. All I can think is that Liam sent me booze I don't even like. Scotch is his thing, and I'm not even sure *he* likes the taste. It's just part of his bullshit persona. The man is a goddamned walking stereotype of a successful middle-aged white guy, from the scotch to the Land Rover and the biweekly golf games. I want to dump the damned bottle down the sink. Fill it with Jack Daniel's. See whether he notices the difference.

I'm pissy with Daisy, too. It's almost ten. Where the hell is she? We had an intruder last night, and she's left me alone past dark?

How much of this is me genuinely being upset that she's still gone . . . and how much is me wondering what she's doing with Tom to keep her out this late? That second part only proves I'm being pissy. Tom calls her a kid, for Christ's sake. I don't think she's noticed him, either. She went over wearing cargo shorts, a shapeless tee and no makeup. Definitely not planning to seduce the local hottie.

Earlier, I made up the spare room for her, deciding we were both better off with her sleeping inside after the break-in. Now I'm reconsidering. That'll teach her. Force her to stay in the back porch, where she's safe from intruders, rather than upstairs where she can help me fend one off.

Stop being afraid. Stop being pissy. Focus on how you can end this once and for all. With Daisy's unwitting help.

I cannot afford to be afraid, and I cannot afford to be kind. There is an anvil over my head.

I cut a deal with Liam, and now that bargain has become an anvil. They always do, don't they? You think you've come to an arrangement, and instead, you fulfill your end of it to discover that it only stopped the anvil middrop. It's still there, waiting for one false move.

I rise and finger the scotch bottle, running my thumbnail along the seal. Then I peer out the window.

It's dark, and there's no sign of Daisy.

Where the hell is she?

She'd better not call and expect me to pick her up.

God, I sound like my mother.

I'm turning from the window when I catch movement in the trees.

Someone's out there. It's not Daisy. She would come from the other direction, and she sure as hell wouldn't be skulking through the swamp.

My hand slides to the end table, fingers wrapping around the gun I set there. Then I ease closer to the window. As soon as I do that, I realize I'm standing in front of an open window, backlit. I might as well wave a red flag over my head.

I step to the side fast and consider closing the cigarette-smoke-yellowed sheers. The movement will be noticed. Also, how will I see outside if the sheer is closed?

I adjust my grip on the gun. From my spot beside the window, I can just make out motion in the forest. That's it. No light. There's a bright moon and floodlights on the back of the house. Whoever's out there doesn't need light.

The movement stops. I imagine someone there, swathed in darkness, staring into the house. I imagine stepping just an inch toward the window, and a bullet shatters the glass, and I drop dead to the floor.

No. As much as I fear death, that is not how this will happen. The man out there is a messenger. A warning that my tormenter is about to make his move. Unless I make sure he doesn't.

All the doors are locked, and I'm not opening them to anyone except Daisy. I should retreat. Go into the spare room upstairs. Pull the blind and wait, the gun on my lap. Or I could run for Tom's place.

I slip out the front door and squint for any sign of Daisy, but the road's far enough from the house that I won't see her unless she's swinging a light. Then I ease into the forest and begin making my way around the house, gun in hand.

I am not as silent as I'd like, but there's little I can do about that. I am careful, moving across the loamy earth, avoiding anything that might crackle underfoot. Thankfully, after three days of rain, there's little dry foliage left, and all I hear are the soft chuffs of my shoes. I strain to hear my attacker moving, but everything is silent.

And then it is not.

I'm nearing the back of the house when I pick up a shuffling sound. I go still, a dozen zombie movies playing in my head. The sound isn't footsteps, though. It's someone moving objects. A faint clatter. A fainter thump.

The sounds come from the shed.

The intruder has boxed himself in a tiny building with a single exit.

As I move around the shed, I put each foot down as if I'm walking a minefield. My approach is silent, though I'm not sure how necessary that is—he's making no attempt to hide his movements inside. He's not bothering with darkness, either, as dim light seeps through the cracks.

I ease to the door. It isn't even closed. When I peer around, I see a figure with his back to me, pawing through Daisy's leftover belongings.

I step into the doorway, gun raised.

Then I clear my throat.

DAISY

When that throat clearing sounds behind me, I jump so high, I fall, and in my tumble, I manage to twist and land on my ass. I also manage to grab my knife from the shed floor. I thump down, knife raised . . . only to realize the blade isn't extended.

That's when I see Celeste standing there, hands behind her back, watching me.

"Jesus!" I say. "You scared the crap out of me."

"I see that." She pauses. "Nice instincts."

I wave the multi-tool. "Yep, one wrong move, and I'd have thrown this at you. Might even have left a bruise." I pull out the two-inch blade. "Even like this, it's better for prying off bottle caps than stabbing would-be attackers."

She eases against the door, one arm dropping to her side as the other rests behind her back. "You gave *me* a scare. I saw you skulking around the forest."

"Skulking?" I raise my brows.

She waves it off. "What are you doing out here?"

"Getting the rest of my stuff." I heft the small backpack. "Not much left out here, but I figured I should bring it in. If we get another intruder, I'd hate for him to steal my"—I reach into the bag and pull out an item—"dental floss."

"You're in a good mood tonight."

Celeste says it with a smile, but a hint of sarcasm slips through, and I hesitate before remembering where I've been and who I've been with.

"I am," I say. "That door was in much worse shape than I expected. I thought I'd be there even later. It's fixed, though."

She relaxes. "Good."

"Tom will be coming by tomorrow to help with the window," I say as I brush off my dirty knees.

Her eyes light up, the distraction doing its job.

She backs out of the shed and says, "I'll meet you up at the house. And next time you go sneaking through the woods at night, please use a flashlight."

I lift the penlight. "I did use a . . ."

But she's already gone.

I sleep with a knife under my pillow. Not the little multi-tool one, but a steak knife from the drawer. I'd much rather have my gun. That's why I went to my shed. Walking back from Tom's, I'd realized how dark and quiet it was and remembered the break-in. Fetching my gun seemed like a fine idea. Right up until Celeste "caught" me, and I could hardly pull my gun from its hiding spot in front of her.

I tell myself that's for the best. I can't risk her finding the gun in my room, either. Better to leave it where it is.

Instead, I have a steak knife and a bedroom door that doesn't lock. Celeste's does. A determined intruder could break it easily, but if someone comes looking for her, I don't want them ending up in my room. So I wedge a chair under the knob.

By now, I'm convinced last night's intruder wasn't random. I'm not the only one here with a plan. I just know how to conduct my business with a little more finesse.

THIRTEEN

CELESTE

I know I'm dreaming. I know the nightmare is nothing more than a memory on replay. That should make it easier, shouldn't it? You're reliving a moment of hell, but it's in the past, and you'll wake up safe in your bed. Somehow, though, it is worse, as if I'm locked in my body, screaming for someone to stop the movie . . . and no one does. I cannot wake myself up. I must suffer through it. Again.

The shot comes first. It always does. A gunshot, and a surreal moment of realizing I now live the kind of life where I recognize that noise. It doesn't sound the way it does on TV. There, you don't feel it vibrate through the air. You don't smell the gunpowder.

The first few times I heard live gunfire, I mistook it for everything that teens like me mistake it for—firecrackers shooting, cars backfiring, even a jackhammer. I no longer make that mistake. I live a life where I will never make that mistake again, and of all the lessons I have learned, this may be the one I hate most. That I know the sound and smell and visceral feel of gunfire.

Then comes the blood. I know that smell, too. The smell of it, the taste of it dripping into my mouth from a broken nose, the hell of cleaning it from a shirt because, goddamn it, I really liked that shirt, and I should have known better than to wear it when Aaron was in a mood.

I am not abused. I hold that delusion high and proud. Yes, he's broken my nose. Yes, I've had to wear sunglasses when there's no sun. But those incidents are few and far between, and I give as good as I get. Aaron may be a man accustomed to solving his problems with his fists, but it takes a lot for him to turn those fists my way, and when he does, I've learned to raise mine back, and he respects that.

So I tell myself I'm not abused, and I'd bristle at anyone who labeled me as such. That does not mean I am happy. It does not mean I am staying. I have a plan, and I will be gone soon. Free of him. Free of this life.

Then comes the shot. And the blood. Shot ringing in my ears. Blood splattering my face, hot and thick and stinking.

He has found out.

He knows I am leaving, and this is his answer, and I am dead. I'm dead, and my body hasn't figured that out yet. A shot in the head, my brain still spinning, my last moments on earth spent navel-gazing on the fact that I know what a goddamn gunshot sounds like.

I am dead, and no one will care. That's what he's told me, time and again. No one will notice. No one will care. No one will shed a tear.

Then someone screams. It's a horrible scream, like a rabbit caught in a trap. A rabbit like me, knowing it's already dead, screaming as it waits for its body to shut down. Waits for the mercy of death and shrieks for it to hurry.

I take comfort in that scream. It will be the last sound I hear as I slump to the floor. Someone screaming for me, proving Aaron is wrong. That I died, and someone *did* give a damn.

A slap comes, hard and fast against my cheek, and I gasp, and the scream stops. The scream chokes off in that gasp, and I clutch my throat as if I'll feel it there. I do, my throat raw and sore.

I was screaming?

That was me?

A wash of despair as I realize no one was crying out for the loss of me. Who the hell did I actually think was screaming? Aaron is right. No one cares. This is the mess I've made of my life in three short years. From a suburban kid running away on a lark to this girl who will die alone and forgotten.

"That's better," he says, a formless voice in the void. "Now help me clean this shit up."

I blink, and Aaron comes into focus, that handsome face I've learned to hate.

I'm dripping blood, cheek stinging from his slap, as I breathe my last, mourned by no one.

Except I am still breathing. Still breathing and feeling no pain except that slap and the rawness in my throat.

"Did you hear me?" he says. "I gotta clean this shit up, and you're damn well going to help, since it's your mess."

I look down at my empty hands. Then I see the body on the floor and the gun shoved in Aaron's waistband.

"Did you think I wouldn't find out?" he says. "Did you think you could sneak another guy into my house and screw him right under my nose?"

"W-what? N-no." I stare at the body, and it takes a moment for the shock to clear, for my mind to rewind and remember who this is and what happened.

"I wasn't—I don't even know—I got up to use the bathroom, and I heard a noise, and he grabbed me. If you hadn't come in . . ." I fall against Aaron. "You saved me."

He takes my chin, fingers digging in as he lifts my face to his. "If you screwed him, tell me. If you tell me you didn't and I find out you're lying . . ."

I meet his gaze firmly. "I didn't have sex with him. I didn't even kiss him. I didn't do anything with him."

The first two are true. The third is not completely true, but in the context of sex, it is, and so I can say it with a clear conscience.

The truth?

The truth is that I had every intention of having sex with the dead boy on the floor. That would be the price I paid for freedom. This boy would help me escape Aaron, and I understood the implicit cost of that. But I had given no advance on that payment, and so I can deny it without fear of Aaron seeing a lie in my face.

Aaron grabs the dead boy by the collar and hauls his body up, grotesquely dangling there, ruined head lolling, a bit of brain caught in his hair.

"You're telling me you don't know him?"

"No, I do," I say. "I've seen him at the park when I walk Lacey. He's talked to me a couple of times and—" I inhale sharply and turn away. "I thought he was just being nice. Friendly, you know? He liked Lacey, and he brought her treats, and he asked about her, not me, so I figured . . ."

"You figured this boy was interested in your *dog*?" A disgusted snort. "Go clean up. Then get your ass back here and help me with this."

I bolt up from the dream, heaving breaths. My gaze darts about the darkness, my heart hammering, hands clawing the sheets, certain I'm back there, in the bedroom I'd shared with Aaron.

I smell mildew first. I have woken in this room cursing that stench so many times, but now I gulp it greedily as proof that I am not with Aaron. I am in my house. My own house. Safe.

Safe?

Not quite, but making my way in that direction.

At whose expense?

I squeeze my eyes shut and try to ignore the voice, the one that doesn't sound like Aaron or my mother, the one that uncomfortably resembles the one luxury I truly cannot afford to possess: a conscience.

I dream of that poor dead boy, the one whose death rests on my conscience more than Jasmine Oleas's. I did not pull the trigger, but I still got him killed. He only wanted to help. Okay, he wanted something in return for helping, but it's not as if he demanded payment in advance. He was just hopeful. A horny, hopeful, decent kid trying to do a decent thing, rescuing a damsel in honest distress. And he died for it.

Now I'm doing the same with Daisy. Pulling her into my problem, and unlike that poor kid, she doesn't have any idea what she's gotten herself into. She thinks she's found a place to hole up, maybe make a few bucks doing honest work, and in return, I am putting her into the crosshairs of a monster, just as I did with that boy.

Except Liam is not a monster. He's just a garden-variety controlling, abusive asshole. For all his fancy clothes and fancy cars and fancy bottles of fancy booze, he's a low-level hustler who pulls in most of his income from a legitimate job. Oh, he'd like to do better. He'd like to be a player, like Aaron. But he's still the guy who's half-convinced I'm his actual girlfriend. The guy who sends me flowers and takes me to parties and always asks, "How was it for you?" after sex.

Not a monster. Still my jailer. Still a threat.

Is it possible Liam was the one who broke into my house? Trying to spook me into coming to live with him? Yanking me out of my den and dragging me into a tighter cage? Yes, and I'm deluding myself if I pretend otherwise. When I thought I spotted someone outside tonight, my gut said it was Liam—or someone he sent to spook me—before I realized it was just Daisy.

I feel under threat, and I am preparing to act . . . and using Daisy to help me. That's what the dream truly means. I fear another foiled escape plan where an innocent pays the price.

I stretch in bed, tilting my head back, and I catch a flicker of light overhead. One flash, and it's gone. I rise on my elbows and stare up at the crack in the ceiling. My first thought is that it's another thing I need to ask Daisy to fix—she'd respectfully stayed out of my room during her assessment. My second thought is that Daisy isn't going to be around long enough to fix it. And my third thought?

Did I just see a light through that crack?

A light in the attic at two in the morning?

It happened so fast that I only had the faintest impression of illumination, but I'd been looking straight at that crack, and I'd definitely seen light.

Daisy is in my attic.

In my attic at two a.m., when she has absolutely no excuse to be up there.

I slide from bed, making as little noise as I can. Then, moving in the darkness, I scoop up my phone, and find my gun and head into the hall.

As I glide along the hall, I pause at Daisy's door. I know her room will be empty, but I still stop to check. The door is shut. I grip the knob and turn slowly. The latch disengages, and I give the door the softest push.

It doesn't move.

I twist the knob again as I crouch to be sure I'm actually opening it. The latch clicks back into place and then retracts when I turn it the other way. Through the crack, I see the faint glow of moonlight, meaning the latch is definitely retracted. The door doesn't have a lock. It'd been my room when Maeve was alive, so I'm well acquainted with the lack of a lock.

I try the door again. This time, it gives a soft thump, as if hitting something. Thumps and stops.

Daisy has jammed the door. I don't know how, but she's a carpenter. She'd know ways to make it stay shut even when she's gone. I'm sure I could break in with a hard shove, but that would only give her time to zip out of the attic and reappear in the hall.

I was just in the bathroom.

I was just downstairs getting a drink of water.

No, I need to catch her in the act. I release the doorknob, straighten and head for the attic. The door is shut, but this one opens easily. I wince as the hinges creak. Then I stand in the opening and squint up into darkness.

All is still and silent above.

Is it possible she got back in her room after I spotted that light? No. It'd taken me ten seconds tops to process the meaning of that flicker and get out of bed. Within twenty seconds, I'd been in the hall, and there's no way she silently fled the attic, got into her room and jammed the door shut before I stepped from my room.

I move my bare foot onto the first step and ease forward. The stairs creak. I know that from when Maeve was alive and I'd needed a place to hide my secrets. The attic had been the one place I could be sure she wouldn't go snooping—the stairs were too narrow for her to navigate.

I know which treads will creak, and I step over them. As I ascend, the attic remains still and silent. When I reach the top, I move even slower, knowing the top of my head will show before

I can see. Once my gaze is at floor level, I stop and tighten my grip on the gun.

I wait for Daisy to see me. She'll spot me, give a startled gasp and then make some excuse.

I couldn't stop thinking about the leak. Insert apologetic laugh. *I wanted to make sure the repair was holding. I hope I didn't disturb you.*

I wait for that gasp. Nothing comes. I climb another step and look around.

Hello? Is anyone up here?

I open my mouth, but I can't get the ridiculous dialogue out. Instead, I grip the gun tighter and keep rising until I'm fully in the attic.

No one's here.

Strike that—no one's here that I can *see.*

That's how Daisy is going to play this. She heard me in the hall and went into hiding. After all, it's not as if I can check her room and realize she's gone. She just needs to wait me out. Plenty of places to do it up here, between the boxes and the old furniture. That's another reason I picked this spot for my box of secrets—no one's ever going to find it in this mess.

I lower my gun. If she steps out, I don't want her to see the weapon. That would be very inconvenient.

After two steps, I pause and crouch with my cell phone flashlight aimed at the floor. My thought is that I'll look for footprints, which I quickly realize is ridiculous—there are prints everywhere from Daisy and Tom fixing the leak, and then from me inspecting it before and after.

I straighten and continue on, swinging my light behind every box, listening for the telltale scuffle of Daisy trying to find a better hiding spot. All I hear is the soft thump of my bare feet on the floorboards.

My light catches something that makes me stop. A box has been moved. It's not near where I hide my things, but I still notice it's moved because I considered hiding my stuff here, amid this jumble of filthy, moldering boxes. Someone has moved a box, most evident by the fact that the damp cardboard tore with the effort.

This spot, at the far end of the attic, is also right over my bedroom. Here the attic floorboards end, leaving exposed rafters and beams.

If that crack in my bedroom ceiling goes all the way through, as I presume it does, then moving a box would explain that flicker of light. Daisy was up here, with a flashlight on, shifted a box, and I caught the light below.

I shine my own light as I look for the crack. I spot the tail end of it. The other end is beneath a box, exactly as I figured.

I move the top crate and then the bottom one. I want to confirm—

I stop. Blink. Shine my flashlight down.

There's something showing between the floorboards. Something fastened to them, right over that crack.

A box.

It isn't big. Maybe the size of a pack of cigarettes. As I watch, it blinks. The single flicker of a dim red light.

There's a moment where my brain screams, *Bomb!* I'll blame that on stress and lack of sleep. It's an electronic device of some sort, and that red light seems to indicate an error. I watch it for at least three minutes before it flashes again, even dimmer this time. Then I bend and shine my light on the device and—

Holy shit.

No.

Tell me that is not what it seems to be.

Of course it is, because "what it seems to be" makes sense for a device poised over a crack in my bedroom ceiling.

I pull it from a plastic holder tacked onto the floor joist to keep the device in place.

And that device?

It's a goddamn camera.

Someone is recording me sleeping.

Oh no, they're recording more than me sleeping. I remember the other night, when Liam slept over.

What the actual *hell*?

It takes all my strength not to start cursing out loud. I stare down at the device. It's definitely a camera, and it's definitely running, that warning light seeming to indicate an error, maybe a low battery, given the decreasing strength of that flash.

I'm standing there, shining my light over the camera, when I pick up footprints on the floor. I go still. Then, keeping my own feet in place, I bend with the flashlight. There are at least a dozen prints, too smudged to make out more than that they are definitely shoe prints of some sort. But there, only a few feet away, are two very distinct prints. Prints from shoes smaller than mine.

I take a cell phone photo of the tread. Then I head down two flights of stairs to the main floor. Daisy's sneakers are there, right by the front door. I check against the photo. It's the same tread.

Daisy set up that camera.

Set up a camera over my *bedroom*.

I want to storm to her room, slam open that jammed door and shove the camera in her face. She'd deny it. I know she would.

Does that matter? It's my damn house. I don't need a reason to kick her out.

But if I kick her out, I can't use her with Liam. If she did this, then am I really going to feel that bad about setting her up? That's a bonus, isn't it?

I turn the camera over, thinking. To use this, she needs it to be transmitting the video somewhere. To another device, like a phone or laptop or tablet. She's been pretending she's tech-free, but obviously, she has something, and if I can get it, I might be able to find out what the hell our Miss Daisy is up to.

She's blocking her bedroom door, but it's open during the day, so I doubt her device is in there. Where else would it be?

In the shed.

I'd checked the shed the night Daisy slept in the lanai, while Liam was here. I'd put on his overcoat and went out into the rain to have a look. I had a stranger in my house, and I had to be sure she at least seemed to be what she claimed. I'd found a few things that supported her story. That utility knife, a wad of protein bar wrappers, a water bottle, even a map of Florida with her route marked.

Staged to look as if she was who she seemed to be, and I fell for it, not digging deeper into the debris. Now I'm out here again, and I'm sure as hell digging deeper.

I take the interior apart, moving each piece and examining the ground for signs that she's buried something. In the end, I don't find a tech device, but I do find something. Something so much worse.

I find a gun.

FOURTEEN

CELESTE

I'm back in the house. I've hidden Daisy's gun, and I've realized there's an easy way to confirm she's using a device. Also, if I'd thought it through, it's proof that such a device wouldn't be at the back of my yard.

To transmit video from the camera storage, she's going to need my Wi-Fi network. It's password protected, of course, but I'm sure anyone setting up spy cameras knows how to circumvent that problem.

What I need to do then is access the router on my laptop and look for devices I don't recognize. I find nothing. A bit of research on the camera shows it has only a low-capacity SSD card. It must download to an existing device on the network . . . like the hard drive of my own damn laptop.

It takes me an hour to find a hidden folder that demands a password when I try to access it.

The camera is storing video on my own laptop. Presuming that folder can be accessed remotely, it's the perfect way to store it in plain sight.

Daisy made that leak in the attic. I gave her an excuse by faking a leak, and she created one, giving her the opportunity to place her camera. Then she needed to set it up on my laptop. As she was doing that, I woke up. She grabbed the laptop, ran and pretended to "save" me from a thief.

Was she aiming the camera at my bed? I don't actually think so. That just happens to be where the crack is. The camera is recording private conversations with Liam or on the phone.

Why store that on my laptop? *Was* it just convenient? Or was it more sinister? Whatever she taped is on *my* laptop. As if I were taping it myself.

I don't know what to make of that. I really don't. I do know one thing: between the gun and the camera, Daisy is not the innocent she seems to be.

Oh, and I know another thing.

I will not feel the least bit guilty about what I'm about to do.

One stone. Two birds.

DAISY

I know where I want to search, thanks to Celeste, my father and Disney World.

Growing up in central Florida, you get tired of Disney World pretty quickly. Or you do if your family has the money to go. If not, then the "most magical place on earth" is an hour's drive away, dangling just out of reach. That changed when I was nine and Dad started doing construction under the table for a guy who gave him two annual resident passes.

That year, Dad and I gorged ourselves on Disney. We had to go on the cheap—sneaking in snacks and eating lunch at our car—but it didn't matter. I was with Dad. Just the two of us. Truly one of the happiest times of my life.

Today, I'm reminded of the first time we went on Splash Mountain. As the raft ascends, the story of Brer Rabbit unfolds. I remember Dad's face glowing with delight at the clever rabbit outwitting the fox and bear.

For guys like my father, that rabbit was their idol, and the predators were the authority figures constantly dogging their steps, keeping them from achieving the American Dream. That's how they were raised, in a world where everyone hustled just to make ends meet.

I know now that the *Song of the South* is problematic, but as a child, I'd been delighted by Brer Rabbit's briar patch trick. As I got older, I used it on many occasions. *Oh no, Brer Keith, please don't make me run errands,* when running errands meant an hour of freedom. *Oh no, Ms. Teacher, please don't make me stay indoors at recess,* where my friends and I were so much happier hanging out and chatting. *Oh no, Mr. Supervisor, please don't make me shingle that roof,* my favorite part of home construction, so peaceful and soothing.

Is there any place in the house you don't want me poking around, Celeste?

Why, yes, please don't go in the attic, Daisy.

In Brer Rabbit's world, that would mean the attic contained absolutely nothing incriminating, just endless boxes that I'd waste my time searching. But I suspect Celeste doesn't know the story.

I really want some quality time with that attic, but Celeste is in a mood this morning. Wary and watchful, as if I sprouted fangs and claws in the night. Normally, she'd retreat to her office after breakfast and shut the door. Today, that door stays open, which means I'm not going to be poking around the attic.

I'll just keep busy, earning my keep and extending my stay while having an excuse to poke around the house, "assessing it." Then I'll get into Sun City and use the library computer. I need to contact someone and do a little bit of online research.

After lunch, I tell Celeste that I'm heading to Sun City for groceries.

"I can cook while I'm here," I say, "if that helps."

Her look suggests I might add strychnine to her spaghetti.

I shrug. "Or I can just cook for myself. Just as easy to do it for two, though."

"I'll buy the groceries, and you can cook. Give me a list, and I'll pick them up."

Now I'm the one hesitating.

"It's a ten-mile walk," she says.

"I was planning to grab the heavier groceries from Tom's store. I was mostly running to Sun City for library books."

"Well, then, I guess I'll be driving you."

"You don't need to."

"I should go into town, too. Pick up a few things." She glances at her watch. "We'll leave in twenty minutes."

CELESTE

"Miss Celeste," the pharmacist says as I walk to the counter. "Don't you look pretty today."

Before he goes to get my prescription, he beams at me, as he always does. I suspect it's because I'm the only customer under sixty. Sun City is as close as a municipality can come to being one massive retirement community. The moment you enter town, signs warn you of its greatest driving hazard: golf carts. They're everywhere, and while they really are a safety hazard, I would happily abandon my car at the city's edge and walk if they passed a law against all motor vehicles except golf carts . . . because that'd mean I wouldn't need to worry about the seniors who still drive cars. After three parking-lot dings, I learned to park as far from any store as possible and get my exercise walking.

I know I'm being ageist. But there's a certain type of person who retires to a place like Sun City, and sometimes I'm seized by the dread of becoming one. Of becoming a person whose golden-years dream is to live in a place where there is, as the name advertises, a lot of sun . . . and not much else. No beach, no salt breeze, no waving palms. Every strip mall has an optometrist and a hearing specialist, but there isn't a single Starbucks, much less a funky local café. If you want coffee, there are donut shops for that. A meal? Expect either a chain restaurant or a cheap buffet.

I fear someday I'll get tired of running and hustling, find a decent guy, settle down and have kids and just . . . breathe. Breathe and relax in a way I can't right now, and I'll be so happy for the security and the stability that I'll just drift along until I wind up someplace like this, waking one morning in horror at what my life has become, all because I got tired.

Tired and scared.

"Miss Celeste?" the pharmacist says.

I flick on my brightest smile as I reach for the prescription bag. He's not holding it out, though. He glances over my shoulder to where a line is forming. He lifts one finger, asking them to wait, and then waves me to the side counter.

My heart starts thumping. Something's wrong.

Of course something's wrong. He's called the doctor who wrote out my other prescriptions. It's begun to nag at him. I have the pills prescribed by Dr. Hoover, Maeve's former physician, but I've added something different this time. A prescription from an out-of-state doctor.

There was a time in my life when I said this was one good thing that came out of my years with Aaron. At least I know how to pull off a stunt like this. If the pharmacist calls that number, he'll get an answering service, apparently for the doctor on the script. These days, though, I no longer pretend those skills are a valuable relic of my past. I accept the harsh truth—if I didn't have that past, I wouldn't need these skills.

"Is everything okay?" I ask the pharmacist once we're at the side counter.

"Oh, yes," he says, reaching a clammy hand to pat mine. "Sorry, dear. I didn't mean to startle you. It's just that I wanted to give you the warnings for this new medication you're taking."

I exhale and listen to his warnings. Then I take the bag and hurry out.

I make my way through the small library and spot Daisy at the computers. I frown, thinking, *You said you were coming for books.* Still, there's a stack of books at her elbow, and I've been gone long enough for her to have found what she needed.

She's running searches, skimming the results without opening any links. I'm walking up behind her when she flips to a different tab, and I stop short, recognizing the face on the screen.

Liam.

She's on his law firm's site. Looking at his webpage.

She's moving the cursor to close the browser when she stops, and I notice my reflection in the screen. I expect a deft flick of the mouse, hitting the Close button, and then she'll start in fake surprise at seeing me there.

Instead, she releases the mouse and leaves Liam's smiling face on the screen.

"Hey," she says.

"Hey." My gaze shifts pointedly to the browser window. "May I ask why you're looking up my boyfriend?"

"I'm not. I mean, I'm not looking him up as your boyfriend. I'm looking him up as a lawyer."

My brows knit as I try to untangle that.

She continues, "Tom mentioned Liam's a lawyer, and I'm kind of in need of one." She pauses, eyes widening, and throws up her hands. "Not like that."

"Not like what?"

"Nothing criminal. It's work-related. I did a big job for a friend, and she stiffed me." Daisy pushes back her chair. "That's actually what sent me on this trip. I needed to clear my head and decide what to do about it. My only recourse is to sue, and she's a friend, and she went through a vicious divorce, so I feel terrible but . . ." She inhales. "It's a lot of money. I cut her a break and lived on my savings and now . . ."

A sheepish smile. "And this is far more of an explanation than you need. The point is that I really should talk to a lawyer. When Tom mentioned Liam, I thought I'd look him up. He doesn't handle this sort of thing, though, and one look at his firm's website tells me he's out of my pay range."

"You could have just asked me what kind of law he does."

"I didn't want to put you on the spot, and I did need reading material." She nods at the books. "But now I've made things worse, getting caught on his web page. That looks creepy."

"No, it just surprised me. He doesn't do that sort of law, but he might be able to talk to you about it."

Her thin face lights up. "That would be awesome."

"Now, if you want to check out those books . . ."

"Already done. The librarians were kind enough to give me a visitor's card." She rises and hefts the stack under one arm. "Ready when you are."

We walk outside, and then I hand her the keys and say that I need to use the library restroom. When I'm sure she hasn't followed me, I slip over to the computer she was using. The browser is still open, now on the library home page. I click the history, and it comes up blank.

Is that the library setting for privacy? Or did Daisy clear it? I want to check another terminal, but there are only three computers, the other two in use by seniors hunting and pecking. I wait as long as I can before I leave with yet another question unanswered.

FIFTEEN

DAISY

That afternoon, I stay out of Celeste's way and putter around the house. Investigate why the basement crawlspace lights don't work. Blown fuse. Investigate why the kitchen exhaust fan won't work. There's a mouse nest in the intake vent. Investigate why the air conditioning doesn't work very well in my bedroom and Celeste's office. The vents have been deliberately shut off to save money. All stuff that a homeowner could fix easily, but I'm guessing Celeste doesn't have much experience in that role, and Liam strikes me as the type who calls a plumber when his toilet just needs plunging.

I got lucky when Celeste caught me at the computer. She only saw his firm's website on the screen. That was a cover while I did deeper digging.

Liam has a distinctly shady side. He makes a habit of defending drug dealers, and he has a reputation for being very good at it. He'd spent ten years working for the Tampa district attorney's office, where he'd been married to a high-school teacher, living in a decent middle-class neighborhood. Then he jumped sides, became a defense lawyer, split from his wife and—despite the divorce settlement—ended up with his million-dollar condo. I suspect the guy spent his time in the DA's office racking up frequent-flyer miles with the people he was supposed to be prosecuting. Then he redeemed those rewards for a solid clientele that won him a partnership at his new firm.

I mull that over as I tinker. As promised, Tom swings by after dinner to salvage that window. We walk there—it's shorter cutting through the property. When we draw near the abandoned house, I recognize it. I passed it a few times, tramping around pastures and swamps.

I was careful not to get too close, presuming the house was occupied. Is that because it's in such good shape? No. It's because half the homes around here are in this state of disrepair, with sagging roofs and broken windows and cluttered yards. This is the face of rural poverty, where you choose between maintaining your home and putting food on the table.

Some will snark about option three: putting dope in your veins or booze down your throat. Yet even for cases where it does apply, like my father, it wasn't a choice. It hadn't been a choice for a very long time, and even when it was, it'd have seemed like an escape from a dead-end life. Stealing one sliver of joy from a world that guards it as jealously as gold. Snatching a few moments where you aren't worrying how you'll pay the bills. And then, one day, you can't pay the bills because the sliver of joy has turned into a devouring monster that always demands first feeding.

After the tragedy, when Mom took me away from Florida, I didn't talk much about my father. Talking about him reminded me how much I missed him, and how much I hated my mother for taking me so far. But talking about him also became a wellspring of shame. None of my suburban friends had fathers with addiction problems—or so it seemed to me. And they had a very definite view of people like my dad, views I'd heard their parents expound on at length. Weak and feeble-minded, lacking the strength and will to overcome their demons.

That middle-class view insidiously infected my memories of my father, and when my mother decided my monthly phone calls with Dad were too expensive, I didn't argue very strenuously. He still sent me cards, each with a handwritten letter, and brat that I was, I saw only the atrocious spelling and cringed and hid them in shame. I replied, but with the kinds of letters one might send a distant uncle who insisted on staying in touch. Matter-of-fact recitations of my life.

I was fourteen when I overheard my mom saying he was in a hospice. Sick and not expected to live much longer. The bubble of my cruelty snapped, and in that moment, he was my daddy again, and I had to see him. She refused . . . so I went anyway. Emptied my bank account and bought a bus ticket to Florida.

I spent two weeks by his bedside. My mother knew where I was, but she didn't come after me. She meant to teach me a lesson. Instead, it was the greatest gift she ever gave me. In those two weeks with my father, all the shame that had cast him into shadow fell away, and the man I knew stepped from it. A complicated man. A man who'd made mistakes. But still the daddy I remembered, who loved me unconditionally, and who'd surrendered his place in my world because my mother convinced him that was best. To him, I now had the life he couldn't give me, the life I deserved. His version of the American Dream: a house in the suburbs, a father with an office job, the bills always paid and the fridge always full, new clothes when I needed them, new bicycles when I wanted them.

I never told him the truth about Keith. Why would I? My father gave me up so I could have that life, and I was sure as hell never admitting it was less than the perfect jewel he'd polished in his mind. However, I did make it very clear that while Keith provided for me, he wasn't my dad. There was still a place in my life for my father. He needed to know that. He owned that spot, and he always would.

After he died, I went home, and my mother acted as if I'd been away at summer camp. We never spoke of those two weeks. There are times when I wonder whether it truly *was* a gift, one she could not give outright.

She let me go to him, and she never punished me for it. I would have loved to have had the kind of mother who put me in the car and took me to my father and waited in a hotel if she couldn't face him. That goes too far, though, and I will instead allow myself to believe that she accommodated my grief in the only way she could—by leaving me to it.

As my mind weaves through slipstreams of memory, Tom and I salvage the window. It'll need a frame to fit, but it's in better shape than the one that broke.

Afterward, I rummage about for other useful bits and pieces while he talks about the people who lived in this house. The couple who'd raised their family here died about five years ago, and the house was in such bad shape that the kids just left it as is, deciding that the cost of bulldozing wouldn't cover what they could get for the land.

Those kids are all middle-aged themselves, off in the world, living the kind of suburban fantasies my dad set as his pinnacle. They're considering returning someday to build a winter retirement getaway here, but they'll demolish the old house first. It's a story that makes me feel less like a thief and more like a recycler, taking from people who wouldn't begrudge me the scraps.

Night is falling by the time Tom fetches his truck, and we load it up. I know Celeste is expecting Liam, but his Rover isn't in the drive yet. We unload the window, and then Tom says, "I've got something to show you," and leads me around the house to where an overgrown garden devours the north wall in a tangle of roses and ivy.

"Haven't been around this side, have you?" he says as he grabs a rusty spade to clear a path.

I watch him chop through the vegetation barrier. "Oddly, no."

"What a mess, huh? However, there is something back here that I think you might like."

He squints, shining his cell phone light over the mess. Then, with a crow of victory, he dives in and wrestles something from the vines.

"Ta-da!"

He flourishes a hand at a bicycle manufactured before I was born. It's yellow, with a torn banana seat and a plastic handlebar basket. I look at it, and a million emotions rush up, all those summer days of running down back roads, Tom pedaling beside me. Summer evenings of us both on our bikes, riding until darkness called us home.

My throat constricts, and I stay back, hiding my expression in darkness.

"I know you're a runner," he says, "but this will be more practical for getting to town. While I'd happily drive you in, you'll never ask. So, if you ride . . ." He waves at the bike.

"It's perfect."

His laugh floats through the night. "It is a *long* way from perfect. However, after a bit of work, I can have her ready to go."

"You don't need to—"

"I want to." He hauls the bike the rest of the way out, shaking off the foliage. "I'll have her done by noon tomorrow."

I want to argue, but that'll get awkward. So I say simply, "Thank you."

He wheels the bike toward me, and I start backing up to give him room, but he comes in close and lowers his voice.

"I'm on your side," he says.

I blink and wonder whether I've misheard. On my side . . . in what? There's an obvious answer, but it doesn't quite make sense.

He studies my face. After a second, he nods, as if to himself, and he wrinkles his nose with a smile as he leans back against the wall. "That came out weird, didn't it? I just mean . . ." He flails his hands. "I don't even know what I mean. I'm a mechanic and an accountant—words aren't really my thing. I just mean that I get the sense you're going through a lot in your life, and I . . ."

"Want to help?"

That nose scrunch again, which is far too adorable. The flailing is also adorable, and something in me melts, seeing him so intent on explaining.

"That makes it sound like you're a defenseless stray kitten. I just . . . I want to be helpful. No strings attached. I'm not offering because I expect anything. I just . . ."

He rocks back and rubs at his mouth, gaze slipping to the side. "I can talk. I can talk and talk and talk, as you've seen. I don't do it with everyone. In fact, I don't do it with most people. But if I'm comfortable with someone, then it's like they pull the string on my inner Chatty Cathy doll. I'm comfortable with you. I feel like there's . . ."

His gaze swings my way, and I'm suddenly very aware of how close he is, the heat radiating off him, the trickle of sweat at his hairline despite the cool evening breeze. Those gorgeous brown eyes meet mine, and his look brings a wave of heat with it as my treacherous body responds.

I swallow, waiting for him to move closer, to take his shot. He doesn't, though. He stays exactly where he is and says, his voice low, "I don't expect anything. It's not that kind of helpful. I just . . . I need you to know that."

I nod mutely.

"I wouldn't do that," he says.

I nod again.

His fingers brush my hip, and I tense, and I expect him to withdraw, but he only tilts his head, looking at me as if trying to determine whether that tensing means "back off." He seems to decide it doesn't, and he stays where he is, fingertips on my hip, correctly interpreting the signal as slow down, proceed with caution. A yellow light, not a red. Not a green, either. He sees that, and he stays in place, close enough for me to hear his breathing.

Then he shifts, his gaze meeting mine, a smile touching his lips, half-shy, half-wry. There's no blaze of the white-hot charisma he gives Celeste. That is a finely honed sword, wielded with almost careless ease. This is the Tom I remember, that smile the exact one that'd played on his lips when he leaned in to kiss me the first time. He makes no move to do that, though, and when his lips part, it's only to murmur, "I'm on your side. That just means . . ."

"I know what it means. Thank you."

I touch his hand, one finger tracing down his, looking up into his eyes with a smile that I hope is friendly and warm and promises nothing. I can promise nothing. Not yet. But after . . . ?

I haven't let myself think of "after." Of when the lies and the deceptions are swept away. I won't think of it, either. Better to just offer a smile that, if it promises anything at all, promises what we had once upon a time. Friendship with the faintest possibility of more.

"You wanna go back to my place?" he whispers with a mock-suggestive wiggle of his brows. "Do a little stargazing?" His lips drop to my ear as he whispers, "I refilled the orange soda."

I laugh as I give him a push, and he leans in to whisper something else and—

A throat clears beside us, startling me, and I stumble, Tom catching me as we look over to see Celeste standing there, arms crossed.

"Did I interrupt something?"

SIXTEEN

CELESTE

It's night, and I am alone in the house again. Because Daisy is off with Tom again. That complicates things. I should have spoken to her at dinner and made it clear that I needed her here tonight. This isn't going to work if she has Tom as her alibi.

It's already not going as planned. Liam was due to arrive long before night fell. He's called three times with excuses.

My last meeting ran late.

Just heard from a client. Need to make one more call.

Grabbing dinner and heading out.

A few minutes after that last text, Tom's pickup sounds in the drive. Voices follow as they unload the truck. I glance through the window and see that it's only starting to get dark, and chide myself for my nerves. I can still do this, even with Tom around. I'll invite him in for a beer and tell Daisy she's welcome to join us.

I throw open the front door with an invitation on my lips. The yard is empty save for a window propped in the garden. I step onto the porch. The pickup is dark, engine off, no sign of its owner or Daisy.

I listen, frowning. Voices come from the side of the house, with a comment about the overgrown state of it. Daisy must have spotted something that needs repair, and she's showing Tom. I'll head back inside and start the popcorn. The smell is sure to add appeal to my offer.

When I return, they're still around the side of the house. Murmured voices slide through the still night.

I trot down the steps. My earlier nerves have flitted away as the prospect of a pleasant evening dances before me. In another life, I couldn't have imagined anything so dull—or Floridian—as sitting on the front porch drinking beer and chatting with a prison-tattooed mechanic.

No, I could have imagined one thing worse: if the mechanic made my pulse race . . . and I was stuck on that porch sharing him with a mousy young woman who he's decided needs a big brother. Right now, though, it seems like the perfect evening. I can enjoy Tom's charms and smiles with the safety guard of Daisy keeping my thoughts from galloping where they shouldn't. That will still leave plenty of time to launch my plan after he's gone. I just need to make sure Daisy doesn't leave with him.

Maybe I'll break out the scotch. I smirk at the thought of Liam showing up to see me sharing his gift with a mechanic who won't know the difference between eighteen-year-old single malt and fresh-from-the-still moonshine.

That's what you get for showing up late. And if you don't show up at all . . . maybe I'll find my company elsewhere. I really didn't intend to sleep alone tonight.

Even as I smile at the thought, my gut twists. No, I can imagine the outcome of that, and it is not what I want. Not at all. I have plans for tonight. Big plans, and I cannot afford distraction.

I head to the side of the house. The voices have gone silent, and I slow. If Daisy and Tom are around back, I don't want to take this route. It was impassable the last time I tried.

As I draw near, though, I see Tom has hacked a path. Enough moonlight shines for me to make out two figures standing very close together. I catch voices then, low and intimate.

Hair on the back of my neck prickles.

They are standing close enough to touch, and when I follow the curve of his arm . . .

Are his fingers resting on her hip? I can't tell from here, and I'm sure it's just the angle. When I look at their faces again, they're still talking, Tom's head bent, his hair hanging to shield his face. Daisy, though, is looking straight ahead, not up at him. He's speaking, and she's listening, and it seems like something she doesn't want to hear.

Sorry, Daisy, I just don't think of you that way.

Possibly, but I've seen no sign that *she* thinks of *him* that way. Her voice warms when she speaks of him, and she will smile, but it's in the way one does if one finds a friendly face in a forbidding world. Nothing more.

I'm about to call a hello when Tom steps closer still, his face right above hers as she looks up into his.

He's going to kiss her. He's lured her into this hidden corner, said a few sweet words, and now he's taking advantage of her vulnerable state.

Except she's not so vulnerable, is she? Not the girl I thought she was. In fact, Tom might be the one in danger here.

She's playing him. I see that now. Her body language had been screaming "No" a moment ago, and now he's moved closer, saying more, and she's looking up at him like a trapped deer, caught in the tractor beam of his charm.

He lowers his lips to her ear and whispers something, and I tense, ready to march down there and—

And what? Rescue her? She doesn't need it. Rescue him? I doubt he does, either.

No, the only thing in need of rescue is my plan, which will be screwed if they decide to slip off into the night together.

When Tom leans in again, I barrel forward and stop a few feet away. I clear my throat, and they both jump.

"Did I interrupt something?"

Daisy laughs softly. "Just Tom trying to lure me into doing more work around his shop with the promise of orange soda and cheese puffs. It almost worked, too."

Tom grins. "What can I say? I know how to tempt a lady. I will raid the store, lay a trail of sweets from your door to mine and trap the wild carpenter in my lair, where she'll work off her sugar high fixing my workbench."

"Wait," Daisy says. "Your workbench is broken, too? Is anything there in *good* shape?"

He flexes a bicep, and she rolls her eyes at me. Either I misread Tom's signals, or he was just idly flirting, more reflex than intent, and she understands that.

Daisy picks up a decrepit bicycle leaning against the house.

"Dear Lord, is that a banana seat?" I ask.

"It is. Tom rescued it from the iron grip of those vines."

He flexes again with a cartoon-bodybuilder grunt. She shakes her head and starts wheeling the bike toward the back of the house.

"I'll take this to your truck," she says. "Fix it for me, and we'll talk about your workbench."

"And that shelf?" he calls. "Before it collapses?"

"Lay a trail of candy bars, and we'll discuss it."

"I will," he calls as she disappears. "Believe me, I will."

He turns back to me, his grin fading into a crooked smile. "I know it looks like I'm stealing your handywoman, but I promise I won't interfere with her work for you. I just . . ." He makes sure she's gone and then steps toward me, voice lowering. "I want her to have the bike for mobility." He pauses. "If that's all right with you."

"It is."

"I won't take up too much of her time. I just know she won't let me fix the bike for free."

"You're good to her."

He makes a face. "She's not a charity case. I just . . ." He shrugs. "I like to help people. It feels right, you know?"

I don't, and regret stabs me at that. I always want to *seem* like a good person, a caring person. That's useful. But for once, I feel genuine regret that I can't experience whatever pleasure comes from helping another person. I've lived a life where that isn't an option. Pause to help someone who's fallen by the roadside, and I'll be mowed down by the life choices I'm trying so hard to outrun.

I open my mouth to agree with him, but instead find myself saying, "I wish I could do more of that."

"You are, by giving her a place to stay."

Real guilt heats my cheeks then . . . until I remind myself that Daisy is no innocent victim. I'm no longer preying on a young woman backpacking through Florida. I'm getting in the first strike in a fair fight.

Tom steps closer and touches my arm and says, "You're helping her a lot. Thank you."

I look up. Earlier, I'd mentally remarked on Daisy being caught in the tractor beam of his charm. It's not Daisy who's in danger. I'm trapped in a web he wove without meaning to, and I'm not sure why I'm so ensnared. I'd thought it was the bad-boy vibe, but the more time I spend with Tom, the more obvious it becomes that there's no "bad boy" here. Mistaking those prison tats for a sign of edgy criminality is like my old teenage friends expecting a pot-smoking dad to know how to hire a hit man.

No, what Tom has is a quality that I never thought I'd find attractive in a man. A quality I've taken advantage of many times. Kindness.

"I should probably go," he murmurs, still touching my arm, and there's a reluctance in his voice that makes my knees weak.

"You don't have—" I begin, my voice a little breathy before I clear my throat and say, lightly, "If you do, you'll miss out on some very fine scotch. That's what I came out here for—to ask if you'd like to share a glass of eighteen-year single malt with me."

"Eighteen years old? Ah, so you're in a hurry to get rid of it, before it goes bad."

I hesitate.

He laughs. "Joking. I know that means it's very fine scotch, but it would be wasted on me. I thought I caught a whiff of . . ." He lifts his nose. "Is that popcorn?"

"It is. Scotch and popcorn, then. Perhaps Daisy will join us."

"Or perhaps we could just not invite her."

His lips twitch, letting me take this as a joke, if that's what I'd like. My choice.

"She *has* had a long day," I say.

"And we ought to be considerate of that."

His eyes dance, and I find myself leaning his way, drawn to him in spite of myself.

In spite of myself? No, I think we're past those games. I want Tom, and if he wants me back, well, we're both consenting adults, aren't we?

"So Liam isn't coming over tonight?" he murmurs.

Reality taps icy fingers on my shoulder, but I shove it aside and reach out to touch Tom's arm. I run one finger over his bicep. His gaze lowers, and he looks at me through long, dark lashes.

"A cold drink sounds good," he says.

"For a start?"

An easy smile. "Sure, a cold drink for a start, and then we'll move on to popcorn."

He's telling me to slow down, and it is delightful. Those lowered lashes. The hair on his arm rising as I run a finger over it.

You're a little shy, aren't you, Tom?

Not what I expected. Not normally what I like. But it shifts me into the control seat, and I do like that.

I rub my finger over his forearm. "Scotch and popcorn it is."

Undergrowth snaps behind me. I turn to see Liam step through. His gaze falls to my hand, still on Tom's arm.

"Should I back up and announce myself first?" Liam says, his lips quirking in a humorless smile. "It seems someone didn't expect me to show up tonight."

Tom doesn't jerk his arm away. He only lifts a level gaze to Liam's. I run a finger down a tattoo that looks like a stylized rabbit.

"I was just asking Tom about this one," I say.

"Ah."

Liam's lip twitch calls me a liar, but he seems more amused than jealous, which puts me on guard.

"And what did he say?" Liam asks.

"Nothing yet," Tom says. "I was about to say it's the trickster, from Seminole stories." He turns to me. "I'll take that cold drink to go, if it's still on offer."

"A cold drink?" Liam says. "Is that what she offered?"

The two men lock eyes, and I have to resist the urge to kick Liam. He's not annoyed with me for flirting with Tom. His attention is entirely on the other man, the trespasser.

"Nah," Tom says. "She offered me scotch, but I told her not to waste it on me. I'm guessing that's more your speed."

"It is." Liam puts out a hand. "Liam Garey. I'm not sure we've formally met."

"We have. You just don't remember me."

Tom steps forward and takes Liam's hand, and Liam's arm muscles bunch under his sleeve as he squeezes hard. Tom's muscles don't even twitch. He sees the game, and he's not playing it.

Tom introduces himself to Liam and then turns to me. "I should be going."

"No, not at all." Liam thumps Tom on the shoulder, and I wince, throwing Tom an apologetic look. Before I can speak, Liam says, "Why don't we all head inside for that . . . cold drink, was it, Tommy?"

"Tom, please. And I really should . . ." His gaze shifts, and I spot Daisy coming around from the front.

"Hey," she says, looking across our faces uncertainly. "I heard voices. I was just coming to tell Tom that the bike is in his truck."

"Daisy!" Liam says, arms outstretched as if she's just returned from a month-long hike in the Andes. "Just who I wanted to see."

Her gaze flits to us. Tom's jaw sets, and he rocks forward, but Liam continues. This isn't going as planned. But can I use it? Maybe.

"I was just asking Tommy to stay for a drink," Liam says. "Now that you're here, Daisy, we have four hands for Friday night poker."

Daisy's brows start to rise, as if certain he's kidding, her gaze going to Tom for confirmation that she's walked in midjoke.

"I should really be going," Tom says, brushing past Liam, who claps a hand on his shoulder.

"Oh, come on," Liam says. "Stay and play with us."

Tom looks at Liam's hand. Liam only grips tighter and continues in that false hearty tone. "Fine, go on. We'll find a three-handed game."

Daisy demurs, but Liam insists. Tom's gaze cuts to her, and then he says, "Sure, let's play a little poker."

SEVENTEEN

DAISY

Why the hell didn't Celeste shut this down? I'm caught in a drama that isn't about me, feeling as if I walked into a theater in the second act, and instead of being allowed to take a seat, I got yanked onstage.

The game started fine. It seemed whatever issue Liam had, he was determined to save face by beating Tom at cards, and yes, that's weird, but whatever. Tom seemed to be willing to go along with it. Let Liam restore his pride through a pointless game.

It *is* pointless, too. Liam proposed stakes, but Celeste vetoed that with a meaningful look my way, and Liam didn't insist.

The drink situation doesn't help. There's that damn bottle of scotch. Tom tries to demur by saying he'd like something cold instead, and Celeste brings him a scotch and soda.

"You mixed eighteen-year scotch with *soda*?" Liam says.

"I gave my guest what he wanted. A cold drink. And as the scotch was a gift, it was mine to do with as I like, was it not?" She turns to me. "Coke, I'm guessing."

"Plain soda, actually, please." When she brings it, I wait for both her and Liam to look away and switch my glass with Tom's. He mouths his thanks.

Celeste serves popcorn, and we settle in to the game. After a few more hands, I decide that either Tom is terrible at poker, or—more likely—he's pretending he is, refusing to rise to Liam's implicit challenge.

Celeste plays decently but, clearly, doesn't have much experience with it. Liam does, and so do I. Keith loved his Friday night poker parties, and when they were shorthanded, I'd step in, at first because the men all thought it was cute teaching me to play, and later because I became a formidable player, thanks to that teaching.

I'd enjoyed those poker nights, and I'd continued by playing with coworkers. That's one thing I can credit Keith with. There are others, too. If I'm being snarky, I'll say he taught me how to avoid guys like him, how to grow armor against charm and charisma, and how to keep my inner books balanced at all times. That's true. Yet he also had some positive influence on me, teaching me skills my parents couldn't, particularly business and financial ones. Life with a stepfather like Keith was not 100 percent hell. I don't think life with anyone can be. Yet it feels as if we need to only remember the terrible parts or else someone will say, "See, it wasn't so bad after all." It was the worst four years of my life, and the fact that I got a few positive things from it doesn't balance the negatives at all.

The game proceeds with Liam or me winning most hands, Celeste popping up with the occasional bit of luck and even Tom taking one or two, probably to avoid Liam realizing he's playing badly on purpose.

The trouble starts right at the point where I've decided we're out of danger. Did Liam sense everyone relaxing?

"Our Miss Daisy seems to have a hidden talent," he says. "Any others I should know about?"

He could say this with sincerity. An honest compliment, paired with a friendly conversation starter where we could all divulge secret talents. He could also make it a lascivious joke, with an exaggerated leer, one that might not invoke a laugh in current company but could be brushed off as frat-boy humor. The way he actually says it . . . ? I can't describe his tone. I only know that I feel he's taken a legitimate compliment and used it to demean me. To remind me of my place in his world.

You're a fine poker player, Daisy. But you're still a woman, and I'm sure you have talents I'd appreciate a whole lot more.

I often worry I'm too sensitive to that. Working in construction, it's a common refrain.

That architect does great design work, and did you check out her tits?

That engineer knows her stuff, and did you see her ass?

It's like we can prove ourselves legitimate experts in our field, worthy of respect, but *still* cannot rise above our biological role.

So, yep, I might be overly sensitive. Even as I tense with Liam's comment, I tell myself to chill. Except Celeste notices his tone, too, her brows rising in a way that says I'm not misinterpreting. But she only shakes her head. Boys will be boys. It's Tom who reacts, his head whipping Liam's way.

"What did you just say?" Tom asks.

"I asked if she had any other talents," Liam says blithely. "Celeste mentioned she's a good cook, too."

Tom's eyes narrow as he recognizes the trick women have dealt with forever. Call a guy on an inappropriate comment, and he pretends you've misunderstood, makes you feel foolish for over-reacting.

"I can also wiggle my ears," I say. "And I can sense snowstorms, which is completely useless in Florida." I turn to Tom. "How about you?"

He relaxes and tosses me a grateful smile. "I am the best karaoke singer you'll ever meet. Outside of karaoke, though, I can't carry a tune to save my life. Celeste? Any hidden and useless talents?"

"Celeste is very talented," Liam says. "But perhaps you already know that, Tommy."

Tom meets his gaze with a level stare. "I'm afraid I don't know Celeste all that well."

"No?"

"No, Liam," Celeste says. "If you doubt that, just come out and ask. But you aren't actually asking. You're just being an ass."

She says it conversationally, as if remarking on the score of a game she doesn't follow. Not the least bit concerned that she's just been accused of cheating on her lover.

"I'm very good at being an ass," Liam says. "I believe that is my hidden talent."

"No, my dear, it isn't hidden at all."

Liam laughs and reaches for the scotch. He pours a finger for himself and one for Celeste, and then moves the bottle over Tom's empty soda glass.

Tom pulls it away. "No, thank you. I've had enough."

"Ah, got a problem holding your liquor?" He points at Tom's tattoos. "Is that what put you inside?"

Tom lifts his gaze to meet Liam's, and if I'd been on the receiving end of that look, I'd have retreated fast. I turn a look of my own on Liam, but he ignores it and shrugs.

"I'm a criminal lawyer, boy," Liam says. "I know a prison tat when I see one."

"Prison . . . ?" Celeste says, her gaze following Liam's. "Oh, is that what that is?"

"Yes, darling, that's what it is. You may have noticed it's not nearly as pretty as the other ones. They give themselves those in jail to pass the time and indicate group affiliations."

I'm not sure what's worse—Liam's patronizing use of *boy* or him casually explaining prison tattoos, treating Tom like a carnival-sideshow exhibit. Tom's jaw sets, but he blinks, too, as if tired, before shaking it off.

"It's getting late—" I begin.

"And the reason you need to know what those tattoos look like, Celeste, is so you don't invite a man bearing them into your house. Or into your bed."

"Okay," I say. "That's—"

"Whatever Tom did," Celeste says, "I'm sure it isn't cause for concern. I'm betting a youthful mishap."

She smiles at Tom. She's trying to be reassuring, but I bristle at that smile, as patronizing as Liam's tone. Tom blinks again, as if he's having trouble following the conversation. I discreetly motion at his glass. He catches the look and shakes his head. No, he didn't accidentally get some scotch.

"Come on, Tommy," Liam says. "Tell us—"

"Money laundering," Tom says. "I did two years for money laundering. I was taking accounting in college and trying to make some cash on the side, and I did something very naive."

"You were laundering money, and that's all there is to it? Just a college kid trying to make a few bucks?" Liam meets his eyes. "Is that really what you're going with, Tommy?"

"Yes, because it's the truth."

"That's not what I heard."

Is it my imagination, or does Tom flinch?

"Liam," Celeste cuts in. "Leave him alone. He obviously doesn't want to tell us what he was in for, and it's his right not to do so."

"He *is* telling you," I say through my teeth. "Liam can look it up, so there's no reason to lie. Now, I really *hate* to break up this *lovely* evening, but I do have an early morning."

Liam grins. "Well, well, our adorable kitten has claws. How many secrets are you keeping from us, Miss Daisy?"

Tom pushes his chair back, legs squealing on the old linoleum. He pauses, as if the sudden move surprised him. I watch him inhale. Then he calmly says, "I also need to call it a night. Regrettably."

"Sit down, Tommy. You, too, Daisy. I will behave myself. In fact, I was just about to make a suggestion to shake up this game. Since Celeste vetoed cash wagers, I thought we'd lay something more fun on the table."

His grin leaves little doubt as to what he's suggesting, and Celeste rolls her eyes. "If you say strip poker, Liam, I am taking that scotch away. Clearly, you've had enough. We aren't in high school."

"I know, which is why I was going to suggest a more adult wager, for a more adult crowd." He takes his keys and tosses them on the table.

"Your car?" I say, and I sit down. "Hell yeah, I'm in."

Tom chuckles, relaxing as he lowers himself back to his chair. "Even I'll wager on that." He takes out his keys and drops them onto Liam's with a smile of challenge. "My pickup is yours if you win."

"I wasn't betting my car," Liam says. "I remember back when I was a boy, my parents would have parties, and all the husbands put their keys in a bowl. At the end of the night, the ladies picked out a set, and that's who they went home with."

Tom reaches for his keys with a disgusted grunt. Liam grabs his wrist so fast we all jump.

"Uh-uh, Tommy, you tossed yours in already. You needn't worry. I plan to rig the game so you'll end up with darling Celeste." He turns to me with a teeth-baring grin. "I intend to discover all Miss Daisy's hidden—"

Tom hits him. All I see is a blur and then Liam's chair toppling. Then Tom's on his feet, grabbing Liam by the collar, and I'm jumping between them—which, in retrospect, is never the smart thing to do when two guys decide to go at it.

Getting between them isn't easy, with Tom gripping Liam by the shirt front. I manage it, though, wedging in with "Enough!"—my hands raised. Tom stops immediately. He wasn't about to hit Liam again—he had him where he wanted him. Liam's the one who's swinging, and his fist glances off my shoulder. Tom lets go, and Liam thuds to the floor. He starts to lever up, going after Tom, but I'm right there, blocking him. Liam exhales, snorting like a bull, and gets to his feet, glowering at Tom.

Liam glances at Celeste, who is sipping her scotch, unconcerned.

"Don't look at me," she says. "You deserved that, and you know it."

Liam rolls his shoulders and finds a smirk. "Seems someone can't take a joke."

"You're angry with me," Tom says. "So take it out on me. Insulting Daisy isn't a joke. It's an asshole move."

"Well, like I said, he *is* an asshole," Celeste mutters.

"I made a joke about playing for keys," Liam says. "Teasing that I wanted Daisy to end up with mine. I think the real insult would be if I said I *didn't* want her." He turns to me. "Right?"

I let my eyes call him a jerk while my lips say simply, "As jokes go, I've heard better." Then I turn to Celeste. "I'm going up to my room. I'll see you tomorrow."

"Walk me out?" Tom murmurs as I pass. I hesitate, but his eyes beseech me, so I nod, and we head for the front door, leaving Celeste and Liam in the kitchen.

EIGHTEEN

DAISY

"I have a pull-out sofa," Tom says when the door closes behind us. "I'd give you the bed, but I know you'd argue, so you can take the sofa."

"What? No."

"You *will* take the bed? Excellent."

I glare at him. "I meant no to going back to your place."

"Not like *that*."

"I know. You're inviting me to stay with you so I won't be near Liam in case he tries something. Whatever you think of Celeste, she's hardly going to let him accost me under her own roof, and *I'm* hardly going to let him accost me. I'm not helpless. But those are moot points because Liam was, as Celeste said, just being an ass. His so-called suggestion was aimed at her, and insulting me was just a bonus because, again, he's an asshole."

"I want you to come back—"

"Are you even listening to me, Tom? No, you're not, because you don't actually give a shit."

"Excuse me?" He moves close enough that I need to lock my knees not to back away. "I'm concerned for you. That's the *definition* of giving a shit."

"I mean you don't give a shit what I think about the situation." I meet his gaze. "You and Celeste did something after I walked away. Liam caught you. He's being a passive-aggressive jerk about it, and I got caught in the crossfire, and you feel bad about that. So to make yourself feel better, you want to protect me. Forget what I want. This is about you."

"It's not—" He bites off the word with a sharp shake of his head. He seems to chew over his choices, and when he speaks again, his voice is lower, softer. "He didn't catch us *doing* anything, Daisy. Not like that. We were just—"

"Don't care."

His jaw works. "I'm trying to explain—"

"And I don't actually care. I'm annoyed at getting caught up in it, but I blame him, not you or Celeste. I will deal with this."

"You shouldn't have to."

"I will. Now, good night, Tom."

He stands there, eyes blazing. Then he stalks off.

I understand why Tom lashed out, but something about it still bothers me. I remember him rubbing his eyes. Blinking. He didn't think he'd had anything to drink. What if Celeste gave me a scotch and soda, too? But wouldn't Tom have noticed the taste?

Maybe I'm making excuses for him. I should go back inside the house and talk to him tomorrow. Instead, I stand there, watching the road long after he's gone. Then I go after him.

CELESTE

Liam has retreated upstairs with an ice pack. I watch out the window as Daisy goes after Tom. She'll be back. This isn't the sort of scene where the girl chases the angry guy and ends up staying the night. I doubt she'll even make it as far as his place before second-guessing and turning back.

And what if she doesn't?

Well, then, despite having launched my plot, I won't be able to carry it through.

I should be furious at that, and yet a small part of me is relieved.

I won't need to kill Liam tonight.

Oh, I definitely want him dead. I'm just not sure I can do it, and that's worse than changing my mind and deciding he doesn't deserve to die, because this is weakness. My weakness. I lack the guts to go through with it.

I remember the night Jasmine died, Mom saying I couldn't have done it—not because I wasn't a monster who'd bully a girl to death, but because I lacked the strength, lacked the initiative, lacked the fortitude.

Seems you were right, Mom.

No, I won't let her be right. I'm not a monster who'd hold an innocent girl underwater, but I *am* a woman who will kill her jailer rather than run again. A woman who doesn't mind framing another woman for the crime, not when that woman will bolt and escape, and even if she doesn't, well, she isn't an innocent like Jasmine.

Liam holds me captive in this house, as a fake girlfriend who has to play that role in every humiliating way. Daisy has invaded my house, targeting me for God only knows what.

Is it possible Aaron *did* send her? Or is she here for another reason? Another ghost from my past come for revenge? Or just an opportunistic grifter, a common con artist, a garden-variety blackmailer? I certainly hope to learn why she was taping me, but mostly, I just want to get rid of her.

I will not say that Liam's crimes deserve death. Nor that Daisy's deserve the possibility of life in prison. But I will say that I am fine trading those fates in return for my freedom.

The night is still young, and there's plenty of time to kill Liam and frame Daisy.

The first part of the plan succeeded. That pill from the pharmacist mixed into Liam's drink fast-tracked him into Drunk Liam. No, it fast-tracked him into *Real* Liam, slamming down his inhibitions. I knew he'd hit on Daisy because that's what he always does when he's drunk and there's a decent-looking woman around he can humiliate me with.

Yes, I knew Tom might also bring out Liam's belligerent side, but I could work with that. Dose Liam's drink to make him flirt with Daisy, and then dose Daisy's with my sleeping pills to make her pass out tonight, opening a black hole in her memory where I can insert Dead Liam.

Daisy? Wh-what have you done?

I won't call the cops and see her marched off in handcuffs. Not unless she forces my hand. I just need to convince her to run. Seed the fear that she killed Liam during a blackout and let her flee, preferably after I confront her with the camera and get her confession there.

So why am I hesitating? Why am I making excuses? Because I'm not a cast-iron sociopath, as much as I need to be.

Damn it, I need a few shots of that scotch myself. Liquid courage.

Liam is in my bedroom. The door is half-open, and as I approach, I see him lying on the bed, staring up at the ceiling.

Staring up at that crack.

I freeze. He's noticed the crack.

I put the camera back last night. I hadn't wanted Daisy to check and see the camera was missing.

Has Liam noticed the camera light?

No, that isn't possible. I'd replaced the battery. Without that alert light, it's impossible to see the camera through that crack.

Except he's looking straight at it.

He's grinning up at it. As I watch, he makes a kissy face, and waggles his brows and then turns, as if jokingly giving the camera his "good side."

"Hey," I say as I walk in.

He gives a start and then covers it with a grin as he extends his arms. "Celeste, come here."

I roll my eyes as I walk toward him. "What the hell was that downstairs?"

"You. Loved. It," he says, punctuating each word with a smack of a kiss. "Especially the part where two hot guys were fighting over you."

"You weren't fighting over me. You were just fighting." I pause. "Did you call yourself hot?"

"I'm totally hot, and I know it, because you cannot get enough."

I move to the foot of the bed, out of camera sight. He grabs my arm and pulls me into bed. When I try to stay on the far side, he tugs me under the camera and tugs my shirt from my shorts.

"You loved it," he says. "And you would have loved it even more if Tommy had gone for it. Cute tattooed mechanic with grease under his fingernails. Perfect one-night-stand material. You get the chance to hit that, you should."

He's laying a trap here, and I'm not naive enough to fall into it. I sputter a feigned laugh. "Didn't you just spend the last two hours being pissy because you caught me touching his *arm*?"

"Nah, I was just giving him a hard time. And if he offers *you* a hard time? Ride 'em, cowboy." He grins. "Just as long as you don't mind me driving Miss Daisy."

I should respond, make some joke, but all I can see is that crack overhead as he peels off my shirt, directly under it.

Daisy.

I'd been so certain Daisy set up the camera.

When his mouth tightens, annoyed that I've stopped playing along, I say, "While I have no issues with an open relationship, *that* pairing would be hellishly awkward."

"Maybe. Still, you can't tell me you wouldn't have been up for a foursome tonight if it worked out that way."

"You are so drunk."

I pretend to roll over, getting farther from the camera's eye. He pulls me back under it.

Daisy did *not* set up the camera. Her footprints had been a few feet away because she'd been up there fixing the leak. She isn't filming me for some unknown reason. Liam's filming me for that most banal of reasons.

He's taping us having sex.

It's the obvious answer, and I hadn't even considered it because I needed Daisy to be evil. Or, at least, I needed her to deserve the cruelty I was about to play, framing her for murder and sending her on her way, running as fast as she could.

I'd decided Daisy created the leak, which gave her an excuse to install the camera. Then, clearly, Daisy got caught installing it on my laptop, so she faked a break-in. And Daisy was obviously storing the video on my laptop to . . . ? Well, there the motivation fell apart, but damn it, how was I supposed to know her motives? The evidence pointed to her, and that was enough.

Unless I have a creepy, controlling boyfriend who'd definitely tape us having sex. Who'd love yet another blackmail-shackle to ensnare me.

Do as I say or I release these online. Some amateur porn site. Maybe I'll even make a few bucks.

Didn't he just give me permission to have sex with Tom? Presumably on this bed? Under that camera lens?

It makes total sense for Liam to save the files on my laptop because it's *his* laptop. He bought it for me. He set it up. He set up my whole damn network.

I can pretend to think Daisy faked the break-in, but that's just me being paranoid. I saw a figure running. I heard the thump of the intruder smacking into her and her falling. She ran through glass, for God's sake.

But someone created that leak in the roof.

Someone who knew I'd supposedly *had* a leak. Someone with enough access to the attic to set up a damned camera, likely months ago.

"Celeste?" Liam says, mouth tightening in irritation. "If you're just going to lie there, princess, I'm going to need to get some rope and make this fun."

"I'm looking at that crack," I say.

He follows my eyes and visibly tenses.

"I was thinking of having Daisy fix it."

His expression is almost comical—that moment of "Oh, shit!" when he realizes the downside of encouraging me to hire a renovator.

I continue, "But it's not a high priority. It's not like it's a leak or anything." I slant my gaze his way. "Weird thing, but when I told

Daisy I had a leak, I thought it was over the bedroom here. Instead, it was over my office."

He shrugs. "It's an old house. I'm only shocked it didn't float away in that storm."

"Hmm. I was just wondering . . . Well, I don't suppose a certain boyfriend might have . . . poked an itty-bitty hole in the roof to persuade me to take in a certain backpacking handywoman who might be willing to work for free?"

"That would be a very considerate boyfriend."

"It would be."

"And such a considerate boyfriend would deserve a reward, wouldn't he?"

He takes my hand and leads me down the hall. Then he opens Daisy's bedroom door.

"What do you say to . . . ?" He jerks his chin at the empty bed and waggles his brows again. "Maybe Daisy will come back and join us."

I hesitate. This is better than any setup I could have imagined. I can slip downstairs and lock the front door. Daisy will have to sleep in the lanai. Then I kill Liam in her bed. Plant the gun. Unlock the doors. Spatter a little blood on blacked-out Daisy. After I scare her off and call the police, I'll tell them how Liam drunkenly hit on her last night. I even have a witness in Tom.

Here is the answer to all my problems. Get rid of Liam. Frame a transient who'll have the street smarts to flee. Who had the street smarts not to give me her surname or her city of origin or any identifying information. Hell, I doubt her first name is even Daisy.

She will be fine. The same cannot be said for me.

I need to do this.

And I cannot.

That is the ugly and humiliating truth of it. I do not have the strength—or the stomach—to save myself. Not to frame Daisy, and not to kill Liam. I said I wasn't a cast-iron sociopath, but I so badly need to be. And I cannot.

With his arms still around me, Liam starts backing into Daisy's bedroom.

I dig in my heels. "Slow your roll there, Romeo. I'm in the midst of getting myself some very cheap labor, and I'm not having you scare the poor girl off."

He sighs dramatically. Then he glances over. "After she does the work?"

I pat his arm. "Yes, after she does the work."

"And what about getting you out of here while she does it?" he says, sobering. "My condo is big enough for two."

I try not to tense as I kiss his cheek. "We'll talk," I say, and I lead him to my room.

NINETEEN

DAISY

I follow Tom home. He leaves his truck. He doesn't see me. He doesn't seem to see much of anything. He pauses once to lean against a tree, as if exhausted. I wonder again whether there was alcohol in his drink. Or maybe he's just tired from a long day. Either way, he must be feeling it, too, if he left his truck behind and walked. I make sure he gets into his shop. Then I stand there, watching the lights ignite, telling myself I'm just being sure he gets up to bed safely. Yet the lights go off, and I'm still standing there, still thinking and feeling and wishing.

I'm there for almost an hour before I feel like a creeper and head back. I'm halfway when a figure lurches from the shadow of a live oak. I spin, fists rising.

"Liam," I mutter as he staggers out. His shirt is open and inside out, as if he just climbed from bed.

Great.

He continues forward until I can smell the booze on his breath.

"Frozen to the spot?" he says when I don't move. "You aren't going to scream, are you, Miss Daisy?"

"I don't need to. Lay a hand on me, and you'll be the one screaming."

He grins. "I like the sound of that." He tilts his head and purses his lips. "How am I doing? I've never menaced a woman before, and the dialogue seems a bit melodramatic. I'm not really feeling it, either. Let's switch scripts to the playacting version. I'll pretend to take you by force, and you'll pretend you don't want me to." He grins. "Because we both know you'd be pretending."

I consider the utility knife in my pocket. Consider where I'd like to sink the blade. I also consider vomiting on him instead.

"Am I supposed to be afraid of you, Liam? You're as serious about this as you were about swapping keys. I figured you were just trying to insult Celeste, but she isn't here, so I guess this insult is for me. Not sure what I've done to deserve it. Nothing, probably. You just get off on the faint chance that I'll take you seriously and quiver in my sneakers."

"Get off?" His brows arch in mock affront. "How vulgar. You give yourself too little credit, Miss Daisy. I'd have happily swapped bedrooms tonight, and I would happily indulge in a little fantasy role play right now if you'd like."

He pauses, giving me a chance to jump on that offer. I snort.

He surveys me. "I *would* like to get to know you better. You do indeed have hidden depths. Hidden to Celeste, at least, and that knuckle-dragging grease monkey she fancies. Not hidden to me, though."

"Lovely. Now, if you'll please leave—"

"You don't seem the least bit concerned by my hints."

"I'm not."

"No? Are you quite certain, Miss Daisy?" He pauses and meets my gaze with a shark's grin. "Or do you prefer Ms. Turner? Ms. Celeste Turner."

CELESTE

I wake the next morning to find a hot, sweaty guy in my kitchen. The only thing that could make this picture more perfect is . . .

Tom turns, coffee in hand, and holds it out to me, smiling. "Thought you might like this."

I might let out a sigh of girlish infatuation. Well, no, as a girl, I wouldn't have been nearly as impressed by a tattooed, muscular, dirt-and-sweat-streaked man handing me coffee. As a grown woman, though? Oh, yeah. It doesn't get any better than this.

"About last night . . ." I begin.

He scrunches his nose. "Don't mention it."

"I have to. Liam was an ass. I know I said that, multiple times, but I kind of brushed it off, too, when I should have put a stop to it. I'm not accustomed to hard liquor, and I overimbibed. I'm sorry for the way he behaved toward you."

His cheek twitches, and I replay my apology, wondering where I've gone wrong. Then he says, "I was more concerned by the way he talked about Daisy."

"She's upset, isn't she?" I sigh. "He was a jerk, but he wasn't seriously suggesting bed-swapping."

"That makes it okay? She's a guest in your home. Your boyfriend joked about screwing her, like she's a piece of pie in the fridge that he's welcome to sample."

I flinch. He has a point, of course.

Before I can answer, Tom shakes his head. "I'm snapping at you because the person I'd like to snap at is gone."

I frown. "Liam? He's here somewhere."

"His car isn't."

"What?" I walk to the kitchen window and peer out. "When did he leave?"

"Before I arrived."

I run my hands over my face. "Damn it. I hope he's not in a mood. I figured he'd just come down without waking me, since it's almost"—I check the microwave clock—"noon."

I pull out my cell phone. "No message, either. Wonderful." I tap in a text and send it. "Well, if he took off in a snit, that's one less problem for everyone today. How's Daisy doing?"

"Fine. We're clearing the side weeds." He nods down at the two other coffees he just poured. "I should get this to her before it goes cold."

"Tell her not to worry about lunch. I'll drive into town and pick us up something."

DAISY

I'm clearing the brambles at the side of the house. While they seemed a mere eyesore, they're damaging the wall. Humid climate plus aggressive ivy can do that. This is my house, and I fully intend to restore her, starting with these little bits to slow the damage until I can take back what's mine.

Clearing brambles also gives me the opportunity to avoid the woman who calls herself by my name. That Celeste definitely won't offer her manicured hands to the demon god of weeds.

Today, I feel something I don't want to feel when it comes to this woman. The stirrings of pity. Yet I can't forgive her trespasses. She stole my birthright. I don't mean the house. I don't give a damn about that. But she took away my last chance to reunite with my grandmother. And, possibly, she stole my grandmother herself, rushing along that "inheritance." That is what I am here to find out.

When my story is revealed, the first question will be why I didn't just call the police on her. The answer is obvious. I am not giving her a chance to run. If I report her for identity theft, she'll flee before I can convince the police that she may also have murdered my grandmother.

I need proof. I need ID with the imposter's real name. Otherwise, if she flees, she's a nameless ghost. I also need my grandmother's diary. I know she kept one, and I know she didn't let anyone see it—I only found it myself because I was snooping about as a kid.

Is it possible the imposter found the diary and destroyed it? Or that she murdered my grandmother without Maeve suspecting a thing? Yep. But I wasn't going to find my answers sitting up North, poking around on a computer. I don't trust the justice system. Can't afford a private investigator. There was only one option left: get my ass to Florida.

Come here. Get a read on my adversary while I search the house for her ID.

Was it a perfect plan? Hell, no. But it was the only one I had.

This morning, I snuck downstairs before Celeste woke. I'll keep calling her that, even in my head. It's safer, especially now that I don't need to worry about Liam giving me away.

I heated up a cinnamon bun and took it outside with my coffee. Two hours later, and I haven't seen her. For all I know, she's still in bed as I wrestle with these brambles and vines, and that's fine by me.

"Looks like you could use some help," a voice says.

I glance over to see Tom, looking sheepish. He thrusts out a box. "I brought cinnamon buns, but I see you already had one." He nods toward my plate and mug on the lawn. "I'm hoping that means you like them and you'll take these off my hands, too."

His smile is crooked, tentative, and in my mind, I see a boy holding out a penny-candy bag after we'd argued.

I got you sour balls. You still like sour balls, right?

Even at that age, I'd sensed something heartbreaking in those words. A boy desperate to resolve a fight, terrified that even a minor dustup could cost him a friend. That's the life he led, where a flare of temper earned a week of blows.

That boy still lurks behind the crooked smile and the anxious eyes as he thrusts out that box of cinnamon buns. But we aren't children anymore, and I don't need to worry that I'll scare him off if I reject his peace offering.

So I just look at him, hedge clippers in hand.

He takes a deep breath. "Liam wasn't the only asshole here last night. I screwed up. I'm sorry."

"You weren't an asshole."

He sets the box down. "If I wasn't, then I treaded dangerously close to that line. I was upset with Liam, and I tried to drag you off like some caveman. I was worried but . . ." He rubs his mouth. "I wasn't listening when you said you could handle it. And I'm not sure how much of it was honest fear, and how much was just wanting to get you away from him."

"Take your toys and leave the sandbox."

He winces. "Yes and no. There was some of that, but also just not wanting to leave you behind to deal with him. Which wasn't my call to make." He shoves his hands in his pockets. "Can I help? That's shitty work, and I've finished my morning appointments."

"You don't need to spend your Saturday pulling weeds, Tom. We're good."

"I got this," he says, striding into the mess and grabbing at a weed. "I have a weird idea of fun."

"Unless your idea of fun involves deep hand lacerations, may I suggest . . ." I tug at my garden gloves. "You wear these, and I'll wield the clippers."

As I pass them over, he blinks, and his mouth tightens. I follow his gaze to the faint ring of purple around my right wrist.

"Yes," I say.

His gaze lifts to mine, brows knitting.

I continue, "I could lie, but yes, it was Liam. We had a disagreement last night. Full disclosure—I provoked him. He grabbed my wrist. A threat, nothing more."

"Nothing more? A threat of violence is—"

"Just that. A threat. He grabbed my wrist to show me he's a big, strong man. In return, I showed him that strength is not a prerequisite for self-defense. We parted with a better understanding of each other."

There's more to that story. So much more. But the gist of it is true. Liam grabbed me, and I made sure he'd never do that again.

"I handled it," I say. "And his car's gone. With any luck, he got called back to Tampa on a legal emergency."

"Or he might just be out grabbing breakfast."

"Your realism is not welcome in my fantasy. Now, let's get this cleared, and then I'll take one of those buns."

TWENTY

DAISY

We have lunch midafternoon, and it's nearly as awkward as our poker game. Celeste picked up Chinese in Sun City, and Tom dives in with gusto, saying how much he loves chicken balls. Celeste thinks he is being sardonic and joins in with a few quips about "American" Chinese food and small-town Chinese restaurants.

I try to intercede because I know Tom isn't kidding. Even if he did prefer authentic Chinese food, he wouldn't make such a joke because he's not that guy. My efforts are for naught because Tom also isn't *that* guy, either—the sort who'd be embarrassed by enthusing over something Celeste considers common. He quite happily admits he's never had anything except American Chinese, and that sets her stumbling over herself to backtrack.

If it is awkward for us, it isn't for Tom, who just continues inhaling his food. While I *do* enjoy authentic Chinese, I'm just as happy with the red-sauce-soaked chicken balls that bring back memories of Dad coming into unexpected money and "taking us out someplace nice."

To add to the awkwardness, Celeste keeps checking her phone as if praying for a call to free her from our company. Finally, Tom stops eating long enough to wave his fork at her cell.

"Don't let us keep you from your work," he says. "Daisy will entertain me while I eat. I mean, just listen to her. I can barely get a word in edgewise."

He shoots a grin my way, and I roll my eyes. I'm about to launch an actual conversation when Celeste looks up from her phone, blinking at Tom.

"Hmm?" she says.

He waves his fork at her phone again. "If you have work to do, don't think you need to play hostess."

She sets her phone down decisively. "No, sorry. It's just . . ." A glance at the discarded device as if itching to pick it up already. Then she looks at me. "Did you see Liam this morning?"

I shake my head.

"Was his car in the drive when you went out?"

"I left through the back door to grab the tools. I didn't see the driveway until I went back in, around nine. It was empty."

She huffs in frustration. "Did you hear anything? See anything?"

"No, but I wasn't paying much attention, either. Is everything okay?"

Another check on her phone.

"You can't get hold of him?" I ask.

"No, he texted back earlier. It's just . . ." She trails off and then shakes her head and seems about to drop the subject when she thinks better of it and asks, "When did you last see Liam?"

"Before I went to bed." Technically true.

Celeste taps her long nails on the Formica tabletop and frowns.

"Call him if you're concerned," Tom says.

She keeps drumming her nails, the sound grating along my spine.

"When is he going to Miami?" I say. "You mentioned something about that."

"Tomorrow."

"Maybe he left early?"

When she doesn't answer, I say, carefully, "But is there something wrong with his texts? Something that has you concerned?"

"They're just . . ." She snatches up her phone like a dog finally given the release word. When she opens her messages, disappointment flashes over her face. A moment passes before she seems to remember why she picked it up.

"They're just not like him," she says. "They're short. Abrupt, even."

She turns the phone to face me.

"I first texted after eleven," she says. "It was an hour before he replied with this."

Liam: Client called. Emergency meeting.
Celeste: Damn. Well, I guess I'll need to take a rain check.

It's another thirty minutes before he replies with a simple yes. From there, she responds quickly, and he takes about twenty minutes to answer each time.

Celeste: Everything okay?
Liam: Yes.
Celeste: It doesn't sound like it.
Liam: Just busy.
Celeste: Okay, so I'll see you tonight, then? Should I plan on you for dinner?
Liam: No.
Celeste: No to dinner? Or no to coming over?

He hasn't answered that, though it's been an hour.

Tom shrugs. "Sounds like he's busy, as you said."

"He's texted me from actual court before, and it still didn't sound like that."

"Either he's busy, as he says, or he doesn't want to talk. There was some tense shit last night. Maybe everything seemed fine, but this morning, he woke up in a mood. It happens. He decided he'd been wronged and stalked off, and now he's being snippy, waiting for you to drag the truth out of him." Tom puts out his hand. "That'll be ten bucks."

Her brows arch. "For what?"

"Relationship therapy. I have absolutely zero qualifications. Therefore, you get it cheap."

Celeste looks at me. "What do you think, Daisy?"

"I'm with Tom," I say. "Liam did say he had an emergency and, no offense, but you keep texting. Or maybe he woke up this morning and decided *he* was the offended party when he had a bruise from Tom slugging him."

"I didn't hit him that hard," Tom says.

"You knocked him out of his chair." I turn back to Celeste. "Give him time. If he decides not to come over, that's his loss." I push my chair out. "I need to get back to that weeding, but thank you for lunch, Celeste."

CELESTE

Liam's phone rings through to voice mail. I hang up without leaving a message. After thirty minutes of work, I call again, and this time, I wait through the message. The beep comes, and I take a deep breath.

"Hey, just me. You know I'm not a clingy girlfriend. This is just . . . Well, it's weird, Liam. You've never left in the morning without saying goodbye. You've never even left without . . ." An unsteady laugh. "You do like your good mornings. Also . . ."

I take a deep breath, hearing it hiss along the line. "I woke up last night, and you weren't there. I remember looking at the clock. It was almost three. I figured you were in the bathroom, and I was going to use it after you, but then I fell back to sleep."

I switch the phone to my other ear. "I'm being paranoid, I know. You must have come back to bed after that and got a call this morning."

I inhale. "Okay, I'll stop babbling to your answering machine. Just call, okay?"

An hour later, I open my contact list and pull up someone I've spoken to many times but only texted once, to let him know that Liam and I would be late for a dinner engagement. It's another partner at Liam's firm, the one who brought him into the company.

Me: Hey, Joaquin, it's Celeste Turner, Liam's gf.

It takes ten minutes to get a response.

Joaquin: Celeste! Of course I know who you are, though when you typed "gf" I kept thinking gluten-free. LOL

Me: Sorry to bother you on a Saturday, and I feel a little sheepish doing this, but let me say, in advance, that I am not a clingy girlfriend.

Joaquin: Okay.

I hear hesitation in that, because the moment you say, "I'm not x," people know that whatever you're about to say probably means you *are* x.

Me: Liam stayed over last night and was gone when I woke up. When I texted, he said he had an emergency meeting. A little odd that he wouldn't leave a note or say goodbye, but understandably he had other things on his mind.

Me: I've had trouble getting in touch with him since then. It's been five hours, and I'm getting worried.

I don't mention that he *did* respond to my early texts. I'd seen Tom's expression at that, a mixture of confusion and pity. Liam was answering, so why was I making such a big deal?

Joaquin would respond in the same way, brush me off as an insecure girlfriend and wonder why I'm wasting his time with this.

Joaquin: Five hours?

Me: Yes. That seems long for a meeting.

Joaquin: Unless by "meeting" he meant that a client was being arrested. That can be a lengthy process, especially on the weekend.

Me:	Or maybe his phone died.
Joaquin:	LOL Not Liam. I swear the guy whips out his battery pack if his phone drops below half charge.
Me:	I'm overreacting, aren't I?
Joaquin:	Liam always says you're the most low-maintenance girlfriend he's ever had. You wouldn't worry without cause.
Joaquin:	If he had a meeting, he'd have told Tina. I'll give her a shout.

I thank him and try to go back to work. Tina is Liam's clerk. I'd have contacted her myself, but she's very protective of Liam, and she'd have been the first to give me the brush-off.

Fifteen minutes later, my phone chirps.

Joaquin:	Tina hasn't heard from him. He might just not have needed anything from her yet.

Which is bullshit. Joaquin just said Liam would have told Tina if it was business. That's true. A sudden call on the weekend would have Liam notifying his clerk immediately, who'd have to abandon her plans and her family and get to the office, ready to support him with whatever he required.

So why is Joaquin walking it back? Because he's protecting his golf buddy, having now realized that Liam might have said "emergency meeting" when he really meant "side-dish booty call."

I don't kid myself into thinking Liam hasn't screwed around on me. I do know, though, that there isn't a regular side dish. Still, I don't argue with Joaquin. There's no way a woman can say "my boyfriend isn't with another woman" without sounding pathetically delusional.

Me:	Okay, thanks for that. Last thing I want is to interfere with his job, so I'll drop it and wait for his call. Sorry again for interrupting your weekend.
Joaquin:	No interruption at all. I was doing paperwork.
Joaquin:	It is odd that he isn't answering my texts, either, though.
Joaquin:	I'm going to give him a call. Just hold on.

I lean back in my chair, phone in hand, as I wait. Then, from somewhere deep in the house, comes a familiar sound. The muted opening bars of "Start Me Up."

Liam's ringtone.

TWENTY-ONE

DAISY

It quickly becomes apparent that Tom is going to work as long as I do, and it's supposed to be his day off. So I declare the job "done for now," and also declare that I am in desperate need of a shower. Tom takes the hint and says he'll pop by tomorrow morning with the bike.

I suspect "and to see if you need any help" is the unspoken addendum. I'm not sure what exactly Tom is getting out of this. Companionship is a good excuse for hanging out with a person, but not for spending nearly four hours clearing a bramble-infested yard that allegedly doesn't belong to either of us.

There'd been a moment yesterday when I thought he might be interested in a whole other kind of companionship. But in our hours of work today, he never so much as touched my arm. He'd joked with Celeste about the list of repairs he wanted me to do at his place, but when I asked today, he had nothing.

Should I be suspicious? My brain says yes. It reminds me that I'm basing my trust on a few summers of childhood friendship. A boy who is long gone. A man who doesn't know that I'm *that* girl and therefore has no responsibility to honor the past by treating me fairly.

What else would Tom want?

Clearly, he's after my grandfather's treasure. I smile at the thought. There is no treasure. It's a local legend that no one actually believes.

I have no idea what Tom's up to. My ego would love to think he just wants to spend more time with me. I'm not Celeste, though. If guys want my attention, they offer me a beer and a lift in their pickup. Well, come to think of it, Tom has offered both, but I suspect that has more to do with who he is than what he wants.

I can't let my fondness for Tom blind me. I'll remain aware that he may have an ulterior motive. Beyond that, I'll enjoy his help and his company.

When I go inside, Celeste's in her office with the door shut. I don't try sneaking into the attic. Too risky. I'll make good on my shower excuse—I do need one. I pop into my bedroom for a change of clothing, and I'm collecting it when there's a muffled *beep-beep* from under the bed.

I pause, trying to identify the sound. It's familiar enough that I know I should recognize it right away, but when I don't, it dances at the edge of memory like a word on the tip of my tongue.

I look under the bed and spot a dim glow, but when I shift myself to reach farther, it goes dark.

I grab my flashlight and shine it under the bed. There are thin blankets for winter. Extra pillows, too, and I tug one out and immediately regret it as the stink of mildew envelopes me.

I keep shining my light until it catches a small box. I reach under, steeling myself against whatever filthy thing I might touch. Good thing I haven't had that shower yet.

My fingers close around something cool. I pull out . . .

A cell phone?

An iPhone, no less, and when I lift it, it tries to read my face. I roll from under the bed and peer at the screensaver photo of a sunset. I go to press the Home button, but there isn't one. I've seen people swipe these, so I try that, and the lock screen fills with notifications.

Missed calls from Celeste. That's what the beep was—a reminder of calls missed, the light coming on for a few seconds.

Why is Liam's phone under my bed?

Was he in here last night? Did the phone fall from his pocket before he came out to ambush me?

The phone lights up with an incoming call, and instinct has me slapping my hands over it to muffle the ring. The moment I realize what I'm doing, I wonder why, but that doesn't stop me from hitting Ignore fast, my heart rate slowing as the musical ringtone stops.

Footsteps sound in the hallway.

I dive for the bed and shove the phone between the mattress and box spring. Then I yank it out and switch it to silent before I shove it back in.

"Daisy?" Celeste calls.

I find my poker face and open the door with, "Hey."

"Did you hear something just now?"

"Like what?"

"Music."

I frown and push open my door as I turn to glance at the front-facing window. "I've heard music from passing cars. They like it loud around here."

"It wasn't . . ." She beetles her brows as she frowns, as if uncertain. Then she blurts, "It sounded like Liam's ringtone."

I perk up. "He's here? Good."

"His car isn't in the drive."

I match her frown, mine feigning confusion and deep thought. Then, "Wait! Call his number. See if that's what you heard."

She does, and as we stand there, my heart slams against my ribs. What the hell am I doing? Why did I hit Ignore? I should have shoved the phone back under the bed, and when she came in, I'd be on my hands and knees fishing it out with, "What is this doing here?"

Right. Yes, because finding her lover's phone under my bed wouldn't be the least bit suspicious. It isn't as if he joked about sleeping with me last night.

My gut told me to hit Ignore, and my gut told me to hide the phone, and my gut dissolves in shuddering relief when she shakes her head and hits End on the call without any sound coming from the bed.

"Apparently, I'm losing my mind," she says.

"You probably heard a passing car, and it sounded like his phone." I lean against the dresser. "Is there anyone else you can call to check on him?"

"I tried that. Called one of the partners at his firm—Joaquin."

"And . . ." I prompt.

"He hasn't heard from him. He checked with Liam's law clerk, who doesn't know anything about any emergency client meeting."

"That's weird."

"It is, but now Joaquin thinks Liam is spending the day with another woman, so he's brushing me off to protect his buddy. I'm not going to get any more help there." She glances down at her phone. "And Joaquin just texted to say that his call to Liam went straight to voice mail. He's decided Liam's phone is dead . . . despite the fact that he literally *just* told me Liam never lets it drop below fifty percent."

Celeste sighs and pockets her phone. "So what are my options? Seem like an obsessed girlfriend, calling everyone because I haven't heard from Liam in a few hours? Or tell myself it's nothing when I know this is not normal?"

"But if he's upset about last night, he won't be acting normally, right? He might even have turned off his phone. That'd explain why his friend can't get in touch with him, either."

"I called earlier, and it rang a bunch of times. It wasn't off then."

"Is it possible you left a message that made him decide to turn it off?" I hurry on. "Not blaming you. If that's the case, he's being childish."

"I'm overreacting."

"No, no—"

"I am. This isn't like me at all. I just . . . I got the idea that it's weird, and now that burrows deeper every moment he doesn't respond."

"Maybe you should take a drive to Tampa."

Her brows rise.

I shrug. "Go to his place. Pick up dinner or something, and if he's there, say you thought he seemed upset and you wanted to talk about it. If he's not there, maybe someone saw him earlier. Or just check for his car and be sure he's safely at home."

"That's definitely irrational-girlfriend territory."

"It's worried-girlfriend territory. At the very least, it'll give you something to do. Maybe there are errands you can run in Tampa to make it worthwhile?" *Errands that will guarantee you're gone even longer, giving me plenty of time to root through the attic?*

Celeste squares her shoulders. "No, everyone's right, and he's upset and dodging me. I have work to do. I'm going to do it."

She turns on her heel and marches back to her office, closing the door behind her.

Celeste doesn't go to Tampa. I suggest it again after dinner, offering to go with her. That would hardly give me the time I need alone in the house, but I'm not expecting her to take me up on the offer.

No, no. I can't ask you to do that, Daisy. But . . . maybe I should. You stay here, and I'll be back before dark.

Instead, I get a flat no. She's so afraid of being "that girlfriend" that she won't follow her gut. I don't argue.

How did Liam's phone get under my bed?

TWENTY-TWO

DAISY

I'm out for a run, trying to clear my head and focus. It's dusk, rendering the landscape in soft focus. I'm behind the house, running along trails through the drier parts of the wetlands.

To an outsider, this would be madness. Hell, to most of the locals, it's madness. One only uses these trails for hunting. Or to get, very carefully, from point A to point B. Snakes, alligators, fire ants, even wild hogs are a possibility out here. Tom says the hogs all get hunted as soon as they're spotted and besides, this is my grandmother's place—I grew up here. I know these paths, and I know what to watch for, and I know where to avoid. Also, I like a bit of danger with my evening run. Keeps me on my toes. It's a small price to pay for enjoying the glory of the evening, the humidity settling so thick that fronds rain on me as my footfalls shake the ground.

The buzz of mosquitoes fills the air, the rage of tiny predators temporarily thwarted by a heavy layer of repellent. I cut my own path through the stands of banyan and tangles of lush undergrowth. I'm circling a bush when I nearly bash into a car. There's a flash of mental confusion, as I think I've somehow become so wrapped up in my thoughts that I've run right through someone's yard.

I skid to avoid becoming a hood ornament. My foot slides on the damp earth, and I stumble forward, hands slamming on the hood with a thud that scares off a woodpecker, the bird giving a shrill cry as it flees.

I back up and blink. What I ran into isn't a car but an SUV. I didn't see it because it's black, and the night is already darker than I thought. Behind the vehicle, I see a lane. It's not a private drive—just a set of tracks made by local ATVs.

Then I see the words emblazoned across the hood.

"Range Rover."

A black Range Rover.

Liam's SUV.

There is a moment where I laugh at myself. Silly girl. You have Liam on the brain. Just because this is the same make and color as his vehicle doesn't mean it's his. There must be dozens around here.

Yeah, I've spent too long in the suburbs. This is a luxury SUV in Fort Exile, where Tom's vintage pickup stands out as a cherry ride.

It's Liam's SUV.

I spot a scrape down one side, and I shiver as my fingers graze a deep, fresh gouge in the paint. I bend to the tire. It's sunk into the muck deep enough that even a four-wheel drive isn't getting it out.

Liam did not drive his SUV back here.

My skin prickles.

Something's not right.

Something is very not right.

I try the driver's-side door. I only jiggle the handle, expecting nothing, but it opens.

The keys are right there, on the passenger seat.

I glance about the SUV's interior, but it's only a cursory look as my gut screams at me to get out of here. I shut the door, and I break into a run, slipping and sliding until I find my footing.

I'm running for the house. Tell Celeste. Call the police. Get them out here, because someone has dumped Liam's SUV. Dumped it and left the keys in hopes that if it was found, it'd be stolen.

Why here? Why not leave it in a parking lot, doors unlocked, keys in plain sight?

I don't know. I just know that I need to get to the house and—

I'm more than halfway back when movement to my left has me stumbling and sliding and smacking into a mangrove. Heart thudding, I drop to a semicrouch, fists out. I know how to fight, as Liam discovered last night. A guy on my first construction crew was a retired pro boxer, and he'd taught me to hit. Now the stance comes automatically.

Everything has gone still. Still and silent.

I know I saw movement, and I'm not turning my back on it. I take a step in that direction, rolling my foot. Another step. One more—

A pale shape lunges from behind a fallen mangrove, hissing at me. At first, it looks like a huge rat. Maybe a small hog? I don't want to encounter one of those, even a youngster. When I make out the humpbacked form of an opossum, I exhale in relief. The beast hisses, back arched, warning me off.

I don't see babies on its back, and it's out of season for that. Is it rabid? Opossums can be nasty, but they don't usually initiate attack. I'm ten feet away, giving it plenty of time to run. Yet it stands its ground, hissing.

Then I see dark splotches on its pale snout.

Blood. Opossums are like raccoons. They'll eat anything, including scavenging kills. That's what I've stumbled on. A feeding opossum.

I take one step back. Then I see the shoe. A white sneaker, glowing in the evening gloom.

My heart thuds anew, and I freeze, swallowing. I square my shoulders and lunge at the opossum, making enough noise that it tears off up a tree, chittering in fury.

I take a step toward the shoe. Two more steps and . . . My heart rate slows. It's just a shoe. Mud stained and grimy and left in the wetlands.

I start to turn away . . . and see what looks like a second shoe. I squint and . . . my breath catches.

Not a shoe.

I hurry toward the pale thing lying on the dark ground. With every step, its shape becomes clearer, erasing doubt until I am there, standing over an outstretched hand. A hand attached to a body. A body with one white sneaker and a robin's-egg-blue shirt stained with blood where the opossum had been feasting. Most of the blood is on the face, though. Or what's left of the face. A crater where the left eye should have been, a bloody hole now crawling with insects.

I see that shirt, and I see Liam last night wearing a shirt that brought out his eyes, and I'd imagined some cute salesclerk telling him exactly that. He'd been wearing jeans, pressed and new. His white sneakers had been spotless, and I'd inwardly rolled my eyes at that, too. Middle-aged guy trying to dress down in pressed jeans and sneakers that he probably replaced if they got a speck of dirt on them.

I look at that one shoe, as muddy as the discarded one. I look at the jeans and the shirt, and still I tell myself I am not seeing what I'm seeing. Not seeing *who* I'm seeing.

Because those shoes are filthy. Liam would not allow them to get filthy.

Then I remember us the night before, me walking into a stand of trees behind the house, and Liam hesitating at the edge.

"Yes, you're going to get your shoes dirty," I'd said. "But I'm not taking the chance of your girlfriend looking out and seeing us." I'd waved at her dark bedroom window and kept walking . . . and he'd followed.

My gaze moves to that ruined face. I want to tell myself it's not Liam. Classic movie twist, right? So tried-and-true that the moment an audience sees someone shot in the face, they know it's a trick.

This is too clean of a setup. First, no one is answering his phone. Then I find that phone in my room. Next, I find his abandoned vehicle, and as I'm running to get help, I stumble over a body that I'm supposed to think is his. Shot in the face so I can only ID him based on his clothing.

Except this isn't a movie. And it's not a shotgun blast obliterating Liam's features. Only one eye is destroyed, the rest intact and leaving no doubt of whom I am looking at.

I sway, and my stomach lurches, but before I can follow through on that classic move—dropping to my knees and retching beside the remains—another emotion seizes me. Terror. Blind and absolute terror, caught in a cyclone of panic.

Liam is dead.

Holy shit, Liam is dead, and I found his SUV, and I found his body, and I have his cell phone, hidden in my room, and he is dead. Murdered.

I run. I don't even realize I'm moving until vines catch my feet and my shoes slide and slosh in mud, and somehow, I don't fall flat on my face. I'm running blind, shoving aside anything in my path as panic tightens around my heart, as my brain shuts down in the grip of cold fear.

I thought I was clever. So damned clever. I would not take a chance on Celeste escaping. If she murdered my grandmother, she would pay, with no opportunity to slide into the shadows and disappear unscathed. I bided my time and got mixed up in something bigger than my own personal drama.

Now my footprints are all around her murdered boyfriend, who I had a confrontation with last night. He's been shot in the head, and I legally own a gun, a gun someone took from the shed.

My prints are all around his body. My footprints circle his abandoned vehicle. My fingerprints are on the door handle.

I think I am running to the house. To Celeste and a phone and *oh my God, I just found . . . just found . . . We need to call the police. Now.*

That makes sense. Get help now, while those prints are fresh, proving my story. Get help from Celeste, who will see my panic and tell the police how freaked out I was, exactly like a woman who just stumbled over a corpse. Not like a killer who pretended to find her victim.

I run, and I run, and when I see where I end up, there is only a flicker of "What the hell?" before I realize I was running here all along. May even have been running in this direction before I found Liam's SUV.

I'm in an open field. Ahead, there's a crossroads, and on the nearest corner squats a building, as ugly as they come, but in this moment, it is as beautiful as an oasis.

I race to the back door and grab the knob as if it will open, forgetting that only two days ago, I made sure it would not. I run around, stumbling through gravel until I reach the store at the front. It's closed. Of course it's closed. It doesn't stay open past six, even on Saturday nights.

I step back and stare at the building. There's a door to the store and a big garage door to the shop and then the one around back I just tried. I had a glimpse at Tom's loft apartment as we passed through to the roof, so I know he lives here, but I have no idea how to summon him. There's no bell on any of the doors. I don't have a phone—or know his number. There aren't any second-floor windows, which is a code violation, but no one out here cares. The only window I find is the store one, and it's barred.

I remember the makeshift patio and Tom saying he likes to lie out there as the sun sets. I spin and see the sky, almost dark, only a hint of red to the west.

I tear around the back. "Tom! Tom, are you up there?"

Nothing. The patio is dark, but it'd been the other night, too, Tom finding his way around like a cat in familiar territory.

"Tom!" I shout, so loud it sets my throat on fire.

A thumping from inside. I dance in place at the back door, ready to run around to the front, listening for where he'll—

The back door flies open, and Tom races out.

"Ce—" He stops short. "Daisy?"

I'm still dancing there, springing on my toes, and I know how ridiculous I must look, but I can't stop. Anxiety strums every nerve, and I bounce as if I'll collapse otherwise.

"Liam," I say, breathless. "It's Liam."

His face goes hard, and he stalks to me, taking my arm to pull me inside.

I realize he thinks that Liam has come after me. I yank out of his grip, words tumbling free. "No, dead. Liam's dead. I found him. In the . . ." I wave, unable to articulate any more, just madly gesturing.

"Police," I manage. "I need to call the police."

"Show me."

I shake my head so hard, my braid whips my cheek. "No, I need to call—"

"Daisy. Slow down. Show me first. When we call, any delay is on me. I'll say you wanted me to notify them, and I wanted to make sure he was dead. I know CPR if he's not."

There is zero doubt that Liam is dead. I could say I found a damned opossum feasting on his decaying flesh. But I don't think Tom is doubting that he's dead. He's trying to protect me.

I nod, and Tom follows me. His feet are bare, and I notice that and start to tell him to get shoes, but he only prods me forward. By the time we reach the area, I'm at a jog, and I stumble over a cypress root. He catches my hand, murmuring, "Slow down." And then he keeps hold of my hand to make sure I do. It's awkward walking side by side through the thick snarl of vegetation, but his hand is warm around mine, firm and steadying, and I need that.

We reach the spot. Reach the body. Reach Liam.

Tom sucks in a breath and bends beside him.

"CPR?" I say, and my voice comes out high and thready with a whisper of hysteria.

Tom says nothing. He rises and takes my arm, his hand rubbing up and down it.

"Tell me how it happened," he murmurs.

"I was out for a run. I bashed into his Rover. It's over there, maybe two hundred feet." I point. "The keys are on the seat. I knew that meant it'd been abandoned, so I was running to tell Celeste when I saw an opossum. It was eating . . . eating . . ."

I break off and swallow. Tom's watching me, nodding, his expression unreadable but giving me the impression that my answer was not quite right. I replay what he actually asked.

Not "tell me how you found him."

Tell me how it happened.

"You—you think I . . ." I stare down at Liam. "You think I did this?"

"If you did, we'll handle it."

"Handle it?" My voice squeaks. "You'll help me move a body?"

A laugh burbles up, sharp with hysteria. I slap it down and say, firmly, "I did not do this, Tom."

I'm looking him in the eye so he'll see my sincerity, but he's not meeting my gaze, and my confusion hardens to anger.

"You honestly think I murdered—"

"No, never. Not murder. But you were having trouble with him last night. And then that." He nods at the bruises on my arm.

"You think he attacked me, and I shot him?"

"No one would fault you for that."

A jury certainly would.

Shot him? Really? Couldn't you just kick him in the balls or something?

"Do you have a gun?" he asks.

I consider lying, but instead, I nod. "It's in the shed. Or it was. I saw Liam rooting around in there my first night, and later, it was gone. Oh, God. I hope it wasn't *that* gun, because it's legally registered to me."

"Shit."

"I absolutely did not kill him. I know I'll be a suspect even if it wasn't my gun. My footprints are all around his Rover. My fingerprints are on the door handle. My footprints are here. That's why I want to report it *now*, while my story makes sense, while they can test my fingers for gunpowder or whatever it is they do. Because I didn't kill him."

He nods, head down.

I swallow. "My story won't make sense, will it? Who walks back here at twilight? Who jogs back here *ever*? They won't believe me."

He says nothing.

"*You* don't believe me," I say.

He glances up. "No, I do. And you're right that you need to report it. However, that is going to bring up another problem, isn't it?" He looks me straight in the eye. "How good is your ID, CeCe?"

TWENTY-THREE

DAISY

"Wh-what?" I stammer. Then I try to recover with, "CeCe?" and a short laugh. "Getting me mixed up with Celeste?"

He locks gazes with me. "Never."

Oh, shit.

"You honestly thought I fell for that?" He shakes his head. "You seemed to think I did, but how the hell could I?"

I say nothing, just stand there, my voice gone.

"You really thought I didn't recognize you, CeCe? That a new hair color and contacts would keep me from recognizing you the *moment* I saw you?"

"Twenty years," I croak. "It's been—"

"Twenty years. And I'd know you after fifty. I know your voice. I know your expressions. I know the way you walk, the way you speak, the way you think."

When I don't speak, he says, "How long did it take *you* to recognize *me*?"

I say nothing.

"Would you have known me if I were bald? If I were wearing sunglasses?"

Yes. That's the truth of it. His hair color didn't tell me who he was. His eye color didn't, either. I saw his face, his smile, and I knew him, and my cheeks heat as I murmur, "I didn't want to presume you'd remember me."

He throws back his head and laughs, the sound ringing in the silence. "Okay, I gotta give you that, because it's exactly what *I* thought when you seemed to figure you'd tricked me. Huh, maybe she *doesn't* know who I am. I mean, sure, we're in the town where I grew up, where your gran lived, but Tom's not an uncommon name. She's probably forgotten me altogether."

"Never."

"And I didn't forget you." He looks toward the house. "You know, there are easier ways of getting your inheritance."

"I didn't want that woman getting away with it. She took something from me."

"Your gran's house. Your birthright."

I shake my head. "Not that. I think she took . . ." My gaze sweeps down and sees Liam, and I give a start, as if his body appeared from nowhere.

"I'll explain later," I say. "Right now, we need to call the police."

"Do you think she did it?"

"Celeste?"

He winces at the name.

"You know who I mean," I say.

"Do you have a real name for her?"

"Not yet. I've been looking for it in the house. She must have kept some ID. Real ID." I look up at him. "Keep calling her Celeste, please, even when it's just the two of us, so we don't mess up. She's welcome to the name. I never used it."

The first time we met, I told him my name was CeCe, and it took nearly the entire summer for him to realize I was the granddaughter Maeve Turner called Celeste. I'd used CeCe at school, and eventually, that's who I became with everyone except my mom. Dad used to call me Skye. Celeste, Celestial, Sky, get it? Yeah, it was half pet name and half because he didn't like Celeste, either, thinking it sounded prissy. I always thought it sounded too pretty, too fancy. It fits the woman in the house more than it ever did me.

Daisy comes from my first construction job, when I showed up in short cutoffs and a shirt with a daisy on it and the crew dubbed me Daisy. After that, I'd go to a new work site and introduce myself as CeCe, and they'd say, "Oh, you're Daisy, right?"

I am a woman of many names. It's certainly made this last week easier.

"Do you think she killed Liam?" he asks again.

I shake my head. "She was genuinely freaked out by him taking off."

"So . . ."

"Someone broke in the other day."

He goes still. When I meet his gaze, he ducks away, cheeks darkening.

"Tom . . ."

"That was me." He blurts the words and then presses his palms to his eyes. "Shit. I'm sorry. I feel terrible. I didn't mean to knock you down. Certainly didn't mean to make you run through glass. I barreled into you in the dark, and I didn't even realize it was you. Just got the hell out of there. I am *so* sorry."

"I could tell no one came in through the window, which made me wonder whether it was Celeste or Liam. But you know where Gran kept her key, don't you?"

"Yeah, from helping her out. I—" He takes a deep breath. "I wanted to help. I know that sounds like the wrong way to go about it—it *was* the wrong way to go about it. I recognized you and figured you were here to get dirt on fake Celeste before turning her in. The best place to find that dirt would be her laptop. So I quietly broke the window to fake a break-in. Then I used the key, got her laptop and . . ."

"Smacked into me making your escape."

"I didn't even manage to hold on to the damned computer. I am the worst spy ever. I'm sorry. Again. I would never have done it if I'd had any idea you could get hurt." He takes a deep breath. "I also went poking around the shed. I thought I saw you on the road, jogging in the rain, and I wanted to check, to see if you were at the house. I saw the shed, with signs of repair. I didn't expect you to be in it, and I think I spooked you. I'm sorry."

I remember that first night of the storm, someone outside, someone in worn jeans and work boots. Which is exactly what Tom wears, but I never made the connection.

"You startled me," I say. "But I understand. That means Liam's death isn't linked to either that or the break-in." I look down at the body. "He confronted me last night. He knew who I was, and he threatened me, but we came to an understanding. I'll explain all that later. For now, let's just say Liam's hands weren't exactly clean."

Tom snorts. "Hell, yeah. I tried telling your gran that. So now he's dead, and that makes this whole mess even messier. You could report it and then lie about your identity, but I'm sure you don't plan to keep lying so . . ."

If I lie now, how guilty will I seem when I reveal that I'm the real Celeste?

Once the police know who I am, unless they've already caught whoever killed Liam, I'll be their prime suspect. I came back to find my grandmother's lawyer conspiring with the woman who stole my inheritance. I confront him with a gun, and we argue and . . .

I look down at Liam, with a bullet hole where his eye used to be.

"We'll report the Rover," Tom says. "Well, you will. If both of us were out here, it'd seem odd. You were cutting through here and found his SUV. While running back to tell Celeste, you spotted a light on at my place."

I'm still staring down at Liam.

"CeCe?"

"Daisy," I say, still looking at Liam. "You need to call me Daisy."

His bare feet squelch in the mud, as if he's shifting his weight, uncomfortable.

"You want me to end this," I say. "Come forward. Let her run."

No answer.

I look over, and there are frown lines around his mouth, giving me a glimpse of what he'll look like in ten years. Ten years plus a bushel basket of regrets heaped on his shoulders, things he got mixed up in when he couldn't afford to, lies he told when he didn't want to.

"I didn't kill him," I say.

His chin jerks up, as if he's been startled from a reverie. His brow furrows more, anger now. "I know. You said so, and I believe you."

"I wouldn't let you help me if I did this."

His mouth tightens at that, and I'm the one frowning, but he only sighs and rocks back on his heels.

"I don't like this," he says. "I don't like the entire situation. Only one thing keeps me from insisting you step forward and just get rid of her." He rubs his mouth and looks sidelong at me. "You *are* her. She's you, at least."

"You mean whoever killed him might come after me?"

"She doesn't belong here," he says. "Not like we do." He pauses and makes a face. "Sorry. That sounded like an insult to you. It's not. I just mean . . ."

"Why *is* she here?" I say.

What is a woman like Celeste doing in Fort Exile, pretending to be me? Before I arrived, the answer seemed obvious. A house. An inheritance. Maybe even a phony treasure. But I remember my surprise on seeing her for the first time. I expected . . .

Well, I expected someone more like me if I'd followed in my dad's footsteps. An ordinary woman, with edges and issues. I expected her to be the living embodiment of the role I've been playing, a woman down on her luck and living rough. Then she met my grandmother and saw an opportunity. Get a roof over her head and a bit of money to boot.

Except there's no money. There's barely a roof. And Celeste is a cultured and attractive woman, one that Liam had no problem introducing to his friends.

"You think she's in trouble." I look at him. "Hiding."

He makes a face. "Please don't give this woman a tragic backstory that makes me feel sorry for her."

When I don't answer, he says, "Daisy?"

I only dimly hear him, and it isn't until he says, "CeCe?" that I snap out of it.

I squeeze the bridge of my nose. "Sorry, I'm . . ." I look down and give a tight laugh. "Standing over the body of a murdered man and trying to figure out what his girlfriend is running from. Not important, obviously."

"It's a shock. But, yes, you need to report the Rover. The more time . . ."

"The more time that elapses between leaving Celeste and making this call, the more our timeline doesn't work. Yes, call, please."

He waves for me to follow him.

I hesitate. "Our footprints—"

"—will be gone in an hour or so. The ground's too wet to hold them. Now come on, and let's do this."

CELESTE

"I don't understand."

It's the third time I've said that, the repetition buzzing in my head. I want to take it back and find a new way to word it.

As a child, I dreamed of being a comic-book creator. I could draw, and I could tell stories, and someday I'd do exactly that. Instead, I do graphic design, creating logos and social media banners, and if I ever get the chance to write, it's on the rare occasions I'm asked to provide copy. More often, I'm given the copy, and then I show off my writing skills.

You've repeated sale *three times in thirty words. Let's try a synonym.*

Your wording is overly complicated here. Let's simplify.

"Ms. Turner?"

I look into the dark eyes of the young officer, and without thinking, I flinch. My gut seizes, seeing a cop, my defenses thrown up.

He's not here for you.

He's here about Liam.

"Ms. Turner?"

I stare, uncomprehending.

Turner. That's your name, remember?

"I'm sorry," I say. "I'm . . ." I give my head a sharp shake.

"In shock," he says. "But there's no need to be. We only found his vehicle. There's no sign of foul play."

Foul play? I almost laugh. Cops actually say that?

Focus, damn it. Focus.

Instead, I hear myself say, "Foul play?" my voice squeaking a little.

That squeak is a laugh at the absurdity of the phrase, but thankfully, he mistakes it for panic and rushes on with "There's no sign that anything happened."

"Except that you found his very expensive vehicle abandoned in the swamp, with the keys on the seat."

The officer squirms.

You're very new at this, aren't you? Just a baby cop. Give it time, and you'll have no problem telling me to expect the worst. No problem telling a seventeen-year-old girl that you'll overlook the drugs in her backpack in return for a few minutes spent on her knees. No problem brushing off a nineteen-year-old girl when she asks for help escaping her boyfriend.

"We didn't find any traces of blood," he says, and then his face spasms in horror, as if realizing what images that last word could conjure for a woman like me.

"So what do you think happened?" I ask.

That is cruel. I know it is. This baby cop doesn't deserve it, but I must ask, even if I know the answer.

The young man's face spasms anew as he tries—and fails—to find a suitably optimistic expression.

Finally, he clears his throat and says, "I cannot speculate, ma'am, but without signs of, uh, violence, it's possible his car was taken for a joyride and abandoned in the swamp, with the keys on the seat, in hopes someone else would take it."

"Why not leave it in a public place?"

"I—" He squares his shoulders. "I cannot speculate, ma'am. I can only say that criminals don't always behave in a logical manner."

"Then where is Liam?" I ask. "The car wasn't taken from my driveway. He had the keys, and now he's missing."

"We don't know that. We've sent a car to his place of residence."

Yes, because clearly, he returned to Tampa, where someone stole his Rover and drove it back to abandon it on an ATV trail outside Fort Exile.

I know this officer doesn't believe that. He's been tasked with talking to "the girlfriend," and his job is to keep me calm.

I am always calm, kid.

I've learned to be.

This young officer is sweet and sincere, and I cannot cling to my prejudice any longer, so I let him off the hook with, "Hopefully, he's there."

The officer nods. "Yes, now, if you don't mind, I need to ask you a few questions about the last time you saw him."

The last time you saw him.

Those words hit hard, and tears threaten. I let one fall and then blink the rest back. The young officer wants my story. So I give him one. Not my life story, of course. That wouldn't help his investigation. It's pertinent, though. In a way I hope he'll never know.

Let's start at the beginning, Officer . . . Coleman, is it? That's what your name tag says, though you introduced yourself as Montrell, so let's go with that.

When did I last see my lover, Montrell? Here's the version I will tell you.

"Last night. At about . . . midnight, maybe? We'd gone to bed, and we'd both had a bit too much to drink, and we . . ." My cheeks flame at the memory, or I hope they do. "Let's just say we'd had too much to drink. So, there was *that*."

I continue, "That's the last time I saw him. I woke at three, and his side of the bed was empty. I figured he was using the bathroom, and I fell back to sleep."

"So he may have left after you two . . ." Officer Coleman clears his throat. "After you initially fell asleep. That was the last time anyone seems to have seen him."

"I don't know about my houseguest. She says she didn't see him this morning."

"So she last saw him before you two went to bed?"

"If she says so."

Officer Coleman frowns. "You have reason to believe otherwise."

"No, I just . . ." I hesitate and then shake it off, and his frown deepens.

"Ms. Turner? If you know something—"

"I don't. I just . . . I got the feeling they'd spoken at some point after that."

"In the morning, you mean?" He pauses. "I thought you hadn't spoken to Mr. Garey after that night."

"I hadn't. Sorry. It's just . . . When I spoke to Daisy, my impression was that she'd seen Liam after I had. Maybe passing in the hall to use the bathroom or something. I must be wrong."

When did I last see my lover, Officer Montrell?

Rousing in bed, to a kiss on my ear and a breathy whisper.

"Wake up, Elizabeth. We have a problem."

TWENTY-FOUR

DAISY

The police are gone, and I'm trying very hard not to run to the toilet, stick my head in the bowl and puke. Withholding the fact I found Liam's body should bother me most, but perversely, I can justify that because I didn't lie. I just omitted information. I suppose one could say I lied when I answered the question "When did you last see him?" but I interpreted that as "When did you last see him *alive*?" and I was relatively honest there. I admitted I'd seen him after Celeste went to bed. I said he cornered me outside, drunk, and made inappropriate comments, and I turned him down and walked away. Which is technically true.

I *had* walked away after he confronted me. I just hadn't gotten far. That's when he'd grabbed me by the wrist, leaving those bruises.

"Uh-uh, Miss Daisy. You don't want to walk away from this conversation."

"Let go of my arm."

His fingers tightened. I wheeled, slamming his arm up, the surprise making him let go enough for me to wrench free. When he bounced back, he was facing the blade of my utility knife.

"Miss Daisy has teeth," he said. "What a surprise."

He grabbed at me midsentence, as if talking was supposed to lower my guard. He caught my wrist, nails scraping before I slashed my knife at his arm. A gash opened, blood welling, and he pulled back, hand to his injury.

"It's a paper cut," I said. "Touch me again, and I stab, and that'll do some actual damage."

His eyes flashed, jaw setting in a way that was supposed to make him look tough, but it was a little boy's pout.

"You think you hold something over me," I said. "But you're going to need to explain it, in small words, so my tiny brain can follow. You know who I am, and you're threatening to do what exactly? Tell the police that I'm the real Celeste Turner? Thanks. You never struck me as the type to do pro bono work, but I'd appreciate it."

His lips twisted in a humorless smile. "If you wanted that, you'd have done it by now. There's a reason you're playing this game, and I think I know what it is. You want her punished."

I shrugged and fixed on my poker face. "Maybe, that'd be the cherry on top, but the ice cream sundae is getting her out of my house, and you doing that for me isn't exactly a threat. What do you want, Liam? And what are you offering in return?"

He hesitated at that. He'd thrown my name at me, thinking it gave him the upper hand, but he hadn't worked it through. Yes, I'd prefer not to step forward until I knew whether the imposter had murdered my grandmother, but I *could* do it now, if I had to.

He rolled his shoulders, tugging back the mantle of control. "We both want revenge. She conned me. Seduced me. I only realized that today. Something about you kept nudging at me. I finally figured it out. You remind me of Maeve. Your facial shape. Your chin. It nudged at me until the answer popped. That's why I was late getting here tonight. I was doing my research. Digging up a photograph of you as a child."

Did I believe that? Not for one moment. The second part may be true, where he just figured out my identity, but being conned by the imposter? Seduced? Liam Garey as the victim here? Nope. Still, I only nodded, accepting the lie as offered.

He continued, "If the truth came out, I'd be professionally embarrassed."

"And you think I can help with that."

"No, I can resolve that on my own." He was amused by my offer, relaxing as he pushed me back into my box. Silly little Daisy, the earnest child who honestly thought *she* could help *him*. "There's another matter that I would like to discuss, and I would prefer not to do it on this road."

I sighed. Then I said, "Lift your arms and let me pat you down."

His brows shot up. "What?"

"I'm agreeing to go someplace private with you, but I'm sure as hell making sure you're unarmed first."

His lips twitched—more amusement. Then he lifted his arms and said, "Pat away."

He wasn't armed. I didn't expect him to be. Liam Garey considered himself permanently armed by the double-barreled rifle of privilege and intellect. He was better than all of us. He was smarter. That's all he needed.

I led him around the backyard on the other side of the property. He wanted to stop there. I kept going until we reached that stand of trees, where he balked about dirtying his shoes. Once we were just inside, I said, "Let's try that again. What do you want, Liam?"

"How much do you know about Bill Turner's treasure?"

I coughed. It was the only way to cover up a burst of laughter. I bent over, hacking, hand to my mouth, and he patiently waited for me to get it under control.

"Bill Turner?" I said. "My grandfather?"

"Yes." The slightest twitch of his lips, satisfied that he had the upper hand. Poor Daisy didn't even know the story. How convenient. "My father represented your grandfather in several legal entanglements. Theft charges, none of which resulted in convictions, thanks to my father's work."

No, thanks to my grandfather's cunning.

He continued, "Your grandfather liked to work alone. One day, though, he agreed to join a job bigger than he could tackle on his own. Three men who needed your grandfather's particular talent."

Safecracking. I knew this, but I frowned as if I found it all terribly confusing. My grandfather? A thief? Liam must be mistaken.

"They brought your grandfather in and pulled the job. Theft from someone unlikely to report the loss. While they got the money, the waiting driver was spotted, which tipped off the homeowner, and they had to split up. One of the men took the money while the other two ran in different directions. They were supposed to reconvene and split the profits. Except the man with the money didn't show up."

"And that was my grandfather?"

"No, Daisy," he said, as if speaking to a small child. "They would hardly have entrusted a newcomer with the money. The ringleader had it. When he disappeared, the others thought they'd been tricked, that he'd intentionally let them be spotted so he could take the money and run. But a month later, his body turned up in the swamp. The money was never found."

"People think my grandfather murdered him and stole the money?" My voice rose in horror and outrage, and if it was a little thick, Liam didn't notice. He was too caught up in his story.

He continued, "Two years ago, after my father died, I found notes in his file. Cryptic notes that took me some time to decipher." He paused for me to appreciate his brilliance. "At the time of the robbery, my father suspected Bill Turner had done exactly what you just said—killed the ringleader and taken the money. He tried to speak to your grandfather, as obliquely as possible, to ensure that if he'd killed the ringleader, he'd properly covered his tracks. Bill pretended to have no idea what my father was talking about, but the case went cold for lack of evidence, suggesting he took my father's advice."

Or, maybe, suggesting he hadn't killed anyone or stolen any money.

"I figured this out last year. Your grandmother's health was failing, and the Celeste-imposter had not yet appeared, so I broached the subject with Maeve. I told her what I'd found. I wasn't asking whether she had the money or not, but I implored her, if she did, to use some for her own benefit. I strongly suggested a retirement home—there are excellent ones in Sun City—or, at least, a healthcare aide. I assured her that I could help with the disbursement of the funds to avoid suspicion."

Yeah, I bet you could help with disbursement.

He continued, "Like your grandfather, Maeve was a cagey old fox. Acted as if she had no idea what I was talking about. Then the next time I visited, she was doing better. She suddenly had the money for the medications she required. Not that she always took them, mind you, but they were there. Which proved the money existed."

Or that Gran had the extra money I'd been sending her, and Liam's little chat convinced her to use some for her health.

"Then along came the imposter," Liam said. "By the time I found out, she'd been here for weeks. I accepted that it was Celeste Turner. It wasn't my place to ask for identification."

Not until she inherited the damn property, with you as executor. You were *the executor, right, Liam?*

"I accepted that she was you, and to my relief, she seemed to help Maeve. While Maeve was buying medications, she wasn't always taking them, or she was running out of them and not getting refills. There were also other medications the doctor suggested that Maeve believed she didn't need."

I mimicked Gran's voice. "Damn doctors and drug companies, as bad as leeches, bleeding you dry."

"Yes, we both heard that lecture. But the imposter was able to convince Maeve to take the medications, and it seemed to help."

Here's where I couldn't sit back and listen in silence, because this was the information I wanted.

Tell me how my grandmother was before her death. Tell me exactly how she died. Give me data to help me figure out what happened . . . and whether Celeste was involved.

"The medications *seemed* to help?" I said. "But it didn't, obviously, because she died. Heart failure, right? That's what I heard."

"That's only what they put on the death certificate when someone's heart stops," he said smugly. "It's the actual cause of death for *most* people. Maeve's heart stopped beating."

"So the doctor didn't know exactly how she died?"

"Everyone knows how she died. Old age. She rallied with the medications, but the damage was done. Diabetes, hypertension, heart disease—it's a wonder she survived as long as she did. One cannot stay alive through sheer obstinacy, as hard as Maeve tried."

"Did she suffer long?"

He turned a look on me, and that look was pitying, but it was a sneering pity for a young woman who wasn't nearly as tough as her grandmother. I might have been quick with a utility knife, but deep down, I was a child sniveling over her lost granny, completely ignoring the fact that he'd just told me there was more to my inheritance than a rundown house.

"No, she didn't suffer long," he said. "She started her decline on a Saturday morning. Celeste—the imposter—called me, and I came over as quickly as I could. Dr. Hoover checked in and thought Maeve would have a few more days, but she was gone before sunset."

I remembered Doc Hoover from my childhood. A good small-town doctor. He topped my list of people I needed to speak to, but I had to figure out how to do that without giving myself away.

"I'm glad the end came quickly," I said.

"It did. But before Maeve passed, she gave me something for you. Her granddaughter's true inheritance." He paused for effect. "Bill Turner's money."

I frowned. "Why give it to you? Wasn't the imposter with Gran?"

"Maeve wanted her to have the money, and she didn't want her—you—to know where it came from. I was to arrange for it to come through me as an inheritance."

"Okay . . ."

"Maeve gave me a safety deposit key. Said not to go there until she'd passed. When I did, I found a note. It was for Celeste. For you. It said that, to find your inheritance, remember how you liked to spend your time at her house. The real key is there."

His voice lowered with each word, drawing them out as he watched my face for a flicker of recognition. Surely, I would understand my grandmother's words, and he would see that understanding in my eyes.

"How I liked to spend my time at her house?" I said.

"A special place, obviously," he said, voice snapping with impatience. "A secret spot? In the house or the forest or the swamp?"

"I had a few special spots," I said. "But I also had a bunch of hobbies, and she could mean one of them."

I managed to say this without even a hint of stifled laughter.

Ah, Gran, even from the grave, you can drive me to distraction, but I do love you. Crafty old fox? Nope. Crafty old rabbit, leading this puffed-up predator on a merry chase.

Now let's see if I learned anything from you, Gran. I'll keep this fox running in circles while he gives me what I need.

"I suppose *that's* what you want from me," I said. "A list of all the places Gran might have hidden Grandpa's money, and a promise that I won't beat you to it."

"I don't need a promise. I know who you are, remember?"

I bit my tongue against reminding him how utterly useless that information was.

Not such a smart fox, are you, Liam? Well, that makes it easy for me to play along.

"Right," I said. "But that doesn't quite seem like a fair deal. You get the money—*my* money—and I get your silence."

"I will give you a third of the money," he said.

"No."

He pretended to consider before saying, "Fine. Half."

I promise, fingers crossed behind my back. Let me find the money, and half of it will be yours, and you can trust me to tell you how much I found.

I *could* trust him to tell me. Because I already knew the number. Zero.

Gran had *Liam's* number. She'd thought he was useful, and she'd thought he was charming and handsome, but she'd also known he was out to screw her over. So she was leading him on this merry chase from beyond the grave. I hoped she was looking down and laughing her ass off.

"I don't want any money," I said, my chin lifting. "A man died for it. Blood money. You can have it all, on two conditions. First, you don't ever bring my grandparents into this—wherever you got the money from, it's not connected to them."

He tried to keep from smiling. "I believe I can agree to that. And condition number two?"

"When I'm ready to come forward, you'll do it with me."

His brows rose.

I continued, "You want to salvage your career, right? You'll come forward with me, and we'll pretend that you were trying to expose the imposter all along. Hell, you can even say you tracked me down and brought me here."

His eyes glinted. *Oh, you foolish girl. Giving me all the money in return for two things that help me more than they help you. Yes, I'll happily leave your poor dead grandparents out of this. Yes, I'll happily take the credit for uncovering the imposter.*

"Oh!" I said. "There's one more thing."

He tensed.

I dropped my voice. "This may sound silly to you, but I want to know more about Gran. About how the imposter treated her. About how Gran felt about her. How Gran died. Anything you can tell me. I just . . ." I lifted my gaze to his, blinking as if holding back tears. "I just need to know, for better or worse. I torment myself thinking of how that monster might have treated Gran. It keeps me awake at night."

"I'm sure it does," he murmured, trying hard for sympathy and looking as if he was holding in gas.

"That's the deal, then," I said. "I'll compile my list of places in the morning. Then we'll talk about Gran. Agreed?"

"Agreed."

TWENTY-FIVE

DAISY

That's not the version I told the police, of course. Just that first part, where Liam confronted me, drunk and horny, and I walked away. They didn't press further. No "Are you sure you didn't discuss anything else?" or "Did he follow you?" Somehow, even knowing that it wouldn't stand up in court, my conscience feels clean on that count.

The part that has my gut twisting is that I lied about my identity. Again, that seems ridiculous. I've been lying about it since I arrived. Now, though, I have given my false identity to the police. No actual ID—the young deputy didn't ask for that. If they do, I'll be screwed. I don't have fake ID, and the real one is in a safety deposit box in Tampa—I'd been paranoid about someone finding it and realizing who I am.

I'm freaked out for the same reason I'm not carrying fake ID. When my suburban friends shoplifted lip gloss and candy bars, they made me stay outside. Even though I wasn't lifting anything myself, the guilty look on my face would have given everyone away. I don't jaywalk. I don't drive after a single beer. I once lost a good job because I refused to use stained poplar when a client paid for black walnut.

Maybe my extreme law-abiding is like Tom refusing to drink. Through my veins pumps a hereditary disregard for the distinction between legal and illegal ways to make a living. Yet I don't judge my father—and grandfather—and great-grandfather—for their choices. They needed to put food on the table. And, yes, in Dad's case, he needed to feed addictions, but the grocery and rent money still came first.

Perhaps *that* is where my true aversion to criminal behavior lies. Unlike my ancestors, I don't have an excuse. As a teen, I could afford the candy bars and lip gloss. My skills pay my bills, and I have no dependents—or dependence—to feed. Whatever the reason, now that I've lied to the police, I'm a little freaked out.

A lot freaked out.

Tom said I could come by later and talk to him. I'm resisting that urge. It feels like when we'd come here in the summer, and Gran would fight with Mom. It always happened at night when they thought I was asleep and Dad wasn't around to run interference.

Mom and Gran hated each other, which was weird because they both wanted the same thing: to get Dad clean and straight. I guess it's like having two master carpenters working on one house. You'd think they'd be thrilled to find a partner who'd make the job easier, but instead, it becomes a battle of will and ego.

Under the surface, they were as alike as mother and daughter, hard in their love and hard to love. So they fought over who could help Dad and who was dragging him down, and on those nights, after I'd gone to bed, they'd clash like titans of old, the house rocking with their frustration and rage.

I think back on those days, and I wish I'd been old enough to jump between them, hold back the force of their personalities and negotiate peace between the two women whose love for my father still couldn't save him. Maybe that could have saved us. Or, perhaps, it wouldn't have mattered how old I was—they'd still only see a child who didn't understand.

Back then, I only understood that their rage scared me. I'd sneak out, run to Tom's place and tap on his window. He'd keep me company until I felt safe enough to go home. Tonight, I am that girl again, desperate to run to Tom and wake him up to soothe my fears.

Eventually, I do sneak out. Celeste has gone to bed. We didn't speak beyond me asking how she was doing and praying she didn't want someone to talk to. Thankfully, she did not and retreated to her room.

When I first planned this mission, I expected to hate Celeste, even if she didn't murder my grandmother. This woman stole my identity. She found my grandmother in seriously poor health and took advantage. She insinuated herself into Gran's life and robbed me of any chance that Gran would, on her deathbed, finally reach out and reconcile. Worse, Gran thought we *had* reconciled. Her granddaughter had returned, and the past was wiped away. My dearest dream come true . . . except it happened to someone else. Someone who hadn't loved Gran. Someone who'd only seen her as a mark to be conned.

Then I'd realized that the best way to do this was to just stay cool. Play my role of wandering soul and hope to get information that way. Get access to the house. Find Gran's diary and the imposter's ID.

It's going to take some time to see this woman as Celeste again, and I need to return to that place if I'm going to follow through on my plan.

I slip out of the house and into the yard, heading to Tom's place. I've gone maybe fifty feet past the property when I catch voices on the breeze, and I drop to one knee, extinguishing my flashlight just as a brighter light cuts through the darkness. My heart hammers as two male voices talk, only their tones reaching me, rough and abrupt. I catch Liam's name and freeze.

What the hell were you mixed up in, Liam?

More than just shady legal work. I know that from our conversation last night.

I wish you weren't lying dead out here, Liam.

I wish you were still alive so I could sue your ass for everything you're worth, get you disbarred and see you locked behind bars. I want to see you in a prison cell looking down at a tattoo you didn't give yourself, marked for life as exactly the sort of person you sneered at with Tom.

I wish that for you, and instead, you are dead, and I'm not satisfied. I only hope that whoever pulled that trigger looked you in the eye when they did it. I hope they were someone you screwed over, and the moment before that bullet hit, you realized every step that brought you to that point was a choice. Your choice.

If I had my phone, I could sneak up and take a picture of the men in case they are Liam's killers. The thought makes me stifle a laugh. Yeah, no, it's probably a good thing I don't have my phone, or I'd end up alligator-chow, all for the sake of a blurry, dark photo.

I should flee. Get the hell out before I'm seen or heard. Yet here is an opportunity I cannot resist. Not a photo, then, but information. A lead. A snippet of conversation.

I stifle another laugh. Okay, maybe hoping for case-breaking information is a bit much. I might hear *something*, though.

I creep in their direction, following the beacon of their conversation and their movements, lumbering through the swamp. Finally, words come clear.

"You do realize this is a complete waste of time, right? Also dangerous as hell. It's after dark, and we're in the *swamp*."

"The swamp is over there. This is dry ground."

"You know what I mean. We shouldn't be out here."

"I just—"

"You want to see your first dead body."

"No, I want to find a man who I'm sure is out here, murdered."

"You mean he *didn't* just abandon his vehicle with the keys on the seat? Isn't that what you told his girlfriend?"

A grumble that I now realize is the voice of the younger deputy sheriff, Coleman. It's the police, out looking for Liam's body.

Shit.

Yes, being found by his killers would be worse, but this is equally dangerous.

I take one step backward. Then another. I'm in the middle of a third step when the flashlight beam swings my way, a voice saying, "Did you see that?"

I crouch there, holding my breath as the beam cuts a swath through the darkness.

"Something moved," Coleman says.

"Mmm, yeah. See, the thing is, city boy, that this ain't the city. Whole lotta stuff moves in these swamps, and the only real question is whether you can eat it . . . or it can eat you. Which is—may I repeat—why we shouldn't be out here. They'll send dogs in the morning."

"What if the body isn't here in the morning? What if an alligator or a wild boar hauls it away?"

The older deputy—Mazur—gives a deep sigh.

"What?" Officer Coleman says. "Didn't you just remind me there are things out here that eat people?"

As they talk, I creep backward. My shoe slips off a fallen log, thumping into a puddle.

"There!" Coleman says. "You heard that, right?"

"Son, did I mention how many critters live out here? I'm humoring you, because you're a good kid and I hate to squash your enthusiasm, but we need to get our asses back to the station before they need to send dogs looking for *us*."

"I just want to check this out."

Another sigh, but the older deputy doesn't stop him. I look around wildly. There's thick vegetation to my left. I start over there, but with each step, my shoe squelches, and I know I'm leaving a trail. Also, I can't see. I can only make out dim shapes and—

I stumble over another fallen branch and look down—

The branch has five fingers, curled inward. It's Liam's outstretched arm.

My chest seizes, panic burbling, the deputies heading my way as I stand beside Liam's dead body.

One of them spots me and crashes through the undergrowth. I wheel to run even as my brain screams that this is the worst possible idea. Stand my ground. That's the best course. The only course. Pretend I just found him now and pray for the best. I didn't kill Liam, so there's no reason to run, and I'll only make things worse.

All that goes through my head . . . as I run. My brain screams instructions, logical instructions, and my legs do their own thing, brain drowned out by instinct. I get three steps before my brain shouts fresh information, information that my body actually hears.

The crashing isn't coming my way.

"Get the hell back here!" the older deputy bellows.

"He's running!" the younger one replies.

"Who? The dead guy? Get the hell back—"

A squeal sounds. The squeal of a very angry opossum. The deputies' voices grow incoherent with distance. I freeze there, waiting to be absolutely certain they're gone before I—

Mud squelches behind me. I spin, fists going up, but before I see more than a shape, a hand slaps over my mouth. I swing, my fist hitting just as I see Tom's face, his mouth opening in a hissed "It's me."

Or that's what I think he was about to say. A fist to the jaw knocks his words away. He staggers and reaches out to steady himself on my arm, but I step away. I stand there, silent, as he recovers and glowers at me.

"You're welcome," he mouths.

I arch my brows. He gestures toward the deputies and pantomimes throwing something. In other words, that opossum didn't just happen to tear out at an opportune moment. Tom had set it running.

I turn my attention toward the deputies. They're farther in now, the older one snarling because he's calf-deep in mud.

I catch Tom's eye, and I don't apologize. I put a hand to my mouth and shake my head. Understanding sparks in his eyes. However good his intentions, sneaking up on a woman and covering her mouth never says, "I come in peace."

He considers and then nods, mouthing, "Fair enough" and "Sorry."

I gesture at his jaw, and I mouth, "We're even," and he chuckles under his breath, and I relax. There'd been a moment, seeing him, when his intentions had *not* been clear, when I wasn't sure he really did come in peace.

A moment when I doubted. When I wondered what the hell he was doing here. I still do.

He motions for me to follow him. He picks his way through the swamp more expertly than I could, and in the distance, while we can no longer hear the deputies' words, it's obvious from their tone that they're in retreat.

It's only when we reach the back of Tom's lot that he speaks, answering my questions before I can ask them.

"I was coming to see you," he says. "I couldn't sleep, and I thought I'd check in on you. I was cutting through when the cops spotted someone, and I sent that possum running, in case it was you."

He pauses at the back door. "I didn't mean to spook you."

"Let's get inside, and I'll tell you how it went with the police."

CELESTE

After tossing and turning in bed, I decide to go downstairs. I pause at Daisy's door. I turn the knob as quietly as I can. The door opens enough for me to peek in and see an empty bed.

I check my watch. It's past one. Where's Daisy? I glance up toward the attic, remembering my earlier suspicions, but I already know she wasn't behind the camera. I still open the attic. It's dark.

I head downstairs to more darkness and silence.

"Daisy?" I call, but I know I'll get no answer. If she couldn't sleep, she'd be reading. I suppose her love of reading suggests I may be wrong about her intellect. Still, it's not as if she reads high literature. It's basic airplane material, quick and unchallenging.

Which is also the sort of book I prefer. I've been known to roll my eyes at women who brag about only reading "literature," and yet here I am, insulting Daisy's reading material when it matches my own.

God, I want to shake myself sometimes.

When there's no sign of Daisy on the main level, I recall an easy way to check whether she's in the house. She always puts her shoes at the door, like the nice girl she is.

Daisy's shoes aren't at the door. Knowing she's been distracted, I check both doors and her room. I also check outside in case they're muddy from being behind the property.

No shoes here, no shoes there, no Daisy-girl shoes are anywhere.

I open the front door and step onto the porch, staring into the blackness.

Snuck out in the night to visit Tom, Daisy?

Huh.

Not what I expected.

Not at all.

TWENTY-SIX

DAISY

We're on Tom's roof. Not his rooftop patio, but the actual sloping roof of his shop. We're perched up there, me with a beer, Tom with a soda, a bag of pork rinds between us.

"Remember doing this at my parents' place?" he asks. "Sneaking up on the roof to watch the stars?"

"I do."

He stretches out. "That's why I set up my patio. A grown-up version of that." He grins my way in the moonlight. "It's nice to be able to talk without pretending I don't know who you are."

"Sorry."

"I didn't say that to needle you. I just think I deserve a gold star for not blowing it. You would not believe how many times I started to say, 'Hey, remember when . . .'"

He sets the soda bottle precariously to the side and folds his arms behind his head. "I've thought about you a lot, over the years. You were different."

I choke on a laugh. "Is that a nice way of saying I was kinda weird?"

"Nah. I meant our relationship was unique. I had plenty of friends, but with you, I felt more like myself. I didn't need to be tougher than I was. Didn't need to worry if I got upset or cried or just"—he shrugs—"admitted stuff I couldn't admit to others. Once I got older, I'd think about you, wonder where you were, wonder why we hadn't kept in touch. That seems weird now. It felt like you moved to another planet."

"We were kids. Our parents made all the choices for us, including where we lived. I eventually lost touch with all of my Florida friends. You're right—it might have only been halfway across the country, but it felt like halfway across the galaxy."

He nods. "I wish we'd kept in touch, but maybe it's better this way. You got to skip my wild and misspent youth."

"And you got to skip my very boring suburban one. I was quite the little stuck-up snot for a few years."

He laughs. "Somehow, I think your version of stuck-up is wearing designer jeans and occasionally failing to hold an elevator door."

"And I suspect your version of a wild and misspent youth is wearing a leather jacket and smoking the occasional joint."

"Maybe," he says with a smile. "Though wearing a leather jacket in Florida is kinda badass."

I shake my head. "So, now that we're not pretending anymore, I finally get to ask how your mom's doing."

His smile broadens. "Very good. She left that sack of shit when I was fifteen. By then, she'd gotten her GED and added a few college courses. She got an office job and moved us to Tampa. Now she's an office manager in Miami, remarried and living in Big Cypress. My stepdad works for the national preserve there. Total straight-up guy. I'm too old to need a daddy, but he's there for me, you know? Encouraged me to continue mechanics after I got out and then helped me get set up here. They bought this place as a so-called investment, but what they were really investing in was me."

"That is awesome." I look his way, meeting his eyes. "Really awesome."

"Even more awesome that I bought them out a few months ago. This is my place now, free and clear." He takes a drink from his soda. "And your mom? How's she doing?"

My expression must answer because he quickly says, "Or we can avoid that subject."

"She's gone. Cancer. Ten years ago."

"I'm sorry. I know your dad passed, too. I'm *really* sorry about that. Just like I was sorry . . ." He inhales sharply. "What happened before you left. I never had the chance to say how sorry I was. I tried to send you a card, but I'm guessing you never got it."

"I didn't, but I did hear that you'd sent one. Thank you."

"About your dad, I was glad you got to be with him at the end. I know how close you two were."

My brows arch.

"Maeve," he says. "Right up until she died, all anyone had to do was mention your name, and they got that story. How you defied your mom and emptied your bank account to take a bus down here and stay by your dad's side until he passed. She was so damned proud of you."

My eyes fill, and I sit in silence.

"And that's not quite what she told you, is it?" he asks softly.

I shake my head, tears falling, chin turned to the side so he won't see them.

"Shit," he mutters. "Do I even dare ask what she said?"

I take a deep breath and wipe my eyes. "It was fine, up until he died. Then she told me to go. Get my ass back home. I wanted to stay in touch. I was old enough to do that, and she wouldn't have it. Told me to git gone, so I did."

"Damn her."

"I still reached out now and then. Sent cards. Sent letters saying I'd like to come see her. When I was twenty, I got two cards in a row marked 'return to sender,' and I panicked, thinking something had happened to her. Nope. She was alive and fine and living in the same house. She just didn't want to hear from me anymore."

"Screw you, Maeve," he says into the darkness. "I understand that she thought she was doing what's best, but really, screw her." He sits up and turns toward me. "You know she didn't mean it, right?"

When I don't answer, he sighs. "Of course you don't know it. How could you? Fourteen years old and you travel across the country to be with your dying dad, and your grandmother sends you packing the moment he's gone."

I say nothing.

He stretches his legs. "After Mom took me to Tampa, I didn't come back to Fort Exile until they bought this place for me. I got to know Maeve a lot better then. To see her as a person, adult to adult."

He pauses. "Well, no, she never did see me as an adult, but that's another story. Point is that I'd come around, deliver her groceries, do odd jobs, and you know why she liked me? Not because I helped out. Because I'd been your friend. She had a soft spot for me, so she tolerated the help. And I tolerated her bullshit. She told me once that it wasn't my fault I went to prison and that I was right to avoid alcohol because those things were bred in my bone. And she *wasn't* referring to my dad's side."

I sigh. "Sorry."

"Why? You didn't say it." He meets my gaze. "She loved you, CeCe. Loved you more than anyone else, after your daddy. Maybe even more than him. For Maeve, the best way to show her love was to chase you away. Make sure you stayed in the big city, leading a big-city life with big-city people. She knew you sent her money."

When I blink, he says, "You did, right? Deposited it into her account?"

"Not a lot. Just enough that she wouldn't realize it."

"Maeve always knew exactly how much should be there. She told me someone was putting money into her account, and all the bank would say was that it came from out of state, so she knew it was you. She said the bank wouldn't let her send it back, so she was stuck with it. That's how she put it. *Stuck with it.* She grumbled about how she didn't need no charity, but you should have seen her eyes shine every time she told that story. And she told it *all* the time, making sure everyone knew her grandbaby from up North was sneaking money into her bank account."

I pick at the label on my beer bottle. "And when the imposter Celeste showed up, Gran thought *she* was the one who did all that."

I hear the hurt in my voice, and it chafes. It's like giving an anonymous donation . . . and then finding out someone else took credit. Sure, you weren't claiming credit yourself, but somehow, the theft saps the gesture of its joy. I did this thing for my gran, despite how she'd treated me, and Celeste got to bask in Maeve's pride and what passed for her love.

When Tom doesn't reply, I say, "Sorry, that's petty and churlish. The point is that Gran appreciated the money."

"It's not petty. It's not churlish. If I'm quiet, I'm trying to figure out how to broach this topic without losing my temper."

He cracks open another soda. "First, there are a few things you need to know about the situation, to explain why Maeve thought she was you. And selfishly, to defend the fact that even *I* accepted she was you." He looks at me. "That last part is really tough."

"It's okay."

"No, it's not but . . ." He inhales. "Your gran was in rough shape. Really rough. She should have been in a home, but we both know she'd have swallowed a bottle of pills before she allowed that.

Cataracts meant she wasn't seeing well. Untreated diabetes meant she wasn't thinking clearly. A year ago, we had a really bad falling out over you."

"Me?"

He nods. "I could see she was on a downhill slide, and I wanted her to contact you. At first, she said she didn't know how, which was true, but when I offered to start looking, she refused to give me even the barest details. She accused me of wanting to track you down for my own sake. And that's where things got ugly. She didn't want me in contact with you. I'm an ex-con mechanic, and one of the best things about you escaping this life is that it meant you'd never end up with a guy like me."

"She said that?"

"Yep."

"God*damn* her. I'm so sorry."

He shrugs. "Part of me says she's not to blame—it was mental decline. But it's like when people talk shit after they've been drinking. It doesn't come from nowhere. It's just stuff they wouldn't normally say out loud. I said yes, I would like to see you again—to catch up with an old friend. I don't exactly need help meeting women. Which led to her opinions on the type of women guys like me attract and that I should stick with them because you deserved better."

"Damn her." I look at him. "I'm sorry. She was a million miles out of line. I hope you knew that."

"Yeah, I did, but I'm also sensitive about it. Especially when it comes to you. All those afternoons you and I spent talking about how we'd get out of places like Fort Exile, and where did I end up?"

"It's not that simple."

"I know. Still, she struck a sore spot, mostly by insulting my integrity, saying I was only thinking of myself. So we fought, and she ran me off, like she did you. I was busy with the shop, so time passed quickly. I still made sure she had what she needed. Glory used to drive her into Sun City for her appointments, and I'd sneak over and fix stuff up while she was gone, and Maeve pretended not to notice her faucet suddenly worked again."

"You shouldn't have done that after how she treated you."

"I wanted to. Anyway, time passes, and one day I nearly run over this woman jogging on the road. Last person I remember jogging in Fort Exile was you, and that made me smile. Never thought much of it until I saw her again, and I asked someone who she was, and they said it was Maeve's granddaughter, Celeste. So, the next time I saw her, I said hello, and she obviously had no clue who I was, and I figured . . ." He shrugs. "I figured I just hadn't made as much of an impression on you as you did on me."

My brows rise. "You thought I forgot you?"

"Hey, you thought I didn't recognize *you*."

"But you did think Celeste looked like me."

"I thought she could be you. When I actually saw *you* again, out jogging in the rain that day, that lightbulb went off, and now I wonder how I ever made that mistake. I *did* realize she wasn't you sooner, though. During Maeve's funeral, I looked over at that woman playing the grieving granddaughter, and I knew. So I started searching for you."

He smiles at my expression. "It was a shitty effort. I had no idea where to start, so I hired an investigator, only to discover how expensive that is. I had to pull the plug fast, and I kept digging on my own. I was doing that, slowly but surely, when you showed up and saved me the trouble."

He chomps through two pork rinds before saying, "Someone else was looking for you, too."

"What?"

"My investigator got a lead on where you used to live, growing up, and one of the neighbors said someone else had come looking for you a few months earlier. He couldn't give me more than that. I figured it must be fake-Celeste. She couldn't have gotten far, though, because she obviously has no idea who you are."

Liam did. I don't say that. I've dragged Tom into this enough already. Admit that Liam ID'd me, and that's motive for murder—another secret for Tom to keep.

I sip my beer in silence. Then I ask, "How did she treat Maeve? I know you weren't close with Gran at the time, but did you get a sense . . . ?"

When he doesn't answer, I say, "Does that mean you don't want to give her any credit? Or you don't want to upset me by admitting Celeste treated her poorly?"

"Door number one. If fake-Celeste mistreated Maeve, I'd have stepped in. So would Glory and others." He chews over his words before spitting out, "Maeve needed looking after, and fake-Celeste did it. Because that was in her best interests, obviously. Maeve would have kicked her ass out otherwise."

I want to tell him what I suspect. That Celeste may have played a role in Gran's death, either through intentional neglect or outright murder. If I say that, though, how's he going to react when I want to go back to that house? Live under that roof with a possible killer?

No. I will get to that, but for now, that part's mine and mine alone.

CELESTE

Morning comes, and I wake to the smell of bacon frying. Daisy is in the kitchen making breakfast. Bright-eyed and humming, she's busy flipping eggs, and I watch her as I drag my sorry ass into the room.

I await a surge of jealousy that doesn't come.

So you and Tom, huh?

Can't say I saw that coming, but good on ya.

"Hey," Daisy says and reaches to pour me a coffee. When I move to take the mug from her, she waves me toward the table. "Sit. Relax. I'm sure you had a rough night."

"Hmm." I take the full mug from her. "How about you? Seemed quiet at your end of the house."

"I went out after the police left. I couldn't sleep."

"You must have been out for a while," I say as I sip my coffee. "I didn't hear you come back in."

"I walked past Tom's place and saw a light on, so I popped in to talk about finding the Rover. He's going to get the word out, see if anyone noticed anything suspicious."

"And you spent the night, I take it?"

Her brows rise in genuine surprise. Then she laughs under her breath. "Uh, no. We just talked. I was back by two."

Silence, then she asks, "Have you heard anything from the police?"

"No. They're bringing dogs into the wetlands out back today."

Not one twitch of surprise crosses her face. Only discomfort and concern, and she says, "It's just a precaution."

"Do you really believe that?" I ask.

She turns back to the stove. "I believe Liam could be okay."

"But he's probably not."

She doesn't answer that, just arranges my breakfast on a plate and then launches into questions about the house, about the order of repairs. I'm not distracted, but I play along as I wait for a knock at the door.

TWENTY-SEVEN

CELESTE

It's the young cop, his dark skin shining with perspiration as he stands on my porch, struggling to keep his face impassive.

Don't ever play poker, Officer Montrell Coleman. You'll lose your shirt.

I glance behind him for his older partner, but again, the young man is alone, his colleague abandoning him to this task.

"Yes?" I inject a note of hope in my voice, and when his face spasms, I regret the cruelty of letting him think I might actually believe he's come with good news.

"We found Mr. Garey," he says.

I must perk up even more . . . because his face contorts in fresh spasms, his eyes widening.

"No," he says quickly. "I mean, we didn't find . . ." He squares his shoulders. "May I come in, Ms. Turner?"

I step aside, and he walks into the cool, dark house.

"What did you . . . ?" I trail off and swallow.

He faces me, meeting my gaze. "I regret to inform you that we've discovered Mr. Garey's body."

"W-where?"

His gaze slides to the rear of the house. Then he says, "I'm not at liberty to say, exactly, ma'am, but it was in the wetlands out back."

"What happened?"

"An autopsy will be required to determine that."

"Is there anything . . . ? Anything I need to . . . ? Should I be going somewhere to ID the body? He doesn't have family in Florida. His ex-wife lives in Tampa, but I'm not sure that's appropriate."

"We may need you to identify him, but we're examining our options right now. Hopefully, you won't need to do that."

"It was . . . bad, then?"

He assures me that he simply meant viewing any dead body can be traumatic. I note that he does not say the body *isn't* in bad shape. I can only imagine what snacked on it during the twenty-four hours it lay out in the wild.

No open casket for you, Liam.

Young Montrell is still fumbling with vague reassurances when his partner shows up, having allotted enough time for Officer Coleman to do the shit job of telling the grieving girlfriend.

Asshole.

There are more questions then. The same ones I answered yesterday, allegedly to see whether I've remembered something new, but also checking whether my answers have changed. I stick to the facts of my story, but I add a few details that I've remembered since.

After they retread the ground preceding Liam's disappearance, they launch into the new questions. Had he argued with anyone recently? Complained of trouble? Mentioned an unhappy client? I answer as best I can. Liam was a lawyer who practiced criminal law and took on the worst his firm had to offer because he wasn't easily spooked.

"I worry—" I swallow. "*Worried* about him sometimes. The sort of people he defended. He always said that's where the money is."

Officer Coleman nods.

"I guess he was right," I say. "He certainly was doing well for himself. I know he never complained about paying alimony. He bought the Rover a few months ago. He has his Tampa condo and an oceanfront place in St. Pete Beach. He sent me a hundred-dollar bottle of scotch the other day. Definitely good money, even if his clientele made me nervous."

The officers exchange a look.

Officer Coleman asks more questions, prodding further into Liam's finances while his partner finger-taps with impatience.

Sorry, Officer . . . I read his name tag. *Mazur, is it? I fear, Officer Mazur, your young partner's career is going to shoot past yours. I suspect that's the way you like it, though. Train the new dogs and watch them zoom on to bigger, better—and more stressful—jobs.*

As for the questions on Liam's finances, I equivocate as much as I can, same as I did about his clients. I'm just the girlfriend, after all. Not Liam's partner in crime. I inwardly laugh. He might have called me that, but I knew what I was. His tool. His captive. His victim. For now, I play the role of a graphic-designer girlfriend, innocent and perhaps not terribly bright.

I have no idea where you're leading with these questions, officers, but I'll answer them as best I can, which is not very well, I fear. I will, however, nudge you in a direction that'll reveal a lot about Liam Garey.

The interview is winding down when voices sound outside the kitchen window. I look through to see Daisy and Tom walking past, his head tilting her way as he talks.

The cops follow my gaze, and Mazur asks, "Who's with Ms. Moss?"

"Tom Lowe," I say. "He owns the garage on the corner."

He grunts. "He's the one who found the vehicle. Friend of yours?"

"Friend of Daisy's." I slip them a smile. "Possibly more than a friend. You know how it goes."

"Mr. Lowe was here with you and Mr. Garey the night before Mr. Garey disappeared, right? He's on our interview list for today."

"He's a good guy. He won't be thrilled to talk to you, but he'll do it."

"Doesn't like the police?" Mazur says.

I hesitate. Then I say, "You'll get this from his background check, so I might as well tell you. He's spent some time in prison. When he was younger. Like I said, though, he's a good guy. Pillar of the community."

Mazur snorts and mutters under his breath, "They always are."

Coleman shoots him a look, but Mazur shrugs, unrepentant.

"What was he in for?" Mazur asks. He peers at Tom, still visible outside, deep in conversation with Daisy. "Assault would be my bet. Looks like he'd be fast with his fists."

Coleman sighs softly but makes no effort to rein in his partner, only shakes his head.

"It wasn't anything like that. Although—" I stop short.

"Yes? You were about to say something," Coleman presses.

"I . . ." I shift uncomfortably. "We didn't discuss that evening much when you were here last night. It didn't seem relevant." I quickly add, "It still isn't. But now that Liam is . . . is gone, and there's going to be an investigation . . ." I swallow. "There's a bruise on Liam's jaw. That isn't from a killer. I'm sure Tom will tell you about it. I just . . ." I trail off and fidget. Then I say, firmly, "It's not connected."

"Lowe hit him. Over the poker game."

"Over Daisy. Liam had too much to drink, and he was being a jerk, joking about playing for keys."

Coleman's brows knit. "Wagering cars?"

"Women," Mazur says. "House keys."

"Right," I say. "It was a joke, but Liam was out of line, and Tom hit him. That has nothing to do with Liam's murder. It just means that the bruise on his jaw isn't from whoever killed him."

Mazur mutters something I don't catch. Then he says, "You never answered the question. What was Lowe in for?"

"A nonviolent crime," I say firmly. "Money laundering. He was training to be an accountant and got in over his head."

"Money laundering?" Mazur repeats, and he straightens for the first time since this interview began. "Did he know Liam before last night?"

I see where this is going and hesitate again, twisting my hands in my lap.

"Ms. Turner?" Coleman prompts.

"Liam worked for my grandmother," I say. "Maeve Turner. She owned this house. He was her lawyer, which is how we met. Maeve lived in Fort Exile for fifty years, and I think Tom grew up here. He was helping out with Maeve before I came along."

"In other words, yes, Mr. Garey and Mr. Lowe knew each other."

"Not well," I say. "Just through Maeve."

"As far as you know."

I pause and then give a reluctant nod. "Yes, as far as I know."

The cops are reinterviewing Daisy. They've warned Tom that he's up next, and he doesn't seem the least bit surprised or alarmed. He says he'll head back to his shop, and they can meet with him there.

I retreat to my office. I can still hear Daisy's interview. The male half of it, at least. Daisy's voice is a soft whisper.

I sit at my desk and stare into the swamp, and as the sun disappears behind clouds, I don't see a sun-bright morning yard. I see a night-dark one. It's Friday night, and I've just woken to Liam nudging me.

"Wake up, Elizabeth. We have a problem."

"A problem," I murmured.

Did Liam just call me Elizabeth?

I bolted upright. He put a hand on each shoulder and held me in place. "Shh, shh. We don't want to wake Miss Daisy."

"What did you call—?"

"Elizabeth. That is your name, isn't it? Not Celeste. We both know that."

"You aren't supposed to call—"

He pressed his finger to my lips. "Take a moment to compose yourself, Lizzy. Nothing wrong with wide-eyed and breathy, but I've come to appreciate cool and savage so much more."

Savage? I flinched at the word. I didn't want to flinch. I longed to own it. *Hell, yes, I'm savage.* Liam didn't mean it to be flattering, though.

Savage. Wild. Feral.

Not who I wanted to be at all.

Cool, yes. But cool, composed, collected. Dangerous. I'd take dangerous.

He'd chosen the word well. It threw me off-balance and ensured, no matter what he claimed to want, that I'd remain just a little wide-eyed and breathy, out of my element.

I tried to gather my pride like a cloak. It was lopsided, barely covering one shoulder, leaving me feeling more exposed than if I'd abandoned it altogether.

I brushed his hands away, as regally as I could, and I looked at him and waited.

"You're wondering what's wrong," he said, conversationally.

I didn't ask for answers. He would have his moment. I must understand that; he was in charge.

I looked at him, and I saw Aaron, sitting in that same spot on a bed so long ago, when I'd been a seventeen-year-old girl, crying for my family. He'd caught me trying to escape, and he'd beaten me.

A savage beating.

Wasn't that the phrase? *Let's talk about savage, shall we, Liam? Savage is a beating that leaves you unable to move for days. Savage is a man who delivers that beating as casually as he'd waggle his finger and lecture you for being a naughty girl. Not cold fury, not white-hot anger, just simple annoyance that he has to expend the effort, which is very inconvenient, and shit, would you look at my knuckles? That's going to leave a mark.*

Aaron, sitting on our bed afterward, telling me how stupid I was, how silly and childish to want to go back to a family that didn't want me.

You made your bed. You lie in it.

Aaron telling me he was my family now. My husband, at least in spirit, and if I was a very good girl, maybe he'd make that a reality someday. For now, I must treat him like a husband. Love, honor and obey. Especially obey. That's the one girls like me never understood. We heard the word, and we balked like pretty poodles expected to accept a leash. But that leash kept us safe. Dogs obeyed because they knew they had it good. They were cared for, pampered even, and in return, they granted obedience to a master.

Did I understand what he was saying?

Oh, yes. I understood. Every broken bone and bruised inch and bloodied cut understood.

Be a good girl, and bide your time.

But I had bided my time, hadn't I? First with Aaron. Then with Liam. Bided my time, plotting to kill Liam, because my experience with Aaron taught me that fleeing was never enough. I needed to get rid of Liam, permanently. Then I couldn't go through with it, and this was my punishment. The universe was slapping me down for my failure of will.

You made your bed. You lie in it.

Why was Liam pulling this now?

Was it Daisy?

That evening, when he said he wanted to sleep with her, was I supposed to snarl and rage and send him on his way? Is that when he planned to pull the trigger?

Mmm, no, Celeste. Sorry, but that isn't how this is going to work. Remember, I know your real name . . .

"You said we have a problem." My voice was quiet, as if I feared the answer. "What is it?"

"Not here," he said, with a meaningful glance toward Daisy's room. "Outside."

I followed him into the hall. Then I hesitated.

I should have killed him last night. I had the chance, and I couldn't go through with it, and this is my punishment, rightly so. My punishment for not being strong enough.

"I'm not going into the forest in my underwear," I whispered. "Let me put something on."

I scurried back into the room, tugged on a loose shirt and then opened a drawer.

"Looking for this?" said a voice from the doorway. It was Liam, twirling a gun. My gun.

I audibly swallowed.

"Come along, Lizzy."

He turned and strode out. I eased open the drawer, reached up to the tape and pried off the gun I'd really been reaching for. Daisy's gun. I pulled on my jeans, stuck the gun in the waistband, and followed him out.

TWENTY-EIGHT

CELESTE

We were past the shed. I tried to stop there, in sight of the house, but he kept walking. When I called after him, he pretended not to see me. I jogged in his wake.

"Liam? I understand that you don't want to have this conversation in the house. But there's no need to go all the way out there. It's not safe."

He kept walking. Drawing me into the wetlands out there. It was both taunt and threat. Taking the reins of control. Seeing how far he could drag me against my will.

"Leave the gun behind," I said. "You took it away from me. You proved your point. If you really just want to talk, put it down."

His jaw flexed, but he wasn't the sort to threaten with a gun anyway. He didn't need weapons to control people.

He set the gun on the ground. Then he waved for me to walk past it. Once I did, he followed, and I could still see the gun behind us.

He may have put it down, but he was pissed. I was going to need to give him what he wanted. One part, anyway.

"What's this problem about?" I asked. "Me playing Celeste Turner, I presume?"

He only smirked. I didn't push—I needed to let him feel in control again. Something had pushed him to the edge. He'd been happily skipping along with our arrangement, and then something had changed, and I was in as much danger as I ever was with Aaron.

Liam was Aaron's lawyer. One of them, at least. I may have left Aaron more than a decade ago, but he's never stopped looking for me. When he hired Liam to defend him a few years back, he decided to toss his new lawyer this bone, too.

Find my ex. She stole from me, and I want back what's mine. Her and the money.

The money. Right. Two thousand bucks. See how far that goes when you're in hiding, unable to use your ID, unable to get a job. I was sure Aaron had told Liam it was more money. I was sure he'd also told Liam he wanted me back. Both lies. He just wants me punished, and he'll pay far more than two grand to do it.

Aaron hired Liam to find me. Liam set his investigator on the task. It took a while, but when it comes to vengeance, the Bank of Aaron throws open its vaults. Liam found me, and I threw myself on his mercy. From a five-minute acquaintance, I could tell how much he'd like that, so I'd gone all in, hoping to lower his defenses with sex and then flee.

While he certainly took the sex, he wasn't letting me get away that easily. He had another idea. A way for me to hide from Aaron. See, there was this old woman, a client of his, half-blind and on her deathbed. This client wanted him to find her long-lost granddaughter, and he wasn't having much luck with that, but I was about the right age, and I did superficially resemble this granddaughter. If I nursed the old lady through to the end, I'd get a new name and a house.

Look after a dying woman? How hard could that be? I found out soon enough. By then, it was too late to back out. Liam had only to make a phone call to Aaron, and I'd be on the run again. I mistook Liam for 50 percent gullible savior and 50 percent useful tool. And maybe, just maybe, a desperate part of me mistook him for a potential partner, in crime and out of it.

No, the real Liam wanted me afraid and vulnerable and trapped, and my only way out was to kill him, which I'd failed to do earlier that evening. Which I was still failing to do, even in that forest with Daisy's gun in my waistband.

"You mentioned a problem," I said.

"Aaron's tracked you down. He's contacted me. He wants me to bring you in."

Liar, liar, pants on fire.

I wanted to sneer and call him on his bullshit, but I was too infuriated. He couldn't even bother coming up with a believable story. He didn't care whether I saw right through it. That was part of the control game. I was so thoroughly trapped that I didn't even dare call him on his lies.

"So what are we going to do?" I said.

"You need to go into hiding. I'll find you a place to hole up, and then I'll tell Aaron that I investigated, and I don't think this Celeste person is you. I'll send photos of Daisy at the house and claim his investigator mistook her for you."

"And then I can come back?"

"No, I don't think that's safe. You'll need a new name, new life."

In other words, surrender everything again. Give up my name. Give up my house. Yes, neither was mine, but they provided shelter, and he was ripping that away. Dragging me from my den. Taking my home and my identity and my job with its small roster of clients who were finally paying my bills. All gone. And for what? For a lie. For control.

I reached out and ran my fingers down his bare chest. "Are you sure there isn't another way?"

He stepped closer. He didn't touch me. He was just putting himself within reach. Telling me to show him how much I wanted to stay in this house, keep being Celeste Turner.

Convince me.

I ran my fingers over his chest, light enough to make him shiver. Then my tongue, tickling and tracing over every sensitive spot. I considered continuing to make my way down, to drop to one knee and then the other.

He'd have liked that. He'd have liked that very much. Yet I was not quite certain it was the right move. I'd refused to take that particular position with him. That was for Aaron, my way of appeasing him, even when I might have preferred being beaten into submission.

I knew I might need to do that for Liam. But I was going to try to avoid it. Keep that one sliver of control.

As I traced my tongue up his chest, he laid his hands on my shoulders, subtly pushing down. At first, I pretended not to notice, but then his grip firmed, and I had to respond. So I looked up with a teasing smile and a coquettish "Soon" that was meant to placate him. Instead, his lips tightened in annoyance. I resumed my ministrations, and he seemed to forget the deflection as he relaxed and groaned his pleasure.

I continued the kisses to his lips, and he grabbed me then, kissing me hard enough that a thrill of satisfaction rushed through me, the certainty that this problem was not insurmountable, that I could keep my den until I was ready to properly defend it from him.

He'd shown me the way tonight, with this stunt of his. Blackmail. I just needed to prepare my offensive before I launched it.

As we kissed, his hands rose to my throat, encircling it. His touch was gentle, thumbs stroking, and I allowed it, even if I knew the gesture wasn't tender. When his grip tightened, I forced myself to stay relaxed. Like getting me on my knees, this was something he wanted. To wrap his hands around my neck and, ever-so-gently, squeeze until I couldn't breathe.

He'd managed it once, in the middle of sex, and later, he'd had to admit that, as much as he'd enjoyed it, that brief moment of pleasure wasn't worth getting kneed in the stomach.

I let his grip tighten until it impeded breathing, and then I slid my hands up, disengaging him as gently as I could. His lips tightened, the kiss pausing. I opened my eyes to see his annoyance flare brighter.

He gripped my throat again, thumbs digging in. Again, I stopped him without breaking the kiss. A growl under his breath that told me he was not happy. Not happy at all. I looked up into his eyes, and my gut sank.

This wasn't going to work. The price would be too high.

I was still willing to give a little ground until I found my footing. I lowered my hands and let Liam keep his around my neck, but it was too late. The illusion had broken. He knew that I was in control, that I would "let" him have this. What fun was that?

I might not have been able to give him what he wanted, but I knew other tricks, and I employed them, and within minutes, he'd forgotten his disappointment, and he was lowering me to the ground, kissing me, fingers yanking my shirt hard enough to rip the fabric.

Then we were on the wet earth, and he was stretched atop me and—

He stopped. He broke the kiss and lifted his head, one brow raised. I didn't know what the problem was until he slid one hand between us, and I felt something cold against my bare stomach.

Liam pulled the gun from my waistband.

TWENTY-NINE

CELESTE

"Whoops," I said, with a laugh that sounded a little too nervous. "Forgot about that."

A single brow rose higher as he held the gun between us.

"For protection," I said.

"This is bigger than the protection you usually carry in such situations, Lizzy."

I laughed again, too hard now, at his joke. "Oh, I have those, too. That was just extra." I propped onto my elbows. "You took my other gun, Liam. I wasn't sure what you intended, so I armed myself."

He turned Daisy's gun this way and that, his hand around the grip, finger poised beside the trigger.

"Can you put that aside, please?" I said.

He only moved it out of my reach.

"Liam?" I said. "Please? You're making me nervous."

I tried to say it jokingly, but a wisp of actual worry slipped out, and his smile twitched as his eyes glittered.

"Liam," I said, firmly, and that too was wrong, damn it. I sounded as if I were reprimanding a small child. His mouth tightened before he found that smirk again, holding the gun out of my reach. When the barrel swung my way, he made it look accidental. It was not accidental.

"Please, Liam?" I said, and I granted him the satisfaction of my fear. "There's a reason I have more than one gun." Deep breath. "This isn't the first time a lover has pointed a weapon at me. You know Aaron. You know what he's like."

Something flashed behind his eyes, and while I couldn't identify it, that look hit me square in the gut, and I knew that was not the reaction I wanted. Not at all.

"Aaron pointed a gun at you?" He took a firmer grip on the pistol. "Like this?"

It was aimed straight at my chest. My heart seized. I forced myself to whisper, "Yes. Now, please—"

"How about this?"

He raised the gun to eye level, and I was staring down the barrel, and I saw Aaron's face, and my bladder spasmed.

"Liam?" I said, as calmly as I could. "Please. This isn't funny."

"Take off your jeans."

"Liam," I said, sharper. "This isn't—"

"Take. Off. Your. Jeans."

I swallowed audibly and undid the button. As I shimmied the jeans over my hips, he relaxed, and I sprang, grabbing his gun arm and slamming him backward to the ground. The shock of it relaxed his grip, and then I had the gun, and he was on his back, and I was pointing it at his face.

"Elizabeth . . ." he said, his voice unsteady. "Put down the gun."

"How about a please?"

"This isn't funny."

"Is there an echo here?" I tilted my head as if listening. "Could have sworn I said the exact same thing when *you* were holding this gun to *my* head. And how did you respond? Told me to take off my jeans so you could rape me at gunpoint."

He flinched. "It wasn't like that."

I moved the barrel closer to his eye. "It was exactly like that."

"I was playing," he said, a whine touching his voice. "I thought you were, too."

"Bull. Shit. I was scared, and you liked it."

He shifted under me and cleared his throat. When he spoke, the lawyer had moved in. Brisk, firm. "Yes, I went too far, but don't embarrass yourself by pretending you're going to pull that trigger."

"*Embarrass* myself?"

"Did I mention how poorly you bluff? You're keeping your trigger finger on the grip. That means you have no intention of shooting me."

I moved my finger to the trigger, just barely touching it. "Better?"

His face spasmed once, terror quickly masked by a smirk so tight a flinch would shatter it.

"You want to shoot me, Lizzy? Go ahead. Just know that the game is up. You—"

He grabbed the gun barrel and tried to yank it aside, but I held it in both hands, and it stayed pointed at his eye.

"Let go," he said.

"Uh, why? I'm not the one who'll catch a bullet in the face. Let go, and I'll lower—"

He smacked the gun with his palm, and it jumped in my hand, and he fell back, and there was blood. Blood spurted from his eye.

Blood spurted from where his eye *used* to be.

There was a moment where I was confused. I was straddling his chest, and he was poised there, still up on one elbow, and there was a bloody hole instead of a blue eye, and I did not understand what I was seeing.

His mouth worked once. Opened as if in speech, and then his jaw dropped, and he slumped onto his back, and I still didn't understand.

That was when I heard the shot.

No, that's wrong. It's all wrong. The sequence played that way in my head, but it wasn't correct, and my mind scrambled to fix it, like a puzzle where you must place the panels in their proper sequence.

Liam's mouth opening, as if to speak.

A shot instead of words.

Blood spraying.

A hole where his eye should have been.

So much blood. More than blood, too. Bits of bone and gray.

His jaw dropped. His elbows collapsed, and he fell on his back, staring up at the sky.

Dead.

Liam was dead.

THIRTY

DAISY

I am no stranger to grief. My entire family is gone. I hesitate even to think that, partly because it's terrifying, and partly because it makes me sound like a girl from a Dickensian novel. I actually do have a living grandparent—my mother's father—and an aunt with assorted cousins, but that side disowned Mom when she married Dad, and I've never had any inclination to reopen that channel.

What I understand of grief is this: that people try to cushion your feelings by avoiding talk of the dead, when all you want to do is talk about them. You long for fresh recollections to squirrel away with your own, and you want to pull out and polish up shared memories—*remember the time we . . . ?*

Maybe it seems like picking at a healing sore, but for me, it was the salve that kept me going. Avoiding any mention of the lost felt like saving others from the discomfort of struggling for a response to my grief. I didn't need responses. I just needed to talk about those I'd lost.

I'm torn between wanting to help Celeste through her grief and reminding myself of who she is, what she may have done. I settle for cooking comfort food—gooey grilled-cheese sandwiches with potato chips—and I bustle about the kitchen, letting her fix a plate and retreat. She sits, instead, and I join her and skate around mundane topics, seeing whether that's where she wants to go, fill her brain with idle chatter. She doesn't. She just eats.

After we're done, I clear her plate as she stares at the peeling wallpaper. She looks lost. Confused. As if she's not certain how she got here and what she's supposed to do next.

"Are you planning to work this afternoon, or rest?" I ask.

"Work, I think."

"I'll keep the noise down, then."

"No need. I don't notice anything when I'm working."

I wash dishes as coffee brews, and she just sits there, like a child who hasn't been released from the dinner table.

"I'm making coffee," I say, as if that weren't obvious. "I also baked brownies earlier."

A strained smile, though she doesn't turn my way. "I thought I was hallucinating the smell of chocolate when I woke up."

"They're just from a mix," I say as I peel back the wrap over the scratched glass pan. "I hate doing that, but if you're only making one batch, it's cheaper than buying all the ingredients."

"Then you'll have to make more batches so we have the excuse to buy the ingredients." She twists in her seat. "We'll go grocery shopping this afternoon."

Her face lights up, and I know that look. It's her numb brain latching on to something she can do, something to get her out of this house and out of her head. Then her smile freezes, and she deflates a little against the counter. "That will look strange, won't it? Me going shopping so soon after . . ."

"One, it's groceries. Not like you're buying new shoes. Two, the news probably hasn't hit yet, and even if it has, it's Sun City. Half the residents can't remember what they had for breakfast."

That's cruel, but it makes her laugh, choking on her mouthful of coffee. "Fair point."

"Three, if it really bothers you, we can go to Tampa, instead."

She brightens again. "Let's go to Tampa. I can get a cappuccino. I have been dying for a decent capp." Again, that smile falters, the light dimming. "That sounds awful, doesn't it? Liam's gone, and I'm getting excited about coffee."

"Don't beat yourself up every moment you're not lying in a puddle of grief. He was an asshole, wasn't he?"

Her shoulders convulse in a silent sob. I hurry over and put an awkward arm around her shoulders, and she collapses into it, crying for a moment before backing up, sniffling.

She wipes her eyes as she stumbles over apologies even more awkward than the hug.

I suppose, if this were a movie, I'd look at Celeste, nibbling her brownie, and I'd think, *In another life, we might have been friends.* That isn't true. At best, she'd have been the sort of classmate I wouldn't cringe at being assigned for a lab partner. She reminds me of so many girls from my suburban high school. Pretty enough, popular enough, smart enough, confident in their future of a post-secondary education, a job with benefits and a 401(k), and a handsome and successful spouse to share it with.

A spouse like Liam.

What happened to you, Celeste?

That's what I want to ask. That is the true mystery here. Not how she wriggled into my grandmother's life and passed herself off as me. She comes from a background rungs above mine. I hear it in her speech, see it in her face, feel it in her confidence.

She comes from that background, and yet she'd played nurse to a difficult old woman in return for a rundown house. She may even have killed her for it.

Who are you, not-Celeste?

And how did you end up here?

Neither of those answers is forthcoming. I do hope to get them before this is over. For now, though, I am going into the city with a woman who is pretending to be me, and I am pretending everything about that is okay.

CELESTE

When we return from Tampa, I pull into the driveway to see state police cars blocking my spot. As I slow, the two officers from earlier—Coleman and Mazur—climb out of one. Two more uniformed officers get out of the second.

"More questions?" I mutter as I turn off the ignition. "How many rounds with the beat cops before they send in the actual detectives?"

"Those are deputy sheriffs," Daisy murmurs, her voice soft, almost reluctant, as if she hates correcting me. After a pause, she says, with equal reluctance, "The regional detachment is small, without any full-time detectives, so the deputies will handle it unless the case requires pulling in someone with more experience."

A quick glance my way as she adds, "I didn't know any of that, either. Tom told me."

"Deputy sheriffs. Right." I take my empty coffee cup and climb out as I call, "Deputies. You're back."

"Sorry to disturb you again, Miz Turner," Coleman says.

Daisy pops open the trunk and pulls out a grocery bag. The young officer—deputy—jogs over with, "Here, let me help," earning an eye roll from his older partner.

"We're not here to play bag boy for the ladies, Montrell." He walks up to me. "We're here to search your house, ma'am."

I blink. "What?" I collect myself and straighten. "My boyfriend is"—I flush—"*was* a lawyer. He told me never to allow a search without a warrant."

He pulls an envelope from his pocket and holds it out.

I pause.

"Your warrant," he says.

"On what grounds?"

"We received an anonymous tip, one that provided cause for searching your spare bedroom, back shed and lanai."

I frown. "I don't use those rooms."

Daisy freezes, poised there, bags in hand, eyes rounding as she realizes what those three things have in common. They're all places she's slept.

"This is ridiculous," I huff. "Daisy is my guest."

"Are you left-handed, Miz Moss?" Mazur says as he walks toward her.

"N-no. Right-handed."

"Huh. Strange that you wear your watch on your right wrist, then. My wife does that because she's left-handed."

Daisy rubs at her watch and then stops. She hesitates and then, slowly, removes the watch, showing a fading circlet of bruises.

"Yes, I got these from Mr. Garey," she says. "But I can explain."

"You will. Like you'll explain the fact that you were seen together after midnight, having a heated argument."

"I mentioned that," she says. "I told you that I spoke to Mr. Garey Friday night. He ambushed me on the road." She glances my way, and her cheeks color. "He was intoxicated and made comments. That's how I ended up with this." She lifts her wrist.

"You told us he made a pass at you."

"A drunken pass," she says quickly. "He wasn't serious. He was just . . ."

"Being an ass," I say, and she shoots me a grateful look. "If Daisy already admitted they had words that night, then I'm not sure what the problem is."

"The problem is that she says he made a pass at her, and yet they walked away together."

Daisy shakes her head. "It was a half-hearted pass. He grabbed my arm. We had words. He apologized. Then we talked."

"After he accosted you?"

"Like I said, he was drunk. I was trying to defuse the situation, and I didn't want Celeste involved. We parted amicably."

Mazur stares at her, laser eyed, as if he can bore through to the truth. Daisy stands her ground, and he wheels toward the house. As he passes, he shoves the warrant into my hands. Coleman shoots me a sympathetic look and follows his partner.

THIRTY-ONE

DAISY

My plan to resolve this has fallen apart, one big screwup, fueled by grief and ego and a hunger for vengeance. After my mother died, I went to group therapy for adults who'd lost both their parents. At first, I seemed fine. Resilient—that's the word a friend used, and that's how I felt. I'd watched both my parents die in hospital beds. I'd nursed them through the end, and I hadn't broken.

People always expect me to be fragile. When I'm quiet, they see shyness. Where I have a slight build, they see a waif. Where I prefer solutions to confrontations, they see timidity. I fit a stereotype, and that stereotype screams neither inner nor outer strength, and so, when people praised my resilience, I'd been pleased.

Then came the guilt. Guilt that I hadn't defied my mother sooner to be with my father. Guilt that I hadn't stayed with Dad and Gran, and let Mom leave by herself. Guilt that I had breathed a sigh of relief after her death. Others might tell themselves they were relieved she "wasn't suffering anymore," and of course I was happy for that, but I was also happy not to *be* the one suffering, sitting by her bed, nursing her, hoping it would win me the gratitude and reconciliation my soul longed for. That moment when she would look in my eyes and say, "I know I wasn't always the best mother, but I love you, Celeste. Thank you for being here."

She never said those words, and I hate her a little for that. Looking back, though, I realize that she was, in her way, saying them every time she drove the nurses off, insisting her daughter would look after her, every time the pain had her clutching my hand, begging me not to leave, every time she woke in a panic because I'd stepped out.

That guilt is what drove me to therapy. Mom was gone, and I was free, and I wasn't sure how to deal with that, caught in a maelstrom of comingled grief and relief. Joining that group felt like accepting failure. Then I looked around at the people in that group, and I didn't see weakness—I saw the strength to admit they were floundering.

What I learned is that, for some, like me, grief manifests as guilt. A focus not on what I lost but on what I failed to do. Because, again, I gravitate toward solutions rather than confrontations. I want to fix things, whether it's a sick parent or a crooked door.

I couldn't tell my father how I'd secretly wanted him to follow us to Pennsylvania. How I dreamed of him striding through our door and rescuing me from Keith. Then I was at his bedside as he was dying, and he was so happy to see me, so confident that he'd made the right choice letting me go.

Same with my mom. I needed to tell her that I loved her for leaving Keith when she caught him in my room. But also tell her how hard it'd been to spend the next five years watching her mourn a failed marriage and subtly blaming me.

I'd poured all my pain and anger into caring for them, and when they were gone, that left a void of things left unsaid, things that I felt selfish for needing said.

Then there was Gran. She wanted nothing to do with me, and that hurt so much. I relied on solutions instead of confrontations. Sneak her money, and then, in a year or two, I'd reach out again.

That never happened. One day, I deposited money and was told her account had been closed, her estate settled. That's how I learned my grandmother was dead.

I dug deeper, reached out discreetly and discovered that her prodigal granddaughter had returned home. The woman who may have killed my grandmother was still living in her house, passing herself off as me.

I came here to find out whether this imposter murdered my grandmother and to discover her true identity. Yet I feel no closer to finding that information than when I started.

What have I done? Well, I've gotten as far as checking the prescriptions in the imposter's bathroom and writing down the names so I can investigate further, see whether that could be how she murdered my grandmother.

What else? I found her lover's dead body, but I'm lying about that to the police, who are now searching my room, where they will find his cell phone, because I am in over my head. In so far over my head. Playing private investigator when I'm too clueless to even hide a murdered man's phone.

There's the old adage about digging yourself in deeper with every move you make. I'm not digging. I've purposefully stridden onto a minefield, confident I'm not in any real danger. I haven't done anything wrong. If things go sideways, all I need to do is make that phone call. Tell the police I'm the real Celeste Turner.

Except now I'm standing in that minefield, and the path back has disappeared.

I need to march up to the searching police and declare myself. *I'm Celeste Turner, and Liam found out, and he confronted me, only I cut a deal with him. We had reached a mutually acceptable agreement, and we'd parted amicably.*

It all makes perfect sense, see?

Yes, but there are a dozen other theories that also make sense, including one where, enraged, I shot him.

I didn't kill Liam, but I'm not sure how much that means in the end. I had motive and opportunity.

I don't see an easy solution, so what am I doing? Cooking dinner and baking cookies, and I can pretend that's a cover—*see, deputies, I'm not the least bit worried*—when the truth is that I'm burying myself in work.

The police began their search in the shed. They're now inside, and I'm resisting the urge to check on their progress, see what they've found. There's nothing in the shed. Nothing in the lanai. The incriminating evidence is up in my room, where they've had a young deputy posted since they arrived.

Is that the only evidence?

What about my gun?

Liam took it from the shed. What if he'd had it with him when he was killed? Confronted someone and they got the gun and used it to shoot him? A gun registered to me.

When the doorbell rings. I don't even get to the kitchen door before Celeste replies.

"Hey," Tom's voice slides back to me. "Everything okay?"

Celeste answers, and then Tom asks to see me. I hold my breath, waiting. But Celeste blocks him. Daisy's busy making dinner, and it should be ready any moment if he wants to join us, and in the meantime, would he take a look at something on her car?

He hesitates, but he knows it will look bad if he flies to my side during the search. So he goes out with her. When dinner's ready, I open the window and call to them. They come in together, Celeste sticking close, giving me no time alone with Tom.

We eat a meal I barely taste. The whole time, Tom's trying to get my attention, and I must pretend not to notice.

We're barely done when Deputy Mazur comes into the kitchen.

"Finally," Celeste says, rising. "I trust you can leave now?"

Mazur turns to Tom. "I think it's time for you to go home, son."

"Daisy was just about to serve—"

"She can give you a doggy bag. Now go."

Tom bristles, but it won't help my case if he gets defensive, acts as if I need protecting.

I put a few cookies into a sandwich bag, hoping my hands don't shake. When I hand it to him, he murmurs, "Come by later, okay?" and I nod.

Once Tom's gone, Mazur turns to me. "We found something in your room."

I blink in feigned surprise. "What?"

Even as I say the word, I have my performance ready. First, my brow will crease in confusion.

A cell phone? I don't have a cell phone.

It's Liam's? Wide eyes. *How . . . ?*

Trail off with dawning comprehension. *He must have left it there. Like I said, he'd been drinking. He must have been looking for me in my room.*

Have I ever handled his phone? Oh, you mean fingerprints? No, I don't think . . . Wait, he showed me a photo the other day. I didn't take his phone, but I might have touched it. If you find a print, it'll be one or two. Because I wiped it clean but may have missed one.

Mazur turns to Coleman, who hands him something in a bag. Something that looks cell-phone-sized, but I need to pretend I'm confused.

"What is that?" I say, and then I see it, and my reaction is not feigned.

It's a gun. My gun. My missing gun.

My mouth opens, ready to give a version of my practiced response. *Wherever did that come from?* Luckily, my brain clicks in before I say it.

This is my gun. My legal gun. I could almost laugh at that. I'm on a clandestine mission, living under a false name . . . and I brought a registered gun. Rule following is just so ingrained in me that I would rather risk losing my shot at vengeance than be caught with an illegal firearm.

Admit it. Say it's my gun and pray that's enough—that they won't have any reason to look it up and realize it's registered to my real name.

"That's mine," I say.

"Yours?"

I nod. "It's registered to me. Legally obtained. I live alone. I'm often on job sites alone, and I've been traveling alone."

"You never thought to mention it to us?"

"Honestly, no. Well, not until about an hour ago. I saw you coming in from the shed, and I remembered the gun, and I freaked out a little, because I forgot it was there. Except you didn't mention it, so I thought you missed it. I was trying to figure out whether I should show it to you. I was, uh, going to seek legal advice tomorrow."

I try to look sheepish. "I wasn't sure of my obligations here. You didn't ask if I have a gun, so I wasn't keen to hand it over when Liam had been shot. I wanted advice."

"We didn't find this in the shed, Miz Moss."

I widen my eyes and say, "What? No. It was in the shed."

"It was in your room. Hidden."

"Daisy," Celeste says, her first words since Mazur came in. "You don't need to answer any of this. In fact, I'd suggest you don't speak to them further without legal representation. Deputy? We're done here."

I know she's trying to help, but I shake my head. "I'm fine, Celeste. Thank you. If I need a lawyer, I'll get one. For now, the last time I saw that gun, it was in the shed. I left it hidden under the floorboards. You'd invited me into your house, and I certainly wasn't bringing a firearm with me."

"We had a break-in," she says. "You didn't think to get it then?" She stops short, as if realizing what she's said. "Daisy, you really do need legal advice."

"Just because I own a gun doesn't mean I'm eager to use it during a break-in. I had no idea how you felt about them, and again, I was your guest."

I turn to Mazur. "That's a Glock 19. I'm sure you know that. I'm sure you also know it's one of the most common handguns out there. I'm guessing a nine-millimeter bullet killed Liam?"

"We don't have the results back yet."

"Well, then you have my gun. I'm hoping you have something in your kit to test for residue because I have not fired that weapon since I was at a range a month ago. I will also provide what I was wearing Friday night for further testing."

Celeste makes a noise under her breath, and her gaze warns me I'm giving them too much. I don't care. I nod her way, telling her I'm fine, and then I follow Mazur from the room.

THIRTY-TWO

CELESTE

I watch Daisy as she tidies the kitchen. She's just going through the motions. She washes one plate twice and places another straight into the drying rack, dirty. As she works, I put cookies into a yellowed Tupperware box. When she finishes, I hand her the box.

"For Tom," I say.

She hesitates, and her eyes cloud with confusion as she says, "Didn't I give him some?" as if she honestly doesn't remember.

"You did," I say. "But these are for the two of you." I force a smile. "Breakfast."

She's frozen in place, dishcloth in hand, suds dripping onto the linoleum, like a maid-android with her power cut. By the time she answers, there's a pool around her left foot, seeping into her ankle sock.

"I . . . We're not . . ." She moves then, easing back as awkwardly as that robot-maid trying to look human. "Tom and I are just friends, and even if we were going to change that, tonight wouldn't be . . ." She trails off.

I try to brighten my smile. "Tonight seems like a perfect night. You're upset, and believe me, he's eager to be your knight in shining armor. He saw the police cars and veered in here so fast he tore a strip out of my yard."

"Okay. Sure, I'll take him more cookies. I was going up there tonight. But I won't be staying."

"I think you should."

Daisy flinches so hard her entire body convulses, and when she lifts her eyes to mine, I want to smack the whipped puppy out of them. No, damn it, that's not true. I might *want* to smack the whipped puppy out, to harden my heart and inwardly sneer at her weakness. Yet that look isn't weak or timid or even accusing. It says, "I didn't piddle on the carpet, but I understand why you think I did."

Damn it, Daisy. Don't do this. Just . . . leave, okay? Leave Fort Exile. Leave Tom. Guys like him are a high-risk, low-return investment. Find some average-looking, decent man who'll think he's the luckiest guy alive for winning you. Get married and build your own damn house and fill it with cute Daisy babies.

Just run. That's all I'm asking. Get spooked and run. Let the cops chase until they lose you and close the case.

"I didn't kill Liam," she says. "That's my gun, but I didn't put it in my room."

"Imagine yourself in my place, Daisy," I say, leaning on a scarred chair. "Imagine Tom is dead from a gunshot, and the police find a gun in my room, a gun I never told you about. Would you want to spend the night alone in a house with me?"

Before she can answer, I push on, "I have two choices here. Be tough and bullheaded, or weak and smart. I'm very fond of tough, but I'm even fonder of smart, and I can't pretend I'm okay sharing a house with you tonight."

"You're right."

Part of me wants her to fight. She didn't kill Liam, damn it. But she sees my point, and she concedes it, and that's what I need, isn't it? Drive her out and hope she hits the road to avoid arrest. If she doesn't, I'll work on it again tomorrow. I hate to do this to her. I really do. But one way or another, she must run with the police in half-assed pursuit. It's the only way we both get out of this.

I push the box of cookies at her. She takes it, nods and murmurs that she'll get her things and leave right away.

DAISY

A string of profanities snakes out from Tom's workshop, leading me in to find him cursing over an engine. I open my mouth to say something light and funny, but no words come, and I stand there until he senses me. Then he strides over, stopping a couple feet away.

"You okay?" he asks.

"I'm . . . not sure."

He reaches out and then hesitates, and I move closer, and his arms wrap around me as I fall against his chest. I don't cry. I can't. Everything jams up inside me, begging for release that won't come. Instead, I lay my cheek against his chest and breathe as he rubs my shoulders.

When I step back, I say, "The police searched my room."

"I know. She told me someone called in an anonymous tip about seeing you with Liam. When I find out who it was, I'm going to string them up alive. We don't do that shit here. No one's expected to lie to the cops, but you don't volunteer information."

"It's okay."

"No, it's not. This is a goddamn community. Maeve was part of it, and I might have left, but I've done my damnedest to make up for that. No one who's short on cash leaves without the loaf of bread they came for. No one needs their car towed home because I won't fix it on credit. I see shit. You know how it is. I don't judge, and I sure as hell don't talk. Folks might not know who you really are, but I've made it clear you're with me, and they pull this shit . . ."

He shakes his head. "Sorry for the rant. I'm just pissed off. First, that tip. Then, Celeste blocking me from talking to you. Then, that deputy sending me on my way like I'm twelve."

A deep breath, and his fingers rest on my arm, thumb stroking it.

"We'll figure this out," he says. "For now, I have Liam's phone."

"What?"

He eases back, hands going into his pockets. "Yeah, sorry if I overstepped there. That's what I was trying to tell you earlier—not to worry about the phone. Last night, when you told me about it, I said I'd take it for you, and we never resolved that. Then, today, I had one of those 'Oh, shit' moments, remembering the phone. I went to the house. You two were gone, so I . . . kinda let myself in. I've got it upstairs. You're welcome to it, though I'd rather destroy it."

"We need to move it, fast," I say. "If the police track it here—"

"I removed the SIM card before I brought it home."

I exhale. "Thank you. And thank you for collecting it. Definitely not overstepping. I'm the one who forgot about it."

He hugs me again, tight and quick. "No, you're the person who's been trying to get her life back and ended up embroiled in a murder. But it'll be all right. They didn't get the phone, and I'm presuming you explained away that anonymous tip the police received about your room."

"I did. I'd been careful not to box myself into a corner earlier. The problem, though, isn't the phone or the tip. It's the gun."

"Gun?"

I explain. As I do, he struggles to keep his expression neutral, but horror seeps into his eyes only to be replaced by fury.

"Someone put that gun in your room. The *killer* put that gun in your room."

I raise my hands. "Let's not jump to conclusions."

"Jump to conclusions?" he sputters. "You are the fairest person I've ever met, CeCe. Everyone gets the benefit of your doubt. But this goes too far. Your gun was stolen. Now it reappears in your room a day after a man is found shot to death? After an anonymous tip led the police to you? I've been stomping around, wanting to throttle whoever tipped off the police, furious because I expected better of people here. But they *are* better than that. No neighbor saw you talking to Liam. The gun was planted. You're being framed."

"My gun might not be the weapon that killed him."

He sputters more and then settles for gathering tools and slamming them back on the bench until he's ready to speak. When he does, he says, "I know you're trying to consider all possibilities, but come on. We both *know* that's the murder weapon."

I say nothing.

"Is there any chance *you* put it in your room?" he asks. "Fake-Celeste gives you the spare room, and you hide your gun there and forget you did?"

"No."

"Therefore, it was planted by the killer."

"I . . ." I lift my hands. "Hear me out. I'm not being difficult. But the person I saw rooting around my shed is the person who's dead. I figured Liam was checking out my story to protect Celeste. Makes sense he'd remove the gun."

Tom leans against the workbench. "Is there any chance he shot him— Uh, no. Forget I started that sentence. There wasn't a gun in his hand or, presumably, near his body."

"I figure he had my gun when he went to meet his killer. They used it against him."

Tom comes over and loops his hands around my waist. "You didn't shoot Liam. The cops will figure that out. Who kills a man and hides the gun in their own *bedroom*?"

"Real people. People who exist outside of movies. They panic and shove the gun in their room to dispose of later. Kind of like I did with his damn cell phone. A jury doesn't throw out forensic evidence in favor of 'no one would be that careless.'"

He chuckles under his breath. "Would you believe my lawyer actually tried that one with me? Told the judge that I was a smart guy—pulled in an IQ test to prove it—and therefore I wouldn't do something so foolish."

"Ouch."

"Yep. The judge didn't even nibble. So you're right there. The point, though, is that you didn't do it, and I trust the evidence will bear that out."

"So who did do it?" I say the words slowly, and he meets my gaze with a look that says I know the answer to that. We both do.

"The imposter," I say. "Fake-Celeste."

"Before now, I was trying not to presume that, since it would only freak me out, knowing you're living in the same house with her. But now that the gun was found in your room, it's obvious she's the killer, and since she's framing you for murder, I presume you'll stay here?"

"Yes."

He already has his mouth open to argue. He stops. "Well, that was easy. Too easy."

"She kicked me out. She defended me to the police, but after they left, she told me to come stay with you."

His brows rise. "Please tell me you aren't upset about that. It's the one decent thing she's done."

"True, but . . ." I turn to the car, its hood still raised. "Show me what you were doing when I came in."

"Distracting myself and trying not to wreck an engine in the process."

"Explain what needs to be done." I turn to face him. "Distract *me*."

He hesitates, giving me a sidelong look that has me choking on a laugh. "The car, Lowe. Distract me with the car."

"Of course. What else would I be thinking?"

He looks so genuinely confused that my cheeks heat, and I quickly say, "Construction projects. If you have any of those, though, I'm happy—"

"That's not what *you* were thinking, CeCe."

Now my cheeks flame hot, and he steps closer, fingers tickling down my arm. "Whatever were you thinking?" he murmurs, and he's close enough that I can feel the heat of him. I look up to see his head tilted, my gaze following the line of his jaw to his lips.

I glance quickly down at his arm instead, watching his fingers glide up my forearm, the rough callus of them scraping ever so gently and sending shivers through me. My gaze moves to his fingers, darkened by ingrained grease, the square nails scrubbed to a buffed shine.

I pull my gaze away again, shivering, and when I look up, he's right there, his face over mine. His lips stop two inches away, and he runs his fingertips along my jaw instead, thumb caressing my chin before he eases back, and I'm left feeling bereft, as if the sun has moved on.

"I don't think I ever thanked you for letting me kiss you," he says, one corner of his mouth twitching.

I blink, collecting myself. "What?"

"When we were kids," he says. "You let me kiss you."

I laugh softly. "Pretty sure I didn't *let* you."

His eyes round, and I wince.

"I mean I didn't need convincing," I say.

He relaxes and closes half the gap between us. "That's not quite how I remember it."

"No?"

"No." Another step, close enough that his shirt brushes mine, and he rests one hand on my hip. "As I recall, you *did* need some convincing."

"Only because your proposal was terribly disappointing."

"Disappointing?" His other hand goes to my hip.

"It was the way you asked." I lift one hand over his shoulder, as casually as I can, resisting the urge to twist a stray lock of hair around my finger. "You said you'd never kissed a girl, and you asked if I'd ever kissed a boy. I said I hadn't. You said we should kiss, then, to see what it's like."

"Uh-huh."

"A girl doesn't want to be kissed as a scientific experiment. She wants to be kissed because someone wants to kiss her."

He chuckles. "We were ten."

"Doesn't matter. I might not have been old enough to want a boyfriend, but I was old enough to have an ego."

"And I crushed it."

I scrunch my nose. "Dented it."

"You still let me kiss you."

I put my other arm around his neck, my hands entwining. "I'm a nice person, as you pointed out. I hate to disappoint anyone. Also, I wanted to kiss you."

"Because you liked me."

"Mmm, no. I just wanted to kiss a boy. As a scientific experiment."

He throws back his head and laughs. Then he tightens his grip on my hips, pulling me closer. "Well, true confession time.

My excuse was total bullshit. I was just playing it cool. I had a crush on you."

"Did you?"

"Yep." He moves against me, his body pressed tight, face over mine as he murmurs, "Such a crush," and looks into my eyes with a heat and sincerity that makes me blush. "Is that okay?"

I want to tease and tell him it's fine if he had a crush on me twenty years ago. But I know that's not what he's saying.

"I have a confession to make, too," I say. "You say I needed convincing. I didn't. But I'd been taught that I was supposed to make a boy work for it, even if I wanted it."

"And you did want it," he says, his breath hot against my lips.

"Yes. Also, I'm not that little girl anymore. I'm perfectly fine admitting what I want." I meet his gaze. "And I'm perfectly fine taking it."

I wrap my hands in his hair, pull him that last inch to me.

THIRTY-THREE

DAISY

We're in bed, the sun dropping outside Tom's window. I ease up on my elbows and look at him.

"So that's where kisses lead," I say. "No wonder my mother warned me about them."

Tom laughs and flips onto his side, one hand propping up his head, the other tracing up my bare side. "Well, not always, CeCe. Sometimes, a kiss is just a kiss. But other times, when two people really like each other, in a special kind of way, they *show* it in a special kind of way."

"And that's how babies are made. I think I've had this talk before. No, wait, the talk I got was, 'Don't let boys touch you there, or you'll have a baby.'"

"Touch you where?" His fingers graze over my stomach. "Here?"

"Nope. That's safe."

They slide up my stomach and cup my breast. "Here?"

"Slightly more dangerous territory, but not baby-making."

He tickles circles up to my side, down it, over my hip and between my thighs. "Here?"

I groan and flop back on the bed. "Damn. Now we're totally having a kid. I hope you're prepared for that."

His mouth opens. Then he shuts it and gives me a rueful smile. "I was about to say something that would mark me as one of those creepy dudes who moves straight from first kiss to bended knee."

"Are you asking me to have your babies, Tom Lowe?"

I say it lightly, teasing, but his cheeks flush, and I laugh. Then I lean in to kiss him. I run my hands down his body, and when I ease back, my gaze follows, drinking in the view.

"Genetically speaking," I say, "I must admit, you make an excellent case for fathering babies. You were a cute kid, Tom, but you grew up *fine*."

"Ah, so that's how you ended up in my bed."

"Nah, it's just a very nice bonus. Like the prize in a box of Cracker Jacks. You buy it for the candied popcorn, and you get something extra."

"Uh, I seem to recall that you bought Cracker Jacks for the prize. You didn't much like the candy part."

"Right. Er, well, the analogy didn't work anyway, since we're talking about the packaging as the bonus, not the hidden prize. It's like . . ." I struggle to think of something. "Like knowing a boy when you're kids together, and he's sweet and smart and funny, and then you meet him again twenty years later, and he's totally hot, while still being sweet and smart and funny."

"Now *that's* an analogy." His grin softens to a wistful smile as he brushes my hair from my shoulder. "I keep thinking of how things could have been different if we'd stayed in touch, of all the time we lost. But then I'm not so sure we lost it. That maybe this was better. Gave me time to get my shit together first."

He pulls me against him. "The real tragedy would have been if I'd never met you again."

"Agreed," I say.

He holds me for a moment before murmuring into my hair, "You said Liam found out the truth. About you. That's why he confronted you the other night."

I try not to tense at the change of subject, struggle against the urge to kiss him and distract him because I really don't want to talk about this. But that's the problem, isn't it? I don't want to talk about it. I'm inwardly freaking out, and if I can't deal with that by taking action, I want to just forget about it until morning comes and I can strap myself into the command chair and make decisions and plans.

That is avoidance. It's the part of me that is just tired, so damn tired, sick with grief and anger and confusion and wanting to lose myself in Tom.

I can do that once I've resolved this. Once I know whether Celeste killed my grandmother. Once I am free from suspicion in Liam's death.

"Yes," I say. "He knew I'm Maeve's granddaughter. He said he'd just figured it out. He also claimed the imposter tricked him, too, which I doubt."

Tom wrinkles his nose.

"You think she did," I say. "And that's why she killed him."

"I think the jury is still out on whether Liam was part of this." He shifts back, hand on my hip, head propped on his other arm. "The reason I got sucked into that money laundering is that, like Liam, I figured I was smarter than everyone I was dealing with. I came from a place where I *was* always the smartest guy in the room. Top of my class. Smartest in my family. When I went to college, I got knocked down a peg or two, but still, these guys running their scheme were from back home, and not exactly intellectual giants. I could make money while keeping my hands clean. In short, I was ripe for a fall, and it knocked sense into me. Liam was me before my fall. Always the smartest in the room."

"Ripe for a fall. Ripe for someone he considers his inferior to drag him into a criminal scheme without him even knowing it."

"You presume he knew because he's too smart to have fallen for her game. My own experience says hell yeah, he could have fallen for it. But either way, he knew. So what did he want?"

"Bill Turner's treasure."

I expect Tom to laugh, and then I'll laugh with him, and we'll giggle over this proof that Liam wasn't nearly as smart as he thought. Instead, a look passes through Tom's eyes. A look I can't quite decipher.

"Tom?"

He drops his head onto the pillow and groans. "Please tell me you're joking. The treasure? Really?"

I relax and smile. "Right? I think I deserve an Oscar for not breaking into a fit of giggles. You should have seen him. He hadn't just drunk that Kool-Aid. He gulped it. And Maeve kept refilling his glass."

His brow creases. Then he sputters a laugh. "She went along with it. Encouraged it."

"She did. He told her he wanted her to dip into the money for her health, and she pretended to have no idea what he was talking about . . . while suddenly starting to use the money I was putting in her account, for medicine and whatnot."

"Which proved to him that the treasure existed and kept him being oh-so-solicitous of her health."

"Yep, and on her deathbed, she gave him the key to a safety deposit box, which he was supposed to give to Celeste. He didn't, naturally. He opened it and found a note telling me to remember how I liked to spend my time at her house, that I'd find the money there."

When Tom doesn't laugh, I look to see him hesitating. Then he bursts into that laugh, shaking his head. "She played him."

"She totally played him."

"So he wanted the answer from you."

"Yep. I promised to come up with a list of ideas. What I really wanted was—" I stop there, remembering what I'd really wanted. I haven't shared this with Tom yet. I didn't want him to try to keep me out of the house, but that's no longer a concern.

I meet his gaze. "I'm not here sneaking around figuring out how to expose Celeste. I could do that at any time. I'm here to find out whether she killed my grandmother."

He stares. Blinks. Stares some more. Then he starts swearing.

"Tom?"

He runs a hand through his hair. "Did I just say how I got suckered into that scheme because I thought I was too smart for it? How I learned my lesson? Apparently, I did not, because no matter how much I hated fake-Celeste, I never considered that."

"You think she didn't do it, then."

"No, I think she absolutely might have, and I can't believe I never suspected it."

"Maeve was failing. Dying. Then she died. No reason to question that."

"Not while I thought you were the person nursing her. When I found out otherwise, I should have wondered, but my focus was on finding you. Then you came back, and I should have wondered why you hadn't just turned her in, but I was too busy trying to be helpful."

I tell him what Liam said about the medications, how good Celeste had been about making Gran take them even when she balked. Then I tell him about what I found in the bathroom, the medications I found in the imposter's name.

"You think either she overdosed Maeve with Maeve's own medicine, or she substituted one of her own." He nods. "You should talk to Dr. Hoover about those medications."

"And find out the exact cause of death. Liam says it was heart failure, but that's like saying she died because she stopped breathing. I also want to find Gran's diary. I know she kept one, and I know she hid it, but I can't find it."

"Did you check under the main-floor bathroom sink?"

My chin jerks up, and he chuckles. "I found it once when I was fixing the pipes while she was out. She hides it behind a bag of adult diapers. I had to move them to get to the pipe. I laughed at that, wondering what the hell Maeve wrote in her diary that made her think she couldn't just shove it under the mattress like everyone else."

"Did you look?"

"Hell, no. Whatever she put in there, I did not want to know. But, yeah, unless the imposter found it, that's where it is. We'll go back for your things in the morning and snag it."

It's late now. Almost three, if the clock by Tom's bed is to be believed. The not-so-believable part is that I'm in Tom's bed, with him beside me, one naked leg entwined with mine, one hand on my stomach as he sleeps.

The logical part of my brain screams that this is a terrible idea. The worst in a string of bad ideas. The timing could not be worse, and I cannot afford to be distracted like this.

And yet . . .

I'm *not* distracted. No more than I need to be, for sanity's sake. The timing may be bad, but Tom himself is the best idea I've had in a very long time.

This feels right. It feels so damn right that tears prickle.

Great, I can't sob with grief, but apparently, I *can* weep tears of sentimentality.

I feel emotion. A lot of emotion, and my body doesn't quite know what to do with that. I'm not going to analyze. Not analyze what I'm feeling with Tom, not analyze whether this is a good idea or a terrible one. There are a whole lot of other things I need to use my mental hand-wringing on, because if this all goes to hell, I won't need to worry about Tom, not unless he's okay with conjugal visits.

My gut twists hard enough for me to wince.

The police will try to match my gun with the bullet that killed Liam. When the match is positive—which I'm now sure it is—they'll check to confirm that the gun is indeed legally registered to me. It will come back to a Celeste Whitfield. Of course, that shared first name could be a coincidence. I will need to admit who I am.

Yes, that's my gun. Yes, that's my name. I think it's time to explain a few things . . .

How long do I have? Not long enough.

Do I have time to get the diary? To talk to Dr. Hoover? Or should I just come clean? Save my own ass, and if Celeste slips the noose and runs, well, at least I won't end up charged with murder.

I'm thinking this when I catch the slam of a car door. Then another. That gets my attention. Fort Exile is a rural community, and those slams are so close by that unless they're on the road, they're coming from Tom's drive.

I lay my hand on his hip and give it a soft shake. One dark eye opens.

"Hey," I whisper. "Someone's here. Emergency repair."

He groans and buries his face in my shoulder. "Every goddamn week. If it's not a knock at the door, it's a call on my cell. I don't run a twenty-four-hour service, folks."

The muffled sound of a distant knock, and Tom groans again.

"Ignore it?" I suggest.

"I would love to ignore it. But then I'll spend the rest of the night worrying that it isn't some drunk asshole who drove in the ditch but a neighbor *hit* by a drunk asshole." He swings his legs over the side and pulls on his boxers. "If it's the latter—or anything legitimately urgent—I might be a while."

I kiss his cheek. "You go play mechanic-in-shining-armor, and I'll make coffee."

"You don't need to—"

I plant the next kiss on his lips. "I know, just like you don't need to help someone at three in the morning. It's the 'don't have to' part that makes it feel good."

His lips quirk. "Okay, but hold off for a few minutes, because there's a very good chance I'll be back in five minutes, grumbling about the state of the opioid crisis in Florida."

"I will grumble along with you."

He pulls on his jeans. The knock below turns to a pounding.

Tom's lips tighten. "Scratch that. I will almost certainly be back in five minutes."

He grabs his shirt and strides off. I listen to his bare feet padding down the stairs. Then, at the bottom, they stop. What sounds like a whispered curse, and then his feet pound up the stairs as I scramble out of bed.

"Lights," he says, breathing hard. "I saw flashing lights. It's the cops."

I blink.

"I didn't do anything," he says quickly. "I'm clean. I don't so much as tweak a tax return these days."

"Liam is dead, Tom. Murdered, almost certainly with my gun. There's not a split second where I wondered whether they were here for *you*."

He nods, still breathing hard. "I know. Sorry for the panic." He takes a deep breath, and I realize that isn't from running up the stairs. "I swear I hyperventilate when I see a cop in my rearview mirror. I know they're here about Liam."

"They're here for me," I say as I pull on my jeans.

"Or me. I'm the ex-con. I'm the one who argued with him. I live here. Not you."

"Celeste sent me here. She knows exactly where I am."

He curses. The pounding comes again, this time accompanied by a voice, and he dashes down the stairs to listen.

"They're saying they have an arrest warrant," he says when he comes back up. "For you."

I inhale. "Okay, let's deal with this."

"Up the stairs. Onto the roof."

"What?" I shake my head. "I'm not fleeing the cops, Tom."

"You aren't. I didn't open the door. They haven't served their warrant. Until they do, you're fine."

I hesitate.

"Trust me on this," he says. "In prison, I had a cellmate who educated my dumb ass about my rights. Need-to-know information if your skin isn't lily white."

I still hesitate. "I should turn myself in. Tell them who I really am and face this. I didn't kill Liam."

"No, that imposter did, and she probably also killed your grandmother. If you reveal your identity, you give her time to run." He lays his hands on my shoulders. "We just need to get the diary and talk to Doc Hoover. We can do the first tonight and the second in the morning. I know where he lives. You can be there before breakfast."

The pounding comes again. Tom's right. I know he's right, no matter how much my rule-following soul screams, *Dear God do not run from the police.*

"CeCe?" Tom says.

I nod and run for the ladder onto the roof.

THIRTY-FOUR

DAISY

We are in the forest behind Gran's—*my*—house. I have fled from the police, and my gut keeps threatening to unload at my feet. To calm my nerves, Tom has gone over the plan in detail. Get Maeve's diary tonight. Be at Dr. Hoover's house before he leaves for work. Reveal myself to the doctor and get answers about the prescriptions and about Maeve's death. Then, with all data intact, Tom will drive me to the police station, where I will tell the deputies who I am and give them what I have.

When we've been hiding for an hour, Tom jogs back to see whether the police are still at his place. They're long gone. Then it's on to Maeve's house, where he checks in case the police looped back to talk to Celeste again. There's no sign of them, and he suspects they'll postpone the warrant until morning.

We slip up to the shed. From there, I can see Celeste's bedroom window. Dark, as expected. All the windows are dark. Still, we take turns crossing to the house, the other one watching and listening.

He stays outside, watching Celeste's window while I fetch the key from the planter and open the door. As I creep inside, I pause and roll my shoulders, the prickle of unease settling between them.

Yes, I'm breaking in . . . to a house that is legally mine.

Is that what's bothering me? Or the fact that right over my head lies the woman who is trying to frame me for murder, sound asleep in *my* house. After she may have killed *my* grandmother to get it.

I take deep breaths. Yes, what I'm feeling isn't the anxiety of breaking in; it's a fireball of rage I've been tamping down for days. Until now, I was the predator, stalking her, slipping into "her" home, investigating her under her very nose. I was in control. I was hunting my prey in an elaborate ambush to ensure she had no chance to flee.

Now she still doesn't know who I am, but she has taken the offensive. Tried to frame me for her lover's murder. Kicked me out of my house. She's struck at me, and the anger finally ignites.

I want her out. In that moment, I don't care whether she gets away with murder—two murders, even. I want to storm upstairs and tell her who I am and let her run.

Get out of my life. Get out of my home. Get out of my head.

I squash the impulse. I would regret it later, especially if the police suspect I "got rid" of Celeste in a more permanent way.

No, I will have my revenge, and it will be a satisfying one, with Celeste led off in handcuffs.

Tom comes in, and I stand guard as he retrieves the diary. It is the same one I remember, faded floral cover and cheap key lock. A diary meant for a child who can pretend that the flimsy lock—one you can open with a fingernail—means her secrets are safe.

Tom lifts the diary over his head, and just at that moment, a thump sounds above. Two soft thuds, as if Celeste is getting out of bed. Tom's eyes widen, and he wildly motions for me to leave. I scamper soundlessly to the back door, and he follows a moment later. We pause there until the upstairs bathroom door clicks shut, and then we are gone.

We are back at Tom's place. He's deemed that safe. The police aren't staking it out, and if it's me they're after, they'll check Maeve's house first. Still, I insist on being careful. Come in the back door and keep the lights off until we're in the windowless second-floor apartment.

That apartment is pretty much just a bedroom, kitchenette and a recliner. Bachelor living at its most economical. We sit at the kitchen table with the diary. Then Tom jumps up, as if he's forgotten something, and I pause, but he waves for me to go on as he fixes coffee. I suspect it's not so much the coffee he needs as the fact he's realized I might want privacy for reading my grandmother's journal.

I send up a silent apology to Maeve. Then I snap the child's lock and open the yellowing pages. The first entry is dated twenty-five years ago.

Mikey brought Celeste over today. I think he's looking better. He has a new job, and he's happy and he's sober. Maybe this will be the time.

My heart clenches, and I pause as I run my fingers over the faded ink.

No, Gran, that wasn't the time. Not that time, or the time after or the time after that. I wonder how often you thought those words. How often my mother thought them. The hope that this time, he wouldn't disappoint you, and he always did, and no one felt the crush of that as much as he did.

I flip forward a few pages and see an entry that stops my heart in my chest, and I need to pause there. Absorb it. Remember it, as painful as that is.

She's leaving and taking CeCe with her, and I can't say I blame her. Mikey didn't mean it. Everyone knows that, even her. He was trying to be a good daddy. But when he's on that junk, he's not thinking straight. The doctor says that the blanket might not have been what killed her, but I guess that doesn't matter. It was the last straw.

I touch the entry, and I remember my mother's howls of grief, waking to find my infant sister dead in her crib. It'd been a cold night, and when Dad went to see her, he took a blanket from the shelf and put it over her. Trying to be a good daddy, like Gran says. Yes, he'd been told that increased the risk of SIDS, but he'd been high and, like Gran also says, not thinking straight. All he knew was that his baby girl seemed cold and the blankets were right there.

That might not have caused her death. It could have been pure coincidence. It didn't matter. It was, indeed, the last straw.

Did Mom take me away to protect me? If so, I wish we could have talked about that. I wish we could have talked about so many things.

I take a deep breath and flip to the last page, where the ink is still bright on the old paper, but the hand is shaky, full of stops and starts.

I've missed my chance. I know that now. The end is coming like a freight train, and goddamn it, I'm not ready. I thought I'd have more time. I just needed to get a little better. Let this silly girl nurse me back to health enough for me to get off my ass and hire a proper private investigator to find my CeCe. But it's too late. Made my peace with it. Know I did the right thing. That is enough.

I stare at the entry as my eyes fill with tears.

"CeCe?" Tom says in alarm as he hurries over.

I brush away the tears. "She knew."

"Knew . . . ?"

"She knew the imposter wasn't me. She was using Celeste to nurse her back to health so she'd be well enough to track me down. But she ran out of time."

He puts one arm around me as he bends in a hug.

I lean against him for a second. Then I straighten and say, "Okay, let's turn back the clock. Find out what she knew and when she knew it."

He squeezes my shoulder and returns to the coffee as I flip backward and begin reading. By the time I finish, I have a half-cold cup of coffee at my elbow. He's finished his, and he hasn't said a word. He just sat with me as I read.

Finally, I shut the diary, take a long hit of the lukewarm brew and say, "She knew Liam was after the treasure. She never trusted him, but like the imposter, he was useful. She did, unfortunately, trust him enough to send him looking for me a year ago. She figured if she dangled the carrot of the treasure—implying she had money—he'd dance to her tune."

"And then the imposter showed up."

"Mmm, not exactly. Liam brought her."

"What?"

I open the diary and point out the passage. "Liam brought the imposter and passed her off as me."

Tom thuds back in his chair. "Okay, I did not see that one coming." When he catches my expression, he peers at me. "You did?"

I shrug. "I considered it. You said someone else had been looking for me. If Gran wanted to track me down, it'd make sense for her to hire Liam. As a lawyer, he'd have investigators."

"So he does a half-assed job and then passes off his girlfriend as you?"

"I'm not sure. Did he just happen to be dating a woman who resembles me? Who also didn't mind giving up her own identity—her home, her livelihood, her life—to help him with this scheme?

Maeve thought there was more to it. She got the feeling Celeste was being forced into it, that Liam held something over her. That's why Gran didn't send the imposter packing. She felt sorry for her. Didn't keep her from using her and, I suspect, not being very nice to her, but she let her stay."

When Tom doesn't respond, I say, "You disagree?"

"I think Maeve saw what she wanted to see. What was convenient to see. She was in rough shape, and if this woman was willing to play nursemaid?" He shrugs. "It helped if she could tell herself the imposter wasn't a bad person." He glances at me. "Did her opinion ever change?"

"No. If Celeste did anything, Maeve never suspected it. From this, I know it wasn't a sudden death. Gran was failing, and she accepted that, never questioned that it might not be a natural end." I flip pages. "I do get a couple of references, though, to her grumbling about Celeste making her take her medication."

"Ah-ha."

"However, Liam said that Gran hated taking her medication. Was this the imposter pressing too much medication on her? Or just insisting she take exactly what she was supposed to take?"

"Dr. Hoover will know more." Tom checks his watch. "We can get ready to head over there."

CELESTE

I can't sleep. At one point, I think I hear someone in the house, but when I finally convince myself to get up, it's empty with the doors locked. It's nearly morning before I fall to sleep, and it only lasts long enough for me to tumble into the nightmare about

Jasmine. Except this time, I'm not at home being questioned by the police. I'm in Starbucks, listening to my friends tricking her as I text with Aaron.

As we're leaving the coffee shop, I jolt awake in a cold sweat, my heart hammering. I hover there, hands wrapped in the sheets as I think back to the dream. Why did that part make me jump up in a panic? Was there something I've missed? Some blocked memory where—I don't know—maybe I'm the one who suggested *killing* Jasmine? I know there isn't. I stayed out of their bullying. I didn't like it, so I didn't participate, and there is zero chance that I've edited those memories. I was never that kind of person.

Was never that person, but I am now? Have I become her?

I killed Liam, didn't I?

That was an accident. Yes, I wanted to kill him, but I couldn't bring myself to do it.

So why did that part of the dream leave me in a cold sweat? I was getting into the car and asking them to drop me off before they went to pull their stunt with Jasmine. I'd honestly thought "a stunt" was all they planned. Not murder. Never murder.

And did that make it okay?

This whispering voice doesn't sound like my mother's or Aaron's. It sounds like someone very different.

It sounds like Jasmine.

Like Jasmine . . . and also like Daisy.

I have told myself that I did nothing to Jasmine. I played no role in her bullying and certainly no role in her death. But I did, didn't I? I played the role of bystander.

I saw how my friends treated her, and I didn't tell anyone. I didn't even try to stop them. I kept my mouth shut because I feared losing my new friends. My new friends who were incredibly popular . . . and absolute shit heels. I didn't even like them. I just liked being with them.

For that, a girl died.

Jasmine Oleas died because I wanted to keep these cool new friends that I didn't even like.

Now I'm doing the same to Daisy. No, it's not *exactly* the same, is it? Because this time, I am doing the bullying myself. I'm framing her for murder. Top of the bullying scale, just short of holding her head underwater.

Daisy deserves it as little as Jasmine did. I managed to convince myself she *did* when I thought her responsible for the camera, the leak and the break-in. I had no idea what she was up to, but damn it, she was up to something. That seemed to justify it.

Once she was cleared of the camera, break-in and leak, I had to admit she no longer "deserved" to be framed, so I changed my mind. Then I accidentally killed Liam, and the police started closing in, so I panicked. Told myself she'd be fine and planted the gun and made that anonymous call about seeing her with Liam the night of his death.

I need another solution. I have an idea; I just need to figure out how to do it.

I'm supposed to identify Liam's body this morning, and since I'm not sleeping anyway, I do it early, with the excuse that I couldn't sleep facing such a terrible task. The police know who he is—this is just a formality.

Yes, that's Liam Garey, exactly as I last saw him, complete with a crater where his eye should be.

I don't say that. It's not true anyway. Something had been eating his face, and as much as they've tried to clean him up for me, there's no hiding that. It actually helps—I don't need to fake my horror and revulsion.

Definitely a closed-casket funeral. There's a certain amount of poetic justice in the aftermath of Liam's demise. He had nothing but contempt for rural Florida and everyone who lived on the swamp's edges. I remember him telling me about a client who OD'd in the everglades and got eaten by an alligator, and even the coroner hadn't been completely sure the guy had been dead when the gator got him. Liam thought it was hilarious. Anyone who's reckless enough to shoot up in the swamp deserves to be gator chow. Same for anyone who decides that's the right place to tell their captive that they're about to lock her into an even smaller cage.

Yes, I didn't intend to pull that trigger, but for the sake of my ego, I'm going to start telling myself otherwise. The bastard pushed me too far, and I put a bullet in him.

If the local police have me on their suspect list, they forgot to inform the Tampa coroner's office. I identify Liam and sign some papers, and then the young clerk brings me a bag with his personal effects. She has obviously mistaken me for his live-in partner, but what the hell, sure, I'll take his Rolex and the keys to his condo. High five to me for only leaving his car key fob in the Rover.

I now legitimately have access to Liam's condo and his belongings, with the freedom to help myself to them. And I do mean *freedom*. There's no one else who'd have a clue what should be in his condo. Not his ex-wife. Not the parents he "helped" into a crappy seniors' home three years ago. Not the "friends" he would never let past his doorstep. Just me, the girlfriend who shot him.

I let myself in. After all, I need to collect any belongings I left behind, which amount to a toothbrush and a few pairs of underwear. While I'm at it, I might as well poke about. I have an idea about how to get both Daisy and myself out of this mess, and I'm hoping to set that in motion here. Also, while I'm at it, let's see what else I can find.

Oh, look, here's nearly a thousand dollars stashed in a coffee tin. Really? A coffee tin, Liam?

I also find the unencrypted recordings from that drive on my laptop. It's exactly what I expected. Revenge porn. A little something to hold over my head if I tried to break our deal.

It seems squirreling away revenge porn is a hobby for Liam. I find more with other women, and I erase it. My gift to all those who came before me. As for the ones starring me, I keep those. I have an idea how they might come in handy.

I ransack Liam's place and put together a nice little bag of parting gifts. I finish up in his study, where I contemplate taking his laptop. That's when I realize the local cops haven't even searched his condo yet.

Really, boys? Murder investigation 101.

Yep, I definitely want the laptop. No telling what's on it. I'm picking it up when I notice a photograph beside it. An old one that makes me frown. It isn't like Liam to keep childhood mementos.

It's a black-and-white glossy photo, the kind I've only seen in old people's photo albums. At first, I think it's antique. But then I see the boy in it, perched on a bicycle.

I blink. Is that . . . ?

There's no mistaking Tom's face. So Liam had an old photograph of Tom, and I bet it explains why he'd been hell-bent on antagonizing him Friday night. My guess is this photograph gave him some kind of blackmail fodder.

There's a piece of paper under the photograph. It's the printout of a report from Liam's investigator. Seems Liam asked him to do a quick search into Tom's criminal past. In other words, when he was needling Tom at the poker game, he already knew what Tom had been in for.

I read the report. Then I read it again.

Damn.

Left a few things out of your story, didn't you, Tom?

I'm folding the report when I see the photograph again. This time, I realize there's someone else in the picture. I catch a glimpse of the face and pull back with a sharp inhale.

It's Daisy.

I shake my head. No, that's impossible. I must be just seeing a girl who resembles her.

There's a magnifying glass on the desk. Liam had been examining this photo before he came over. He'd seen what I do, and he wanted a closer look.

I turn on the desk light and move the photo under it.

If this isn't Daisy, it's a very close relative.

I lift the photo. As it catches the light, I notice black marks showing through. I flip it over and read "CeCe & Tom, July 1988."

In my mind, I see Maeve, sitting on the sofa. Liam had just stepped into the kitchen after introducing us.

"Celeste," she says. "You don't go by CeCe anymore, I take it."

I wrinkle my nose. "No, that's a little girl's name."

"And you're not a little girl anymore." Do I detect disappointment in her voice? "All grown up."

"Yes, ma'am."

Maeve cackles. "Well, at least that hasn't changed. You always were a polite little thing."

That was the real trick to assuming another persona. All the research in the world wouldn't help me become the girl that Maeve remembered. Yet I'd learned that when I took on other identities, what mattered weren't the facts of someone's life but the things others remembered about her.

You always were a polite little thing. Time to start remembering my p's and q's, then.

You still run, Miz Turner? You used to run everywhere when you were a girl. Time to take up jogging.

How's that ankle doing, Miss Celeste? You sprained it pretty bad back in the old days. Why, yes, Doctor, it's as good as new—I never get so much as a twinge in it these days. You fixed it up right.

CeCe.

While I didn't need to use the ridiculous little-girl name, I had to be prepared to respond to it, like the real Celeste Turner would have, back when . . .

My gaze rivets on the photo.

Daisy.

CeCe.

No. No goddamn way.

The scene in my mind shifts as I remember a photograph on Maeve's mantle. It's a young man, no more than twenty, good-looking with a killer smile and the slightly unfocused eyes of an addict. That smile, though . . .

He holds a little girl on his lap, and he's beaming like the gods rewarded his sorry life with a gift beyond measure. A cherub-faced toddler, smiling sweetly up at the man.

"You sure did love your daddy, girl," Maeve says as she catches me looking at the photo.

"I did." I sigh, as if in remembered pleasure mingled with regret. "Dad had his problems, but he did his best."

"That he did."

How many times had I seen that photo? I'd watched Daisy walk right past it. The girl in that photo was little more than a baby, chubby, a doll with blond curls and wide eyes. She's not the girl in Tom's photo, thin, with straight blond hair and shy eyes. *That* girl looks like Daisy.

Daisy.

CeCe.

The real Celeste Turner.

THIRTY-FIVE

DAISY

I'm at Dr. Hoover's door. Tom wanted to come earlier, but I insisted on waiting for a reasonable hour. The clinic opens at ten today, so nine is reasonable, especially if I arrive bearing Glory's cinnamon buns. Tom himself isn't with me. He wants to get a read on where the police are with regards to the investigation, and he thinks he knows someone he can trust to give him that information.

He dropped me off and insisted I take his cell phone. We're supposed to meet at the abandoned house where we salvaged the window. From there, we'll compile what we know and plan our next move. Or that's his version. I already know my next move. No matter what happens with Dr. Hoover, I am going to turn myself in as the real Celeste. Either I will bring enough for the police to arrest the imposter for my grandmother's murder, or I won't. I will not keep digging, further endangering Tom as an accomplice.

It takes a few minutes for Dr. Hoover to answer. He's got to be past retirement age by now, but he doesn't look much older than when I knew him, still bright eyed, his curly hair shorn almost to his scalp.

"Well, I know that's Tom's truck," he says with a smile. "But you do not look like Tom."

The smile falters as his dark eyes fix on me. Then they widen, and he pulls on a pair of glasses worn around his neck.

"Hey, Doc," I say. "Been a while."

"It has, hasn't it?" His words come slow and careful, eyes fixed on me, uncertain and assessing. "Remind me the last time I saw you."

"When I was ten. I sprained my ankle jumping out of a tree."

His eyes sharpen. He's not asking because he's trying to place me. He's testing me.

"And who brought you in?" he asks.

I smile at the memory. "Tom Lowe. He doubled me on his bike, racing to your office, screaming 'emergency!' like some kind of siren. He came into the parking lot so fast he wiped out on the gravel, and when you came out, we were arguing—he was trying to carry me, and I was telling him to stop fussing."

Dr. Hoover leans against the doorframe and gives a long exhale. "CeCe." He backs up. "Come in, child. Come in."

I follow him into the trim little house, which also looks exactly as I remember.

"Tom blamed himself when you didn't come back to Fort Exile after that," he says as he leads me into the living room. "He was sure your parents were keeping you away because he let you get hurt."

I wince. "Oh."

He waves me to a seat. "Maeve set him straight soon enough, told him to stop being silly." He sighs. "CeCe Turner. So who the hell is the woman living in your house?"

"Good question. Tom and I are sorting it out."

"She didn't remember that ankle sprain. I asked her about it, just breaking the ice, and I could tell it caught her off guard. I didn't think much of that. It wasn't exactly a traumatic injury, and while you'd always been a quiet child, you'd apparently grown up to be cold and distant, too. It happens. I let it go. I shouldn't have."

"She fooled a lot of people."

"Not Tom, I bet. There was no way she pulled the wool over his eyes. I don't know how she thought she would."

"As far as she was concerned, Tom was just a guy Celeste Turner hung out with now and then when she visited her grandmother."

"I guess so." A deep sigh. "What a mess." His brow furrows. "Wait. Are you the young woman who's been living with her? Doing repairs?"

"Yep."

The furrow deepens. "Didn't I hear that lawyer was found dead in the swamp?"

"Yep. All I can say for sure is that neither Tom nor I had anything to do with that. I'm here to ask about Maeve. About her death. I have questions."

"I'm sure you do, and as her next of kin, you are entitled to answers. Ask away."

CELESTE

I turn into my drive to see it blocked by a familiar pickup, one that would have made my heart skip a few days ago.

It's Tom.

He's brought Daisy back to collect her things. Last night, I checked her room and was disappointed to find that she'd only taken half her things, which meant she wasn't running. Now she's back, with Tom in tow, to collect the rest.

Daisy.

Daisy who is not Daisy at all. Daisy who is the real Celeste Turner.

I'm tempted to reverse and roar out of here. Hell, I was tempted to not come back to Fort Exile at all. But she's known all along that I'm an imposter, and she hasn't called me on it. I sure as hell don't want to tumble into a trap, but nor do I want to scamper off like a scared rabbit, leaving all my belongings behind. She doesn't know anything has changed. I just need to play along for a little bit more and then collect my things and hit the road. Leave Daisy with her house and her inheritance.

And a murder charge?

Guilt stabs through me. This isn't what I intended, damn it. I've done enough to her already, and I am keenly aware of that.

Now what?

This should make me even more determined not to frame her, but while I have an alternate plan, I no longer dare stick around long enough to act on it. I can only get the hell out of Dodge before Daisy summons me to a showdown at noon.

Leave . . . and let her face a murder charge.

I'm sorry, CeCe. This isn't what I intended, and I hope to God you can get out of it okay. I'll help if I can, from a distance. I won't do anything more to hurt you, but I can't undo what I've done, either, on any count.

I want you to be okay, and my flight will help. Let them come after me instead. I won't set them on my own trail—I'm not that selfless—but you can do that. Tell them I stole your identity and let them decide I may also have killed my partner in crime. Then tell Tom who you really are. Fall into each other's arms and live happily ever after.

That's what I want for you. Good things. Only good things.

You deserve it, just like Jasmine did.

I head inside.

"Hello?" I call, a note of concern in my voice, like someone who has returned to find uninvited guests in her home.

No one answers. As I listen, I catch the sound of the shower running.

She's taking a *shower*? Really?

Yes, because it's her shower. Her house. And as long as she's busy, I have time to gather my things and get out.

I'm in the upstairs hall when the shower stops. Two more steps, and the bathroom door opens.

"Hey," a voice says. "I thought I heard someone here."

That is not Daisy's voice. I turn to see Tom. Dripping wet, a towel wrapped around his waist.

"I hoped to be done before you were back. Whoops." He shoots me a bashful smile, but it's a total put-on, as his eyes dance with undisguised amusement.

I stand there, arms crossed. "What are you doing in my shower?"

"Mine's busted," he says. "Daisy asked me to collect her things, so I figured I'd sneak a shower."

"She's not coming to get her own stuff?"

"I get the feeling you spooked her. You are a very scary lady when you want to be."

"Not scary enough to keep you out of my shower."

"Do you want me out of your shower?" He leans one hip against the counter. "Or are you just disappointed that I wasn't still in there?"

"Someone's feeling flirty today. I'm guessing Daisy slept on the sofa."

"Never. That would be inhospitable. Daisy got the full measure of my hospitality."

"The full measure?"

"Nothing less."

"Must have been disappointing if you're inviting me into showers already."

"Did I invite you?" He backs against the vanity counter, resting on it, the towel parting to show one thigh and the enticing shadow of more. "Mmm, no, I think I just asked if you were disappointed that I was finished. Now, if you're inviting *me* back into the shower . . ."

I step toward him. "Let's say I was. What would your answer be, Mr. Lowe?"

"My answer would be that, sadly, I've already washed up. I could use a coffee, though. Otherwise, I might just collapse on your sofa, and I have the feeling that would be unwise." His lips purse, as if in thought. "Still tempting, though."

His glittering eyes meet mine. "What do you say, Ms. Turner? Should I insist on a coffee or risk falling asleep in this towel?"

I flick a finger against his chest. "Tom Lowe, you are an unrepentant flirt. Poor Daisy never stood a chance, did she? Dare I ask where she is? Recovering from the exertions of the night?"

"Alas, no, as much as my ego would love that. She had errands to run. We have about an hour before she shows up."

"An hour for coffee?" My eyes widen in mock innocence. "You must drink very slowly, Mr. Lowe."

He chuckles. "Normally, no. But in this case, that coffee may take a while. I have a proposal for you. One that I think you'll like."

"Somehow, despite your flirting, I have the feeling this proposal doesn't involve showers or couches."

"Not yet."

I flick his chest again, hard enough to make him yelp. "Un-re-pent-ant *tease*. Fine. I'll bite." I turn toward the door. "You might want to get used to that."

His laughter follows me as I head downstairs to make coffee.

I sit at the table while Tom brews a pot for me. He's pulled on his jeans and nothing else, so he's barechested, barefoot and damp haired. A charming picture indeed. The bare chest may be a bit much with the air conditioning, but I get the message. It's like a pretty girl undoing a button or two on her blouse. He's putting on a display, one intended to distract me while reminding me of what I might win if I play my cards right.

As the coffee brews, Tom pokes around the kitchen until—with an *ah-ha* of victory—he finds the cookies. He sets four on a plate and microwaves them, saying, "Daisy's cookies are so good this is possibly gilding the lily, but warm is always better with chocolate chip."

There's no hint of guilt or derision in his voice. He's flirting with me using cookies made by the woman he slept with last night, and he's blithely complimenting her baking.

Yep, CeCe, you deserve so much better. We both do.

It seems our Mr. Lowe is a bit of a player. For me, he is sexy and flirty and bold. For Daisy, he's sweet as sugar, considerate and kind.

Which is the real you, Tom Lowe?

Tom brings over two mugs, mine fixed exactly as I like it. He grins, as if expecting a head pat for it. I take it with a regal nod. Accepting my due.

He nibbles a cookie and closes his eyes, *mmm-mmming* his appreciation. "My mom always said no one baked cookies like Maeve Turner. She guarded her recipe like a dragon hoarding its treasure. One year, at the state fair, someone said it was just the regular Toll House recipe. And she admitted it. Do you believe that?"

"Maeve was unpredictable."

"Nah, she was totally predictable. She admitted it because she was saying that everyone else was welcome to use 'her' recipe and it wouldn't make any difference. It was the baker that counted, not a list of instructions."

"Uh-huh."

"She only ever taught one person how to make those cookies." He takes another bite. "Her granddaughter." He lifts his gaze to mine. "Do you remember making these for me?"

He waves off my answer. "That's right. You barely remember me. That's okay. I didn't remember you, either. I thought I did, but then we met, and it was like looking at a stranger. People change, you know?"

The back of my neck prickles.

He continues, "It's disappointing when that happens. You're so sure that you'd remember a friend, even if they were a kid when you last saw them. You think your eyes will meet in a crowd and your brain will scream, *That's her*."

He might be sitting there, munching on a cookie, sipping his coffee, but in my mind, he's on his feet, backing me into a corner. His eyes glitter with predatory delight, and in that moment, he looks so much like Liam that, if I had my gun, I might put a bullet through one of those brown eyes, and it *wouldn't* be an accident.

Two choices. Retreat or stand firm.

I am done retreating.

My voice low, I say, "How long have you known?"

"How long have I known you aren't CeCe Turner?" He reaches for another cookie. "Since the moment I saw you."

"Yet you did nothing."

A one-shouldered shrug. "I didn't owe Maeve anything. The old bat was a bitch to me. Ran me off when she started looking for CeCe. Didn't think I was good enough for her grandbaby."

"You proved her wrong, didn't you?"

He pauses, cookie to his lips. Ah, he doesn't know who Daisy is? *I have the advantage, sir.*

And the moment I think that, his lips quirk in a grin. "So you figured it out, too. Innocent little Daisy isn't so innocent after all."

"She told you who she really is."

"Told me?" His brows shoot up. "You really do think I'm that oblivious. I saw through both of your charades."

"She doesn't know that you know?"

That languid shrug again. "It didn't seem useful."

I meet his gaze. "So what does seem useful to you?"

He smiles. "Framing her for murder."

THIRTY-SIX

DAISY

My grandmother died of kidney failure. The result of—surprise, surprise—untreated diabetes. She'd had a myriad of issues, including heart trouble, but it was her kidneys that finally shut down, despite treatment.

Dr. Hoover had been her physician to the end. He admitted—grudgingly—that Celeste had been the best thing to happen to my gran. Sure, she wasn't trained as a nurse, and she got frustrated with Maeve, confessing that to Dr. Hoover. But none of her nursing mistakes were dangerous, and her frustration had been with my grandmother's stubbornness, refusing to take medications, refusing to help herself. The same frustrations Dr. Hoover had shared.

So no, Celeste did not kill my grandmother. She didn't even help nature take her sooner. If anything, she kept her alive beyond what Dr. Hoover had expected.

As for the medications in Celeste's cabinet, they're ones he prescribed for her—an antidepressant and a sleep aid.

I remember the night of the poker game. Switching drinks with Tom. His behavior afterward, unsteady and exhausted. Had Celeste slipped a sleeping pill into "my" drink? Making sure I'd be out cold that night while she murdered Liam?

I've been at our meeting spot for an hour now, and there's no sign of Tom. I pick up his cell to . . . call him? It's a testament to my mental state that I sit there with his phone in hand, thinking, *Maybe I could text? Or email?* Yeah, none of those options are working while I'm in possession of his sole mode of electronic contact.

I walk to his place and pop into the store, where Glory is serving a customer.

"If you're looking for another cinnamon bun, they're all gone," she says. "I can offer you this nice pack of jerky instead."

I smile. "Thanks, but no. I'm just wondering whether you've seen Tom this morning."

"Only long enough to say hi. Everything okay?"

"Something's come up, and I need to talk to him, but he left me his phone. He didn't get an emergency call, did he?"

"Emergency?" She stops unboxing jerky.

"A mechanical emergency?"

She relaxes and picks up the sticker gun. "Nope, nothing like that's come in."

I thank her and walk outside, where I look up and down each side of the crossroads. Then my feet start moving, carrying me toward my grandmother's house.

CELESTE

I want to leap up from the table. Grab the edge and throw it on Tom, coffee splashing, mugs shattering. A move I've seen on film so many times, but one that I suspect rarely choreographs quite that way. I'd probably fumble the table, slip on the linoleum and land on my ass.

So I tamp down the rage and panic, look Tom in the eye and say, "I guess this means we aren't going to screw."

I expect a sneering laugh. No, I can't actually see Tom sneering. Not gloating, either. He'll just laugh and shake his head, and let me know that was never on the table.

Instead, he lifts one shoulder and says, "Depends on you, really."

You bastard. You set yourself up as the nice guy. The small-town boy to Liam's rich asshole, and guess what? You're just as bad as he was.

Tom leans over the table, muscular forearms resting on it, hands clasped as if in prayer. "If you think this is where I toss you out on your ass, fake-Celeste, you are misunderstanding the situation. If you think this is where I back you into a wall and rage at you for hurting my girl, you are also misunderstanding. CeCe and I were friends once. But that was a long time ago, and I'm interested in more than a girl who'll sip sodas with me and kiss me behind the barn. Interested in more than a woman who'll let me do pretty much anything I want to her because she's in over her head and needs a big strong man to shield her from the wicked witch."

Rage fills me. So much rage. All of it for Daisy. I clamp it down and manage to say, "What are you talking about?"

"You killed Liam. I don't blame you. I found Maeve's diary, and she said Liam was the one who brought you to her. Maeve knew you were a fake, by the way, but she let you stay on because she felt sorry for you."

I whip back with the sting of that.

He continues, "She had a soft spot for you. But you finally fought back. Killed your captor, and now you're framing CeCe, and I want to help you."

"I don't know what you're talking about."

"Sure you do, but whatever."

"All Daisy needs to do is turn herself over to the police. Admit who she is."

He leans back, stretching his legs out. "I made sure she won't do that. Someone came around last night wanting an emergency repair, and I convinced CeCe it was the cops with a warrant for her arrest." His lips curve in a smug smile. "She's currently holed up in the swamp, waiting for me to rescue her."

"I didn't kill Liam."

"Whatever," he says with a wave. "I don't actually care. I just want a cut of Bill Turner's money." He pauses for a beat. "Maeve did tell you where to find it, right?"

Yes, she did. She said it was where I liked to spend my time at her house, as a kid, and it didn't take long for me to realize she was feeding me bullshit, knowing I wasn't her CeCe.

But maybe, just maybe, I can use that to my advantage. To my advantage and Daisy's.

"Tell me what Maeve said," he continues. "We'll retrieve the money and split it. You can take your share with you."

"With me?"

He rolls his eyes. "CeCe knows who you are. Like I said, I'll help you frame her for murder, but that only buys us time to get the treasure. I presume the police are going to find out her gun was used to kill Liam?"

"I have no idea."

He sighs. "If we're going to be partners, I need a little more."

"So do I. I want what I was promised."

Frustration flits over his face. "You want *all* the money."

"No." I look him in the eye. "I want what you offered me earlier. Upstairs."

His mouth opens, and he's going to say he never offered me anything. Then he looks at me. Gives me a hard, searching look. And he stands.

"All right," he says. "You want a shower or . . . ?"

"Or."

He spins on his heel and heads upstairs. Not a word to me. Just marches up there as if he's been ordered. Which I suppose he has.

"I'll be right there," I say and slip into the main-level bathroom.

I head upstairs moments later. As I pass my office doorway, a floorboard creaks, and before I can react, Tom grabs my arm and thrusts it behind my back.

"Mmm, sorry," I say as I twist to face him, ignoring the pain ratcheting through my shoulder. "I don't do the rough stuff. Not on a first date, anyway."

"Let's both drop the act," he says. "You want the money. All of it."

I keep twisting, and he could put more pressure on my arm, but he doesn't. He can't. This is as much role-playing as the rest. He said he didn't want to hurt me, when the truth is that he can't.

I move toward him, hand on his chest, fingers stroking just below the base of his throat.

"No," he says.

"Yes."

Temper flares in his eyes. "I didn't pull this shit on you. Don't pull it on me."

"Sorry, Tom, but I think . . ." I move my other hand up to his stomach. "I think I'll pull whatever shit I want."

He tenses and exhales a puff of shock as he looks down to see the cold barrel of a gun against his stomach.

"How'd you . . . ?" he begins.

"How did I get the gun back from the police? That's CeCe's. This is mine."

His gaze turns inward, processing.

Not as dumb as you look, are you, Tom? Not as dumb and not as violent, and I'm not sure which is more the pity. Both are just going to make this worse, so I'd suggest that whatever you're thinking, you don't—

"You're the one who took her gun from the shed. Not Liam."

I say nothing. I don't need to. He doesn't wait for a response. "CeCe presumed it was Liam, digging for confirmation of her identity. But you were the one out there that night. You took the gun. You used it to shoot Liam."

"Into the bedroom," I say. "We're done talking."

He doesn't move. Just holds my gaze with that same steady stare.

"You're making a mistake," he says.

I clench the gun tighter. "No, I don't think I am. You aren't who we thought you were, are you, Tom? Liam looked into your prison stint. It didn't quite go the way you say, did it?"

I expect anger, a flash of temper, even shame. Instead, he meets my gaze. "No, it didn't, but I think you'll understand why I make a few creative adjustments to the story."

"Because the truth is that you didn't go along with the scheme of some high-school buddies. You caved to the demands of your high-school bullies. They forced you to launder that money. Paid you, yes, but not as well as you let on. When I read that, I actually felt sorry for you. I don't now."

He gives a half shrug. "I don't need you to feel sorry for me. That's why I don't broadcast that version. I think you know what that's like. Not wanting to be seen as a victim."

"I'm *not* a victim."

"No? Tell me no one has threatened you. No one has ever held a gun to you and made you do something you didn't want to do."

I glare at him.

He continues, "You think you're flipping the tables, but I only flirted with you to get what I wanted. I'm sure you've done that before. Doesn't mean you deserved this." Another nod at the gun. "And I'm sorry if someone made you feel like it did."

Rage wells up in me, white hot. His tone is so soft, firm and gentle at the same time, and it enrages me so much that my finger moves, unbidden, toward the trigger.

"Celeste . . ." he says.

Goddamn you, Tom. You'd be better off being just a pretty face. So much better.

I wasn't going to force you into anything. I just wanted to see you afraid, and instead, I get this look that's worse than pity. It's sympathy.

I look him straight in the eye . . . and I move my finger to the trigger.

THIRTY-SEVEN

DAISY

There are ruts in Maeve's lawn. Tire ruts from someone doing a three-point turn to leave the driveway. The police, probably, having presumed that a lawn in such rough shape was fine to drive on, even wet. I tamp down the edge of a rut as I prepare to face Celeste. I'm still nudging the dirt into place when the door swings open, and I start toward it, my face fixed in the most neutral expression I can conjure.

"Hey," I say as Celeste appears. "Just came to collect my things. Is that okay? I can wait until you're gone if you're more comfortable with that."

"And where would I be going?"

I shrug. "Wherever you want to go so you aren't alone in the house with me."

When she doesn't answer, I say, "May I retrieve my things? We can wait for Tom if you'd rather have him here."

She tenses at his name, and fresh frustration darts through me. Is there nothing I can say that won't upset her more? Put her on guard? Exactly what I do not need.

"Come back later," she says.

"With Tom?"

Her jaw hardens. Goddamn it, does she think I'm taunting her?

She sent me to Tom and *encouraged* me to do more than sleep on his sofa.

"May I get my books?" I ask.

Her brow furrows. "What?"

"My books. I'm stuck at Tom's place with nothing to do. He's out for the day, and I'm bored. While I'd love to grab all my stuff, I'm fine with a couple of books."

She waves to the house. "You have three minutes."

She lifts her watch as if to time me. I walk past her at a normal rate, neither speeding along nor dawdling. Once inside, she follows, and I tense, expecting her to trail me up the stairs, but she only calls, "Three minutes!" and lets me continue.

I open my bedroom door and snatch the first book I see. Then I head into the bathroom.

"Hey!" she calls, as if hearing the door click and lock.

"Using the toilet!" I call back. "I've still got two minutes."

I ease open the medicine cabinet to double-check the prescriptions. Yep, as Dr. Hoover said, they're in her name and prescribed by him.

I need to let her go. Let her run. I don't give a damn if she killed Liam. She did not kill my grandmother, and that's all that matters to me.

I'm turning to go when I spot a sock on the floor. It's a men's crew sock. Not Liam's—he's a dress sock guy. These are the cheap white socks you buy by the mega-pack at Target.

Tom's.

When I undressed him last night, I pulled off a sock that was the twin of this. I turn it over in my hand. Then I ease open drawers and doors until—

"Daisy!"

"Sorry!" I call. "I thought I just had to pee."

A grumble of disgust. I'm crouched in front of the under-sink cleaning cupboard, holding Tom's T-shirt and his other sock.

CELESTE

Daisy's footsteps sound on the steps. I will continue, in my head, to call her Daisy. As ridiculous a name as I once thought that, it's not as bad as CeCe. This old-fashioned country name suits her better. Fresh as a daisy. That's our girl.

Not so fresh right now, considering how long she's been in that bathroom. Though she might be a bit fresher after spending five freaking minutes washing her hands.

"What were you doing up there?" I say as she comes down. "Scrubbing in for surgery?"

"I got grease on my hands. I should have used Tom's cleaning goop. Soap does not do the job."

"Where are the books?"

"I decided to leave them in my room. No sense taking them, really, when I'll be staying here tonight."

She's coming down the stairs, veering to walk past me. Her tone is casual, as if I told her she's welcome back.

"You aren't coming back to my—"

"Not yours," she says, spinning, right beside me, making me

startle backward. She closes that gap in a single step, and before I even realize what's happening, my back is to the wall.

"Not your house," she enunciates. "Not your grandmother. Not your inheritance. None of it is yours."

"CeCe, I presume."

I try to twist the words with challenge, but I can't manage it as shame prickles through me.

I wish this could be different. God, how I wish it.

Daisy just stands there, staring up at me, saying nothing, leaving me struggling against the urge to squirm as I had all those times I stood up to my mother, feeling tough and strong for about two seconds before wanting to shrink into the woodwork, my feeble attempts only embarrassing us both.

"Where is Tom?" she asks.

I try to sidestep, but she's got me pinned here, a scant breath of air between us as she plants herself in my face. I resist the urge to squeeze free. I don't want her to think I *feel* pinned, feel trapped.

When I don't answer, she pulls Tom's T-shirt from her back pocket and holds it up.

"He played you," I blurt.

"What?"

"He conned you. He was only in it for the money."

Her face screws up. "What money?"

"Your grandfather's treasure."

She blinks. Then she bursts out laughing. "Please don't tell me you believe in that."

"I don't. Tom does. He came here to cut a deal."

She shakes her head. "No, sorry. Nice try, though."

I straighten. "So this is how it goes. This is how it always goes. We trust men over each other. I'm trying to help you out here, CeCe. Tom may have been your friend once, but he isn't now."

I can tell she's not buying that for a second, and I quickly say, "Last night, he made you think the police had come for you, right? Said he saw police cars. Said they had a warrant. Made you run with him? It was bullshit. It was just someone with an emergency repair."

"I *saw* the police cars," she says. "I *heard* the officers."

I hesitate. Then it hits. Tom lied. He wasn't setting *Daisy* up. He was setting *me* up. Trying to get me to confess to murder.

"Where is Tom?" she asks. "He was here. He did not leave without his shirt. If you've done something to him—done *anything* to him—"

I lunge. I've timed it perfectly. As she talked, my hand slid toward the gun in the back of my waistband, and as I lunge, I'll pull it out and—

I'm on my hands and knees, staring at the floor. I blink, my brain only able to register the possibility that I slipped and fell, and I flip over to see a gun trained on me.

My gun trained on me.

I see it, and I still check my waistband, as if Daisy's simply holding an identical gun. It's only as I feel nothing there that the last split second comes back to me.

I lunged . . . and Daisy grabbed me by the arms. A knee in the stomach and down I went, and she just plucked the gun from my waistband as I fell.

I look up at her, and I laugh. I laugh too loud and too long, until my sides ache. Then I collapse onto my back and gaze up at her.

"That is one kick-ass move, girlfriend," I say.

Her lips tighten at the last word, and I feel . . .

I feel like when I was twelve, and I had a girl-crush on the twelve-year-old next door. We'd moved in at the beginning of summer, and I didn't know anyone, and Tara took me under her wing. Tara was everything—whip-smart and cool-smooth and pixie-pretty.

I wanted nothing more than to be her friend, and I thought I was until I bought her a BFF bracelet, and she took both halves. Clearly, I'd bought it for her to share with her actual BFF. After all, I was just the new kid next door.

I'm lying on the floor, with Daisy holding a gun on me, asking what I've done with her boyfriend, and I'm hurt—yes, *hurt*. Rejected, yet again.

I laugh, and it comes out as a snigger, which I don't intend. Her eyes narrow, and her grip on the gun tightens. Her index finger, though, remains on the grip.

Daisy has more trigger control than me, too. Not surprisingly.

"I've called the police," she says. "That's why the water was running so long. To cover the call." She holds out Tom's cell phone, the screen showing the last call—to 911 mere minutes ago.

She's speaking calmly, but she keeps adjusting her grip, sweat trickling down one cheek despite the air conditioning. She's thinking of Liam. Thinking of what I did to him and trying very, very hard not to think of what I might have done to Tom.

"Liam was an accident," I say.

Her lips twitch. This isn't what she wants to talk about.

"He threatened me with your gun," I say. "I got it away from him, just like you got it away from me. I only meant to threaten him back."

"And it just went off?"

"I hear the sarcasm in your voice, but yes, it did. I put my finger on the trigger to show him I was serious, and that was a very, very bad decision. He grabbed the gun, and it fired. You probably won't believe that, but I wanted someone to know the truth."

"You tried to frame me. You put the gun and his phone in my room."

"You weren't going to jail, Daisy. The phone wouldn't have had your prints on it. There's no proof that you fired the gun. I just wanted you to get spooked and run. Like a herd of deer when a wolf comes along. Make one doe take off, knowing she'll outrun the danger, and give the others time to escape."

"That's not how deer do it. That's not how any animal does it. They protect each other until they can't."

"Well, I guess that's why I always sucked at group projects. That *was* my plan, though. You run, and they chase, and we both get away." I meet her gaze. "I'm not trying to defend my choices. Accident or not, I did kill Liam."

"And Tom?"

"He's in the basement crawlspace."

Her breathing quickens, coming in short and fast bursts through parted lips. "You killed—"

"No. I took him hostage while I figured out what to do next. I thought he was conning you. Conning both of us. He's alive and well."

Her gaze shifts in the direction of the basement door. Debating whether to trust me. Will she be the panicked girlfriend, running to ensure her lover is alive . . . and giving me the chance to turn the tables? Or will she harden her heart and stand fast just a little longer?

When you first came here, Daisy, I'd have guessed door number one all the way. You'd race off to check on Tom while waggling a finger at me and telling me to stay where I am. You might even have put the gun down in your distracted rush. But you aren't who I thought you were, and I don't just mean your identity.

You'll glance at that door and feel guilty for not checking on him, but you'll tell yourself—rightly—that it doesn't matter. If I'm lying, he's already dead. If he's fine, he'll still be fine in five minutes.

"He didn't con you," I say. "He was trying to trick me into confessing to Liam's murder. Tom's a good guy, and I could say you're lucky to have him. But honestly, I think it's the other way around."

Her lips tighten again as she hears my words and interprets false praise and is insulted that I think she'd fall for that.

I'm not sure we could have been friends, Daisy, but I like you. I really do. You are so much more than I expected.

"You deserve each other," I say, "and I mean that in the least sarcastic way possible. There was a time when I thought the same about Liam and me, though possibly with a little more sarcasm. We deserved each other."

"Like Bonnie and Clyde?"

"You're joking, but yes, I tried to frame it that way. Pretend I wasn't his victim. We were partners in crime, who'd screw over everyone but each other. That was the fantasy. The truth is that the one who got screwed over most was me. Ran away at sixteen to be with a drug dealer. I wanted to escape my proper little upper-middle-class life and release my inner badass. Didn't work out that way. Never does. Which didn't keep me from making the same mistake with Liam. Agree to captivity and tell myself it's my idea."

Two beats of silence pass. Then Daisy says, "Tell me about Maeve."

Still on the floor, I pull in one knee, my hands hooked around it. "Your grandmother was the toughest, meanest old broad I ever met. I mean that as a compliment. God, she was something else. I admired her, and I wish she had been my grandmother, but only in the way most grandmothers are—someone you visit and leave again. Living with her was an entirely different thing. Especially when she was getting sicker by the day, frustrated by all the things she couldn't do anymore."

"And taking out that frustration on you."

I don't answer that. It's a statement, not a question. I've been watching Daisy's face as I talk about Maeve, and I don't see shock or anger there. She knows what her grandmother was, and she loved her anyway. Having known the woman, I get that. I really do. I loved her a little bit myself.

"Were you good to her?" Daisy asks, and there's a note in her voice that I could sneer at, but I don't.

"If I wasn't, do you think she'd have let me stay?" I ask.

Silence. Daisy nods, slowly, and I add, "I wasn't the perfect granddaughter, but I did my selfish best for as long as I could, and in the end, she died holding my hand. You know what the last thing she said to me was?"

I lean back on my arms and look up at Daisy. "You aren't my CeCe."

She blinks, and her mouth opens, but I continue, "Final words. And I've thought about that a lot. At first, I thought she meant I wasn't the girl she remembered. Eventually, I realized she meant exactly what she said. That she knew I wasn't you, and she wasn't accusing me of anything—she was getting in the last word. One final jab from Maeve Turner. She knew I wasn't you, and she'd known for a while."

I laugh. "Here I was, so smug about pulling one over on everyone, and I'm not sure who I actually fooled. Maybe the lady at Tom's shop? Tom knew. Maeve knew. I wouldn't put it past Maeve to have known from the start, just figured if she could get free nursing from me, she'd take it. She didn't die mistaking me for you, if you're worried about that."

Daisy starts to speak, but a distant noise cuts her off. Her head jerks up. She follows the sound. Then she goes still. The sound finally comes clear. Police sirens.

"They took their sweet time, didn't they?" I say. "Here I was, thinking they were ignoring your call, when they were just being considerate, giving us time to chat."

Daisy snaps out of her trance and runs to the front door. She slams it shut and turns to me.

"You need to go," she says.

THIRTY-EIGHT

CELESTE

My brows shoot up. "What?"

"Go. You don't have time to pack. Grab your phone, your wallet, whatever you need. I'll get the rest for you later. Get out the back door. I'll stall them."

"I just admitted to framing you for murder, CeCe."

She spots my purse on the hall stand. In her rush to grab it, she sets the gun down and yanks the purse strap, the whole thing toppling with a crash. She runs back to me and holds out the purse.

"I shot my lover and tried to frame you," I say.

She shoves the purse at me. "Is your phone in there? Do you need your laptop?"

Sirens wail, louder now.

"No time for the laptop," she says. "Just—"

I lift the gun. She reels back, gaze whipping to the now empty side table. She looks at me, hands rising.

"Don't," she says. "Please. I won't tell them anything."

"I'm not going to shoot you, CeCe. You've done nothing wrong. You just wanted what was yours, and you treated me better than I deserved. This?" I waggle the gun. "This has been a long time coming."

I put the gun barrel under my chin. Daisy lets out a yelp and rocks forward, hands out to grab the gun before stopping herself, not wanting to spook me into shooting.

"I'll hold them off," she says, even as the knock comes at the door. "Run."

"I'm tired of running. Tired of needing to run. Tired of being the kind of person who runs."

"But you can. I don't know your real name. You're safe."

"Elizabeth—"

"No!"

"Elizabeth Tara Judd of Indianapolis. You'll find my ID in the attic, hidden in a box marked 'receipts.' Now turn around, CeCe."

"No. You do not have to do this."

"I don't. But I want to. It's this or suicide by cop, and I'd rather pull this trigger myself." I look her in the eye. "I make my own choices. This is a choice. Now turn away."

"No."

She stands there, glaring at me, defiant. Her mouth opens to say something more, make one last argument . . . and I pull the trigger.

I feel something like an uppercut to the chin. Then I'm on the floor, and I see her face, her horror and her pain, and I see one last thing.

Me. At eighteen. Standing in front of Aaron with his gun to my head. Him saying, "Pull the trigger, you dumb bitch. You think anyone cares if you put a bullet in your brain?"

I hear him, and I see Daisy's face, and I think, *Someone cared.* And I start to smile and then—

THIRTY-NINE

DAISY

"You ready?" Tom says.

We're inside the bank. It's been two weeks since I got my life back. A week since Elizabeth . . . Well, that's another story, and this is mine, at least for a little longer.

"I bet it's a stack of birthday cards," I say. "Gran saved all the birthday cards she never sent and put them in a safe-deposit box."

He snorts at that, though I'm not sure whether it's at the idea that Maeve would make such a big deal out of cards . . . or the idea that she ever actually bought me any.

Before my grandmother died, she left Liam a clue: where to find Bill Turner's supposed treasure.

To find your inheritance, remember how you liked to spend your time at my house.

A month later, Tom got a delivery. A safe-deposit-box key in an envelope marked "For CeCe." By then, he'd known Celeste wasn't me. By then, he'd started hunting for me. So he put the key away, and when I returned, he forgot all about it until I mentioned Liam's "clue."

Where did I like to spend my time when I visited Gran? With Tom. Who held the literal key.

I've gone through all the legal hoops to reclaim my identity and my inheritance. This is the final step. The bank, not surprisingly, dug in their heels the hardest, especially considering that Maeve had left specific instructions that, no matter who held the key, multiple pieces of government-issued ID were required for access.

I hold my breath as I turn the key in the lock. The box springs open. Inside is an envelope bearing Maeve's handwriting.

For my CeCe, who always deserved the best. All my love, Gran.

I pause, eyes filling. Tom puts an arm around my shoulders. Then, hands trembling, I pick up the envelope, open it and pull out the contents. It's money. Money and three smaller envelopes.

The first thing I check for is a note, but even as I do, I know I won't find one. My note is written on the envelope, and even that would have felt uncomfortably sentimental for Maeve.

I hold the bundle of bills. Bundles of hundreds.

"Probably fifty grand there," Tom says. "Maybe more."

I nod, still numb from that note.

That's what I wanted, Gran. Your message. I hope you know that. While I'll put the money to good use, what I wanted was the note.

I fold the envelope carefully and put it into my purse. Then I pick up the other envelopes and turn them over. Three, each with a name on the front.

The first is for Tom. Like mine, it has a note, his even simpler, just "I'm sorry," and that, we both know, might have been even harder for her to write than the sentiments on mine. Inside is a smaller stack of hundreds—probably about five thousand dollars.

The next one is marked "Liam" with the words "In appreciation of all you've done." Inside, well, inside there's nothing, and I do laugh at that. Not for long, though, because then I come to the last envelope. No name, just three question marks, but the rest makes it obvious who she meant. It says, "Get your ass out of there." I smile, even as my eyes fill.

Get your ass out of there.

Out of my house . . . and out of Liam's life. Get out. Get free. That's what Maeve meant. Her last words for Elizabeth, along with a thousand dollars to help her on her way.

We pocket the money in silence. Then we leave.

It's later that day. I'm working on the porch. All that remains of it is the foundation, the rotting wood relegated to a bonfire pile out back. Most of the house is salvageable, but some, like the front porch, needs a complete do-over.

There are times—more than I care to admit—when I'm ripping out a board on this old porch or nailing in a new one—and I think of Elizabeth. I wonder whether this is how she saw herself. Beyond repair. Unsalvageable.

"I knew she was a fake."

I look up to see the mail carrier. I brush off my bare legs and rise to take my mail.

"I knew all along," she says. "It was obvious to anyone with eyes. I'm glad she got what was coming to her."

I try not to tense. Just nod. Make a noise she can interpret as agreement.

"We all get what's coming to us," she says, as if to herself, as she walks back down the driveway. "One way or another."

I stand, watching her go and thinking that Elizabeth agreed, and what she thought she deserved was that bullet. I disagreed. I'd managed to grab her just as the gun fired. Knocked her out of its path and left her with a bloodied furrow.

It is remarkably easy to fake one's death. Well, not officially, of course. Anyone who digs isn't going to find a death certificate for Elizabeth Judd. They will, however, find a death notice in both the Sun City and Tampa papers and even a tiny plaque on a memorial wall in a cemetery that hadn't demanded anything more than a pot of ashes and a check.

As for who killed Liam Garey, the police have a very good suspect, courtesy of Elizabeth. It seems there's a certain client with an excellent motive to have murdered Mr. Garey, considering he paid Liam to find his former girlfriend . . . and Liam ended up taking her as his lover and forcing her into a fraud scheme. Liam had even taken hidden sex videos of them together.

Obviously, this client must have found out what Liam did. In retaliation, Liam got a bullet to the head—an execution-style shooting. In checking out a lead, the client—or his employees—must have found my gun in the shed, used it on Liam, and snuck it into a bedroom to frame Elizabeth—the former girlfriend. The forensic evidence cleared me of the crime, as Elizabeth knew it would.

As for Elizabeth, I'd helped her escape. I'd managed to stall the police until she could flee, and later, she provided the tips to set the police on Aaron.

The fake-death trappings won't hold up if the police indict Aaron. He'll find out she's still alive and wanted as a witness, but with any luck, it'll never get that far, and Elizabeth will finally have what she always wanted: her freedom. I'll give her Maeve's message, but I'm not sure she needs it. Maeve wasn't telling her anything she didn't already know. The money might make her smile, though.

As for my money, I have enough to renovate the house and start my own business. That's a sweet, sweet spot to be.

Speaking of sweet spots to be . . .

Tom rolls into the driveway just after five. I set down my hammer and stroll over, and he's out of the truck before I get there. He swoops me up in a kiss.

"Porch looks good," he says as he sets me down.

I glance at it. "Porch looks like crap."

He laughs. "It looks like a work in progress, and I am visionary enough to see the end result, complete with rocking chairs."

"And shotguns?"

"Unloaded ones."

We talk for a few minutes, standing there in the drive. We're good at talking, never seeming to run out of topics. The one thing we don't discuss is Elizabeth. He can't forgive her for what she did to me. I understand that. I wouldn't have forgiven her if she'd hurt him, either.

Tom cares more about what she did to me than what she did to him. I care more about what she did to him than what she did to me. As forecasts for relationships go, that one seems like an excellent predictor of success.

At a break in the conversation, Tom takes my hand and starts leading me toward the house. I pause and point at the pile of equipment in his trunk.

"Taking up lawn service on the side?" I say.

"Nah, that is for a very special, top-secret project." He leans in, lowering his voice. "I'm going to clear a safe path out back for some daredevil lady who likes to jog there."

"Sounds like a very nice gift. I'm sure she'll appreciate it."

"Mmm, she may appreciate it a little less when I ask her to help me build wooden boardwalks over the wet parts."

"I think she'll be okay with that."

"Good. It's all part of my plan to give her reasons to stick around long-term."

I laugh. "Pretty sure she's already got all the incentive she needs."

"True. It is a very nice house. Or it will be, when she's done."

I kiss his cheek. "Nice house. Nice property. Nice boy next door. I might even ask him to move in."

"Seems like he's half moved in already. If you want to make it official, though, he may expect a ring."

"I could probably dig one up somewhere."

He glances over, checking to make sure I'm not just extending the joke. I smile back and give him a kiss meant to erase all doubt. When we part, he holds the front door open for me, and I pause to look back at the road, taking in the scenery.

A place I never thought I'd come back to. Now that I'm here, I can't imagine leaving. When I gaze at the front window, I picture Elizabeth, looking for peace and being trapped instead.

I hope you've found your peace, Elizabeth.

I look out at the dusty road and the empty fields beyond, feel the humidity settling in, the lazy weight of it, and I glance over at the man holding open the door. I walk through, and it feels right. It feels like home. It feels like forever, and I am fine with that.